LEGION OF DORKS PRESENTS: HORIZONS

An Anthology of Epic Journeys

Edited by
KELLY LYNN COLBY

Cursed Dragon Ship
PUBLISHING

For all the explorers on epic journeys of their own in whatever form they may take.

Contents

Introduction

Welcome to the award-winning series *Legion of Dorks presents.* This second anthology, created for the Legion of Dorks Gaming and Giving Charity Drive, promises to meet those same standards. This group of gamers and creatives have once again put together an incredible collection of adventure to satisfy their lust for travel in a time when we're stuck at home.

The best part? Fifty percent of all proceeds will go directly to the chosen charity this year—in past years, it's been Toys for Tots. After the production of the book has been met, *all* of the proceeds will go to charity.

By purchasing *Horizons*, you have awarded children—of greater numbers than recent year thanks to this blasted pandemic—a bit of joy for the holidays. While you're exploring the Old West, sailing the ocean, and fighting bandits, your purchase price buys toys that will feed the imagination of the next generation.

Thank you for your support. Enjoy the journey!

Kelly Lynn Colby

Editorial Director

Cursed Dragon Ship Publishing, LLC

Beyond Reach

Taylor Adel

The waters have been calm, and Sebaison thanks the Sea Mother for the crew's ease of journey thus far. Her sister, the Creator of Wind, is less obliging. The skies lie still, no currents for *Storm Chaser*'s sails to catch and ride here in the open ocean of the Abyson. Yesterday, Sebaison dropped rows and commanded the men to take shifts at the oars so they might make some ground. There were grunts at the demand, but they set to. For hours, the oars stroked the ocean in rhythmic beats that drowned out the sound of the gulls above, a deep gravel of voices risen in chant as the men worked. It was comforting, the constant noise of the instruments breaking down into the water and then back up into the air. If Sebaison was one for words, he might have tried writing to the sound. Fortunately for most, he was not, and so he had taken up in his favorite spot, the main top, and listened to the sound of the waves with the sun on his face.

It's a good distance from Elline to Ascera, and wearing his crew out a few days into their travels would cause angst and anger. So, Sebaison lets them rest to prepare for the morrow. To the left of their ship, he watches a pod of Greytails, their bodies stretching twice the length of his vessel as they slice open the ocean's surface. He grins at the scene, while swell of respect for the Sea Mother and her creatures blossoms in his chest. What would it be like to live in her embrace, to encompass her comfort? There would be less heartache, he assumes, and rubs a hand along the fine stubble of his chin.

A few juveniles swim in the middle of the group, protected by their families. Not that they would need much protection. Even the young ones are monstrous, capable of bringing the *Storm Chaser* to the depths should they get it in their minds to try. They keep a companionable distance, however, and Sebaison, along with members of the crew, enjoy their presence as they dip and dance between the waves.

The balmy flush of sea spray dapples his face and a lightness catches his feet. It builds in his throat and creeps to every orifice within him like a blessing. This place is home—the deck, the men, the ocean an endless expanse on all sides—he doesn't want to leave for any shore.

The briny water tosses and turns with the creatures. It starts out an illustrious steel hue before shooting into the sky to shift from turquoise to seafoam green to bright white, the caps dispersing in a shower of droplets that sparkle in the sun. The whales croon to one another as their bodies arch out of the blue expanse like temporary, salt-washed islands. It's a joy to watch.

Sebaison leans his arms against the bannister of his stoop, then settles his chin in the bridge of his hands. They're spectacular, the animals that the Sea Mother filled her waters with upon Creation. He had seen plenty of whale species during his journeys, from ones with bodies as blue as Elline's waters to others decorated with black and white spots. He'd heard tales of dolphins with horns on their heads, squids the size of mountains, and dragon-fish with wings made to glide through the sea rather than the air, their bodies the size of small towers with teeth to match. Beasts he can hardly fathom, brought to life by her grace.

One of the larger animals of the pod breaks the surface. Water erupts from the hole in its back, spraying up as it breathes in the crisp air, before diving back beneath the crystalline depths. Its tail lifts into the sky as though trying to block the sun from sight, before slamming into the water with a crash. The sea splits, flying up and out far enough to land across the *Storm Chaser*. The ship rocks around him as Sebaison's crew hoot and holler, thrilled with the show. He finds himself laughing as well. For all he's suffered in the name of duty, this reminds him of where he belongs. If he never had to set foot on land again, he would be a happier man.

But helping Syemod makes him a *better* man. He had been riffraff before his ties to the royal family—he owes them everything he has become.

Sighing, Sebaison looks across the main deck to the sanded, driftwood doors behind which Princess Sybelle's quarters rest. From atop the roof, he watches the quarterdeck, men bustling about with rags and mops, keeping the ship as clean as they can manage with the royal aboard. The longer he stares at the barrier of wood and brass between them, the more his heart aches. This can't happen; he won't allow it. So he draws in a long inhale to steady the pitch of his gut. He can't have her, even if she loves him, too.

From above, his second, Oras, meets his gaze. Sebaison waves him over, glancing back to the whales. Oras follows the command, making his way down the deck stairs to where Sebaison stands. "Aye, Captain. What can I do for you?"

Sebaison nods in the general direction of Sybelle's cabin. "If you wouldn't mind telling the princess that we've a scenic show, she might enjoy watching the whales sing and dance. It's been a time since she's smiled... perhaps this will do the trick."

"That I can do, Captain, but wouldn't she prefer the tiding to come from you, rather than your second?"

Sebaison snorts, tapping his palm against the fresh-polished bannister before he turns away from the frolicking pod altogether. Perhaps, if he hadn't crushed the final thread of hope in her eyes on the last night in Elline. At the moment, she'd more likely throw him overboard and leave him to a watery grave than breathe forth an overture. He can't tell Oras as much, though. "If these were normal circumstances, then yes, that would be the cordial approach. The princess is not pleased with me at the moment, however, and would be more inclined to follow your behest. Besides, you've got some elderly charm to you, Oras."

Sebaison grins to the man, lips ticked up just above a grimace. Indeed, gray weaves its way through Oras's close-shaven beard, indistinguishable from his mustache. His skin crackles from age, his pursed lips sit chapped from years with the saline air and salty sea, but never has Sebaison met a man with more youth in his eyes and movements.

Oras bares his teeth back and bellows out a laugh before he claps Sebaison on his shoulder. "I'll take that as a compliment, and I'll have you know, I'm more limber in my old age than you are now, Captain."

Sebaison chuckles, watching Oras's green eyes twinkle in his dark face. "Now that is a truth I can't argue with. Go, see if you can't give our princess a sampling of happiness. She's born of the sea; she should enjoy it while she's surrounded by it."

Oras nods and departs, leaving Sebaison alone once more. He chews his lip. She shall enjoy it before she's left to an unknown land hundreds of miles from the ocean she adores, from the Sea Mother. His shoulders pinch in, the weight of wet sand embedded in his gut. She has every right and more to hate him for this.

To give Sybelle more breadth, he exits the main deck and moves up to the quarter. The *Storm Chaser* beams back at him when he takes it in from this vantage point. Syemod had outdone himself, and Sebaison shakes his head at the lavish renovations.

Syemod had the entire vessel sanded and polished, every inch of the ship gleaming as though it had been built the week before. The barnacles and algae long since having found a home on its bottom had been stripped from the keel and hull, leaving the ship in a much healthier condition than before. New designs had been painted onboard, too.

Whereas the leviathan of House Kept wrapped around the outer wood, Syemod had remained true to the vessel's name on the decks and cabins. Painted wisps of thunder clouds and lightning strikes highlight the interior design, giving it an attractiveness that has not been seen since the beginning of *Storm Chaser's* days.

Kings and their desire to shine, even through others. A dash of fondness flickers in his chest. If only the three of them could return to what they had. But they've become interlocked in a game of betrayal, and the coils in his stomach churn.

Sebaison watches the horizons around them, keeping an eye out for dark clouds. They may not have come across a storm yet, but from the word of other sailors visiting Elline's ports, the change in climate from winter to spring had riled up quite a few tempests in the Straight. They're still a week's time, maybe more, from the entrance to the Tempen, but the squalls could have moved out from the close quarters of the two continents into the Abyson. At the moment, however, the skies are clear and pure with no spots of tarnish, so he settles against a railing.

The pod moves away from them, their infectious joy swimming languidly into the distance. Looking down, Sebaison exhales to see Oras has indeed coerced Sybelle from her rooms. Her hair hangs in a single thick braid down her back, the deep set dusk of her skin vibrant beside the burned tan of her companion. A thin silver crown sits on her head to keep loose strands of the plait from flapping in the sea spray. She's discarded her usual outfits—shear pants and skirts with plunging, bejeweled tops and an array of bangles. Instead, she adorns a simple tunic and trousers unit with seaworthy boots. In her nose and brow sit the ever-present rings, but aside from these items and her crown, she looks as average as every other woman in Elline— yet more enchanting than any other woman he's ever laid eyes upon.

What hasn't changed is her insistence to lean over railings. Sebaison clenches back his desire to yell down caution, to wrap a protective hand on her hip as he so often did before. Instead, he swallows the lump that's built in his throat.

Sybelle hangs over *Storm Chaser's* bannister, gaze on the whales in the distance. Oras leans next to her, gesturing with his hands in what must be a beguiling tale of adventure and courage and heroism. Sebaison snorts and rolls his eyes at his fabled second. Sybelle looks to Oras, laughing, then returns her attention to the pod. Sebaison lurches forward when she releases the bannister with one arm and tips more than halfway over the rail to point as a few of the adult whales leap in the air, the juveniles following suit. He spits out a low curse and runs a hand through his hair.

Sending a prayer to the Sea Mother, he thanks her for the gift of her creatures and for being at Sybelle's side in such a trying time. He wants to return to the main deck, to join Sybelle and Oras as they continue their animation with one another. He doesn't, knowing she would flee from him. Instead, he sneaks into his own cabins, located just behind them.

If Syemod had updated the vessel's outside, Sebaison's chambers were unrecognizable. He had enjoyed the simplicity of his quarters before, with the oversized cot, mismatched tables filled with maps and scopes and instruments of various types. The paint had been peeling, but such things were common on a ship as old as his. The rum was kept in barrels in the corners, open to any of the men who wanted them so long as they asked permission for entrance. He'd had a few decorations set about—a fishing net from his first catch, a seal pelt from a courtier, and souvenirs he had acquired from different continents during his travels.

Now, there sits a feather bed in the center of the room with anti-quated nightstands on either side. A maps table is positioned to the right of the cabin, the Kept leviathan painted into its surface. A pot full of weights posts atop it, available to hold parchment in place as he plots routes. Portraits of sea life hang from the walls, and display cases reside steadfast beside them to give order to his numerous souvenirs. Blues and oranges fill the room, which did not surprise him, but Syemod had gone as far as to add greens and yellows as well, Sebaison's favorite colors. The bed spread was of a forest green with cream sheets, and yellow accents in the form of décor and draw-ings are scattered throughout the quarters. Rather than buckets of rum, shelving stretches from floor to ceiling on either side of the room to hold the bottles, two hundred at least in total.

Sebaison had been baffled when he'd first seen it, stammering to

Syemod that it was more than he could accept. Of course, Syemod had waved him off and laughed, happy that things had turned out fine since he would not step aboard to make sure the plans were captured correctly, and said all he needed in repayment was Sybelle's safe delivery to Ascera.

Looking around now, Sebaison's gut churns. He hadn't changed his cabin in twelve years, and if it weren't for the remains of his antiques and the pelt beneath the table, he would feel a stranger in it now.

Walking to the lines of rum, he removes a bottle from the shelf, grabs a glass from the cabinet, and sits at the table of maps. He must admit, the weights had come in handy. Normally, he would draw out his route, roll the map up, and tuck it into a sack nailed against the cabin wall for safe-keeping until he needed it again. Not the most convenient way of doing things, and other sailors would probably criticize him, but he had worked with what he had.

Now, his route to Acsera is drawn out on an elegant parchment that sits across from him, held in place by the weights and easy to see. Groaning, he leans back in his seat, and releases the cork from his drink. It sloshes in the glass as the ship takes a sudden dip, then levels out. Just as he's to take a sip, there sounds a knock at the door.

Sebaison grumbles and cranes his neck to the door. "Yes! Who goes?"

"Oras, Captain. Might I join you?"

It seems Sybelle's been left to wander on her own. He grunts his approval and his second enters. The man remains cheery, a grin on his face as he shuts the door behind him.

"I see our princess put you in a good mood, Oras."

Chuckling, Oras shakes his head and retrieves a glass from the cabinet to join Sebaison at the table. He fills his mug to the same height and corks the rum. "She's bright, that Sybelle. I'll tell you what, I'm going to miss her in the streets and shores of Elline once she's left to Ascera." An odd look passes over him, casting shadows beneath his eyes and cross dimples around his cheeks. "Might I ask you a question?"

"You might," Sebaison responds, then takes a long sip of the rum.

"I had expected a large party to accompany *Storm Chaser* in delivering the princess to Ascera. But we have just the one ship. There was no sending ceremony or goodbyes, no feast for her departure... it's almost as though her leave from Elline was a secret. My apologies if I overstep, but why? Her sisters had week-long celebrations when they joined unions with their husbands. If I do remember, Choral requested a feast for every year difference between herself and her husband, giving us ten memorable revelries."

Sebaison finishes his glass and pours another. He won't lie to his second. If he didn't give his crew truths, how could he expect loyalty from them? Gesturing to Oras's glass, the man nods and Sebaison pours more rum, corks the bottle, and takes a small swallow of his own.

"You might have noticed Princess Sybelle's... animosity towards her marriage."

"I had not wanted to mention so, but she said as much while we watched the Greytails."

Sebaison purses his lips. The people of Elline adored Sybelle; it would make sense she would turn to them in the hopes they might show disgruntlement towards the marriage. "I believe her betrothal to King Hollow is not to be known to the other kingdoms until they are wed. Why? I could not say, such political matters do not involve me, nor do they require my consent. I believe Sybelle is unhappy with the arrangement, and therefore, did not care for ceremonies or other engagements. Syemod sees this match as the best move for Elline and hopes that he himself might find a wife once the princess is happily and safely settled into Ascera."

Oras nods, grave brows drawn, then beckons for more rum. "Spoken like a diplomat, if ever I've heard one. I see, though. It's understandable why she seems upset. And her aggravation with you?"

Sebaison frowns, but puts Oras's blunt nature to the drinks and answers with a half-truth once more. Her anger with him lies in a heap of ruined trust and shattered vulnerabilities. "I'm taking her to a man she does not wish to be with. It is by her brother's command, but the messenger still receives the brunt force of the repercussions. We all have our duties. You and I, we must be prepared for all manner of tasks, whether it be diplomatic missions or naval attacks. Our duties are to protect and help Elline in whatever way we can. The royals? Their duties are political, and marriages fall into that category quite often. Is this fair? No. But such is the life they have been given."

Oras nods and toasts the air. "Here, here. Such is the life."

The two men talk for a few more hours, finishing off their current bottle of rum plus one more. Oras recollects a time he claims to have spotted a leviathan off the coast of Karsington, near the Shipman Isles. Sebaison listens intently to the story, but puts it off as another exaggeration.

A few years back, Oras insisted to have seen people with tails swimming not too far from Elline's own shores, and Sebaison had forbade him from libations for a week. The man lasted a good day before that restriction ended. Now, he stands as though to grab another bottle.

Sebaison sighs, but goes with him and removes a third casing of rum, handing it to the sailor. "I believe I'm done for the night, but I'll follow you out and see how we fare."

Oras takes the bottle from him and leads the way out of the cabin. A cool evening air hits him, the sun lowered in the distance to cast orange and yellow rays across the edge of the distant ocean, that place where it goes flat and disappears beyond sight.

Most of the men wander about in their tasks that keep the ship in order, but with such an uneventful day, there's little left to do. Assignments for the night crew had been laid out, and already some of the men head below the main deck. He spots Maisone and his brother, Matherson, on their way down from the poop deck. They make their way over, but he waves them off. They've been with him for years; he hardly needs to listen to their excuses. "Go on and take five to ten bottles for the crew, but I'll not have gambling down in the cots, you understand?"

Sebaison narrows his eyes in caution even as Matherson's grin splits ear to ear, and he nudges Maisone in the ribs.

The elder brother shoves the boy off, rubbing his side. "Aye, Captain. No gambling in the bunks."

Sebaison nods and looks out over the Abyson just in time to see the sun slide below the shoreline.

Beyond the horizon.

The Kept words come to him suddenly, and he watches the last rays shimmer above the surface—red and orange and purple ribbons —before they dip out of sight. It's eerie, how quick the light leaves in the middle of the ocean. Already the stars peek out from their daytime rendezvous to watch the *Storm Chaser* crawl across black glass. Aside from the night crew, the decks are clear.

Sebaison's shoulders sag, his eyes ready to droop closed. The sun seeped at his energy throughout the day, and the rum brings his exhaustion to the forefront of his mind, but the thought of returning to his chambers doesn't appeal, so he moves to the upper deck. As he reaches the top of the stairs, he spots Sybelle across the way, her sight on the western horizon. He shouldn't disturb her in the moment of quiet, and he's already turned to leave when her voice rings out.

"Captain Sebaison," she calls to him.

There's no endearment in his name, as there was so often before, but there's no rage either. Instead, it's an uninterested beckon. Hesitating, he twists back around. She watches him, those golden eyes locked on his. The simple crown atop her head is set with uncut embers and sapphires.

Primitive. Strong. Dangerous. A tempest herself in all things. His heart aches at the vision she makes.

"Princess." He swears her eyes flash at the cordial greeting, and he braces himself for the Kept storm, but she turns back to examine the distant darkness.

"We're not children. At least, I would hope not. At some point during this journey, we'll have to be on the same deck together. Might as well start now."

Sebaison hesitates, wondering if she has an ulterior reason

behind giving him access, but he doesn't refuse the offer to join her. Resuming his climb, he walks to stand beside her.

"Beyond the horizon," he states simply.

"Yes," she agrees, "but what happens once we reach it? Nothing, because a horizon is something unattainable. An end destination you can never grasp. Just like the leviathan, it remains forever, a never-ending circle that leads to nowhere. It begs the question, is there truly a place beyond?"

Sebaison shifts, uncomfortable with her words. He's a blunt man, at a loss when it comes to riddles, but there's no choice save to answer. "Horizons are always changing, never the same. They show us how much progress we've made. How far we have left to go, yes, but also how far we've come. Without it, life would be too great an expanse for us. We need the horizon, because it gives us a reasonable goal."

Sybelle scoffs, her eyebrows raised and eyes bright in incredulity. "Reasonable goal? Tell me, Sebaison, how is something you can never touch, never reach, never have, a reasonable goal?"

Sebaison hesitates, the taste of this puzzle on his tongue. Gold eyes scrutinize him, waiting for him to give in, but he refuses. Not this time. He squares his shoulders back and extends to his full height. Even still, he feels small in her shadow. "Because, the horizon itself isn't the goal. The horizon is merely a place marker for where we want to go. It's a guiding point, and if it wasn't there, we'd be lost."

Sybelle shakes her head and her brows furrow in thought. "I suppose we'll take different views on this matter."

Sebaison grimaces, but doesn't argue any farther. Instead, he looks up to where the stars have appeared in full bloom, sprinkled over the ship in a way they never do over Elline. Surrounded by an eternal darkness—the sea and the sky in the night—they shine like burst sparks. Watching them now, he understands how followers of Uriel could think they're souls. They're beautiful, and it's difficult to contemplate how they were hung so high above the land. Even in his own religion, there is controversy as to whether they were molded by the Creator of Land or given birth by the Creator of Fire. Either way, the Gods had made something beautiful.

Sybelle steps forward to rest her palms on the edge of *Storm Chaser*. "What do you see?"

"The stars." Sebaison squints up, an attempt to see more, but there's nothing.

She huffs, a contained quirk at the corner of her lips. His heart aches at the control she's forced upon herself near him, and he clasps his hands behind his back. "A lazy answer. You'd be blind to not see the stars. But what do you *see*."

Sebaison searches yet again for what Sybelle speaks of, but can't find it. Shrugging, he licks his lips. "The moon? The stars and the moon are all that I see."

Beside him, she sighs. "Open your eyes to the world, Sebaison. You'll be surprised what all you find." Pointing up, she draws a circle with her finger. He follows it, but misses what she's showing him. Thankfully, she begins to explain. "There, to the left of the moon. Do you see the five stars brighter than the rest?"

It takes him a moment, but after a time he does realize some of the sparks are a little larger than the others. "I do see them, yes."

"Good, and swirls around them. That's Frayer the Gardener with his two daughters."

"A gardener?" Sebaison asks, laughing a little.

"Yes, a gardener," Sybelle responds, and Sebaison looks over to the slightest of smiles on her face.

The sight brings that same lightness to the balls of his feet and up through his chest. He glances up before she notices. "Frayer the Gardener."

"And his daughters."

"I see," Sebaison starts, "and why would a grouping of stars be named after a gardener and his daughters?"

For the remainder of the night, Sybelle tells Sebaison stories of the images in the sky. Some of them are happy, some of them are sad, but what matters is that they're there, and Sybelle and he are here, and for the first time since he lied and said he didn't love her on the beach in Elline, she's opening her heart to him again. He just prays she won't force him to crush it a second time, because if she does, it'll destroy his as well.

Not even the Sea Mother will have the power to fix it.

Meet Taylor Adel

Taylor Adel is an avid writer and reader who dabbles in baking and drinks more coffee than should be allowed. Ever. She adores her rescue dog, Homer, and finds inspiration in the weirdest places. Be sure to check out her debut novel *Leather and Sage*, the first installment of the Willow Moss and Kindling series, which releases March 2021. Her short stories have been published by all the sins, The Birmingham Arts Journal, Every Day Fiction, and more. To learn what makes her tick and to read more of her work, visit her website at https://ravingwrites.wixsite.com/tayloradel.

Good Stew

Stephen Adams

I'm leaving for Georgia."

Abraham let the statement hang in the air. He was no fan of being blunt, but on occasion it was necessary to get a point across. It was particularly necessary when dealing with someone as hard headed as Jeremiah Cox.

"You've been in that outhouse for nearly about half an hour, and you come out with something as bold as that?" Cox didn't bother to look up from the Bible. "That must have been some shit."

"I'm serious, Jeremiah. I have business to attend to. It just took me a while to come to the decision, that's all. I'm old and tired. Such a thing as a fifteen-hundred-mile journey ought to be pondered for some time." Abraham spit in the dirt, mindlessly shuffling it around with his boot.

Jeremiah sat the Bible across his knee. Abraham knew Jeremiah only read the parts he liked. As he'd never been much for the moral high ground, he enjoyed the Old Testament best. Something about God's righteous judgment coming for those who angered Him appealed to the old outlaw's sense of justice.

"Why on earth do you think you need to go to Georgia?"

"It's complicated."

"Can't be that complicated if you came to a decision in one shit." Jeremiah stood and walked to the edge of the porch. He leaned against a post, glancing back and forth between the horizon and his old friend. "I've known you, God, more than thirty years. If it doesn't darn near slap you in the face, you might as well had never taken notice."

"Mabel's dying," Abraham said, his voice shaking on the last word.

The two outlaws stared each other down as the words hung in the air. Jeremiah wiped his mustache with his old cracked hands. Abraham could only assume that Jeremiah was hoping it was all a joke. That any moment he would laugh that he got one over on his old partner and just wander off in his self-satisfied way.

"Well, get on with it, if you're going," Jeremiah said plainly.

"I am!" Abraham shouted. "I just thought maybe you'd want to know. Ain't like I expected you to care, but I guess I'm a damn fool who hadn't learned nothing over thirty years with you." Abraham rubbed his chin, as he was known to do when he was anxious.

Jeremiah went back to reading as if Abraham had said nothing at all.

"I'm going to need the wagon," he said. Some of the temper had worked its way out.

"You can't have my wagon," Jeremiah said with a tone that did not invite argument. "I'm the only one that gets to drive the wagon."

"I reckon you're going to have to come with me then. We ain't got enough money left for me to get my own."

"I have no interest in Georgia. I think you ought to let it go. No good can come of it."

"I have to, Jeremiah. I don't expect you to understand it, as I don't know that you even have a heart." Abraham paused for a moment, looking over their dusty spit of land in the middle of Texas. "I'd be willing to bet there ain't nothing in you but sawdust."

Jeremiah slapped the Bible on his thigh. "I have no need of a trip to Georgia, and neither do you. You ain't seen Mabel in years. She's probably got a whole family of her own tending to her. She don't need you wandering in and messing all that up. I got no desire to run off on your damn fool adventure. You ought to just set here with me and get old. Hell, I'll even let you deal the cards."

"My God, you are an obstinate old man, you know that?"

Jeremiah sucked his teeth and turned back to his book. "Get on, if you're going."

"Well, I'd say it's been a pleasure then, Mr. Cox. Good luck runnin' this place without me then." Abraham started to the barn to saddle his horse.

He'd won the horse in a game of cards a year prior. The pot was low, but a dimwit gambler from Austin had thrown his horse in just to stay in the game. By the end of the round, the man had lost his horse along with a five-dollar pot. Abraham had taken to calling the horse Worthless to remind him of the event. He had also taken to reminding Jeremiah that the name was not offensive as horses could not speak English.

"Mr. Monroe!" Jeremiah shouted. Abraham turned back to him. "What makes you think Mabel even wants to see you? You ain't never been there for her. I know you visited maybe once, maybe twice in her whole life. Why go now?"

Abraham looked off in the distance, pondering the questions for a moment. "I got a letter from her."

"What did it say?"

"Enough." Abraham started back toward the barn. That was about as much explanation as the old man was ever going to give.

For a horse named Worthless, the black Tennessee Walker rode quite well. Abraham had become quite attached to it and cared for it like he would have a small child. If he'd ever had to care for a small child, that is. He assumed it took a lot of work and patience.

Having never been much of a patient man in the past, he'd spent his later years trying to learn the skill. He still had work to do, but Worthless was helping with that.

Abraham rode into the nearby town of La Flor to gather up what he needed for provisions and to say his goodbyes.

La Flor was a small town. There was a general store, a saloon that doubled as an inn, and a Sheriff's office. The Sheriff never had much work to do on account of no outlaws bothering with the place. If there had been any money, it may have been worth it, but there was a reason Jeremiah and Abraham had chosen such a place to settle down. Less possibility of running into somebody they knew.

Abraham tied his horse outside the saloon, went in to grab a drink and say goodbye to Fiona, the bartender, and get ten dollars back from Buford. The piano player had borrowed the money to pay for time with a sporting woman and had neglected to pay him back.

Yet another opportunity for Abraham to work on that patience he so desperately felt he needed.

"Morning, Abe," Buford said, as Abraham slung the doors open, his spurs clacking as he walked the wooden floorboards.

"Howdy, Buford. You have that ten dollars you owe me?"

"Oh, you know I'm good for it, Abe." Buford fidgeted in his chair.

"I know you are. Now go on and just give me that emergency stash you keep in your hat band. I have need of it."

"How did you know I keep money in my hat band?"

"More than once I've picked your inebriated self out of that chair. More than once your hat has fallen off. You're lucky it was me picking your head up off the table, or you'd be broke ten times over."

Buford bit his lip and nodded, then removed the money from his hat. "Fine, then. Since you're here, how about a game of cards?"

Abraham chuckled as he stuffed the money into the inside pocket of his vest. "Not today, Buford. Some other time."

Buford nodded and went back to noodling on his piano. He was no smart man. He could barely recognize his own name, but he was some sort of virtuoso on the piano. He could hear a tune played once and play it himself without fail.

Abraham slid onto the seat at the end of the bar, his usual spot, gazing at Fiona for a few good seconds before saying hello. She was near the same age as he, but looked years younger. The hard life in this dirty town had not done much to wear her angelic features down.

Her husband had not been so lucky. He passed after a stud kicked him in the head. He wasn't a cruel man, but his patience with horses was not a strong suit. He had given up a lucrative business back east to come out here and try his hand at horse breeding. That had proven to be a fatal mistake.

"Howdy, gorgeous," Abraham said with a slight smile.

"You don't look so bad today yourself, Abe." Fiona polished a glass and returned the same smile. "What brings you in this morning?"

"I was hoping to get a bowl of stew and maybe some polite conversation. Of course, I'd trade either for a kiss."

"Keep trying your luck, old man. I'm saving my kisses for whoever walks through that door and sweeps me off my feet. Maybe they'll take me to California and let me dip my toe in the ocean before this body gives out."

Abraham chuckled. "You know I'd take you to California, if you wanted."

"Not a chance. You wouldn't know what to do without Jeremiah to keep you straight, and Lord knows I'm not up for that job."

"I'd be willing to give you the chance. The job don't pay well, but there's great benefits"

"You don't say?" she grinned. "Let me get your stew, Mr. Monroe."

"Thank you, dear." Abraham looked down at the wooden bar he'd passed so much time eating off of. He had nearly memorized the wood grain. Each ripple was a memory of some conversation, some fight, or some missed opportunity over the course of his life.

All the times he had sat at this bar thinking about Mabel, the daughter he never wanted from the girl he didn't know how to forget. He had walked away when she was very young, but she followed him in spirit. Turns out you can't outrun old debts. At some point, the bill comes due.

Fiona returned with his soup. "There you go, honey. It's not as warm as it was last night. Truthfully, I didn't expect anyone else to come asking for it this early, so it's been sitting over embers."

"This will do fine, thank you." Abraham took his spoon in hand and slurped up a bit of the tomato-based stew. It was over salted, but it got the job done.

"Let me go take care of a few things, and I'll come back to check on you, okay?"

"That's fine," Abraham said, as he ate another spoonful.

The thing about a good stew was that it had a way of making otherwise unappetizing vegetables have a purpose. It surrounded them with something flavorful. It gave off a smell that put a person's thoughts at ease and had a way of saying, "There, there now. Everything is all right." The hungrier a person got, the sweeter its voice.

Abraham reckoned life was a lot like a hot bowl of stew. A whole lot of nonsense mixed in with a bit of good meat. All he had now was to stare into a reflection of his life in the brown bowl in front of him and hope that he had enough good meat in it to make it worth a taste.

Abraham slurped down the rest of his stew and pushed away the empty bowl. He gazed across the bar at Fiona with his tired eyes.

"Thanks for the stew, darlin'," he said with a slight wobble in his voice.

Fiona reached for his bowl. "You heading back already? I usually can't get rid of you," she said smiling. "Jeremiah must be hounding you pretty hard."

"It ain't like that today," he said with a slight smirk. He couldn't help it. Talking to Fiona always brought out something buried deep in him. "Nah, I'm headin' east."

"What's east? Running a herd?" Fiona asked.

By the tone of her voice, Abraham knew that for her this was just another conversation on just another normal day.

"No, my dear"—the words struggled to make their way out—"I'm riding to Georgia."

Abraham had spent the better part of his later years at this bar, eating this stew and talking to this woman. He'd invested more than he intended, and, as much as he gained, leaving would put him right back in debt. He cared for Fiona. He cared for this life, as much as he hated to admit it.

"You're not riding to Georgia," Fiona said, as if trying to convince herself it couldn't be true. She wasn't known to cry. Running a saloon in this part of the country was no task for a soft person. She was anything but.

"I am," Abraham said, leaning back a bit and peeking out the front windows. He didn't make eye contact with her aside from a glance.

"Well, I'll be damned." Fiona's posture changed. She hung her head, tapping at the bar anxiously with her fingers. "You coming back?" she finally asked.

"Yes, ma'am. Soon as my business done, I'll saddle up and be back so quick, you'll wish I was still gone."

Abraham reached out and gently lifted her chin. "You'll always be my girl, Fiona. In another life, we might have had something." Abraham said it with a smile, knowing those were just words. He loved Fiona, but like a dear friend.

She knew it too. "I could never have put up with you," she replied, her eyes watering. "Now get on out of here if you're going. You're old, and if you don't get a move on, you'll be dead before you can turn around." She let out a bit of a laugh mixed with a cry.

"I'll tell Jeremiah to come by more often and keep you company."

That got a laugh out of her right away. "You wouldn't dare. I get more entertainment from staring at a wall."

"You're not wrong. He's no Abraham Monroe, that's for damn sure."

"Nobody is, love."

They let the words hang in the air for a moment. It wasn't easy to get Abraham to stop talking, but if anyone could get him to stop dead in his tracks, it was her.

He tipped his hat and stepped away from the bar. "That's right, darlin'."

At that, the saloon doors swung open, and the clank of spurs broke up the moment. A large man with a black beard stomped in and took a seat at the bar.

Abraham hadn't seen him before, and he'd seen just about everyone who ever came through town.

The man sat down at the other end of the bar, muttering to himself.

"You got business to attend to, my dear. I'll see you around." Fiona just smiled, tears welling in her eyes as part of her life walked away.

Abraham was nearly out the door when he heard it. "What kind of saloon puts a woman behind the bar? Why aren't you upstairs where they keep the rest of the whores?"

Abraham turned around and walked back. He kicked the man's stool out from under him, forcing his face to slam onto the surface of the bar. The stranger's face left a blood splatter as he fell backwards onto the floor.

Abraham put his boot on the man's chest and pulled his gun. It all happened in a space of two seconds. Barely long enough for anyone to have processed what was going on.

"What the... ?" the man shouted, but was cut off by Abraham pulling the hammer back on his Colt Peacemaker.

"Slow down, partner. I would hate to make a mess of this clean floor."

The man spit out a tooth and a gob of blood across the floor. His face and beard were covered in crimson. His nose was clearly broken.

"Now any other day, I might have done you in right here for such a show of disrespect, but you've caught me in a forgiving spell. If you think you can get up and act like somebody, I'm sure my dear, dear friend, Miss Fiona, would be happy to serve you some food or spirits. Now, if you choose to cause any more of a ruckus, myself or one of my fellow peacekeepers will see that swift justice is carried out."

"You can't just kill a man. The law will—"

"It's a small town. It's a close town. The story will check out with the law whether true or not. Now, are you going to behave?" Abraham stared the man down, looking for any reason to pull the trigger.

"Fine," the man said through gritted teeth.

"Good. Let's keep it that way." Abraham lifted his foot off the man's chest, put away his sidearm, and held out his hand.

The man brushed it away and stood up on his own, wiping his bloody nose with his sleeve.

"I'll have a whiskey," he said, as he picked up his bar stool and sat back down.

Abraham holstered his pistol and turned to give Fiona a wink and a slight smile. She was visibly shaken by what had taken place, but she nodded right back at him and blew him a kiss.

"Safe travels, Abe," she said, as he turned his back and walked through the swinging doors.

Abraham stepped out onto the street. "Good meat," he said to himself.

He looked toward the general store where Jeremiah loaded up the wagon. *Well, I'll be damned*, he thought. He walked across the street to greet his friend.

"What made you change your mind?" he asked as the old outlaw threw a bag of corn muffins onto the wagon.

"You and I both know you can't make it to Georgia by yourself. You can't even make it to the Mississippi without somebody to watch your back. Besides, if you get lost out there, who am I supposed to play cards with?"

Abraham laughed. "Well, I'd say you're wrong, but we both know that the great Jeremiah Cox is never wrong."

"Don't you forget that neither," he replied. "Now I've already done most of the work, per usual. I told Smokey to watch over the place while we're gone. He knows it well enough."

"Smokey? We'll be lucky if he doesn't burn the place down. You remember what happened when he tried to make biscuits."

Jeremiah thought for a second and sighed, "Yeah. Yeah, I remember the biscuits. It's just going to have to do."

"Fair enough. You ready?"

"I'm ready as I ever expect to be. You said goodbye to Fiona?"

"I did." Abraham looked at the ground for a moment.

Jeremiah said nothing. He usually didn't in matters of the heart. Jeremiah had never loved nor been loved. The closest thing he was ever going to get was Abraham. Someone to stand back to back with when the enemy was closing in. It was a bond forged in fire and blood.

Abraham always counted himself lucky to have been in such good company in some of the toughest of times. Riding with him wasn't easy, but he was the toughest outlaw there ever was. Jeremiah could read the prairie like a book, and Abraham was sure that he would make it to Georgia with time to spare as long as they rode together.

"Let's saddle up then," Jeremiah said, while tightening the straps on the lead horses. "I'll drive the wagon, and you follow. If I feel generous we may switch off when we hit Arkansas."

"No, we won't. I know better than that," Abraham said, while climbing onto Worthless.

"No. We won't."

The two men rode out of the town they'd called home for the last ten years destined for the east coast. Neither knew what they would find when they got there, but Abraham held on to the hope that he would make it in time to see his daughter. He'd never made enough time when it mattered, but he was bound to try to fix it now.

Jeremiah would never admit it, but he was glad to be back on the trail. He had long worried that his old age would produce a uselessness he could not abide. Just being a glorified escort was enough to prove to himself there were a lot of miles left in him.

They road eastbound for days, crossing rivers, weathering storms, and passing by strangers on a well-known trail. The ride across America was not meant to be exciting, but on occasion, excitement cropped up, and it usually didn't bring good tidings.

Jeremiah and Abraham had spent the better part of their lives crisscrossing the west in search of money, women, and a peaceful life. It took a whole lot of violence to earn that peace, but they'd gotten it for the most part. Once they got the peace, Jeremiah had always felt Abraham was discontent in some way or another. He figured it was lack of action, or that he was getting bored. He never once considered it might be his conscience picking at him over the wrongs he had done. Particularly the wrong of leaving a young woman alone with his child.

The men made camp in a bit of brush that would give them a good view of what was coming and going. Jeremiah started a small fire over which to cook their beans and they looked forward to a peaceful night under the stars.

After sundown, the sound of hoof beats ended their short-lived tranquility. Jeremiah readied his pistol in the event their company was not polite.

"Howdy, gentlemen," the stranger said as he rode up to the camp. He wore a wide, brown hat with a hole in the crown, and had a weathered, but young, face.

Some cowboy, Jeremiah thought to himself.

"I'm a bit turned around I believe, and I was hopin' you could point me in the general direction of Nacogdoches."

"West," Jeremiah said curtly, pointing in the general direction.

Jeremiah noticed Abraham drop his repeater a touch as it seemed there was no threat from this man.

Jeremiah continued to let his hand rest gingerly on the butt of his sidearm.

"Thank you, good sir. Now I hate to be forward," the stranger continued, "but I am running low on rations and it is a bit late for me to be heading in any direction, much less into the great unknown that is west of here. I have only once been past the Mississippi, and I'm sorry to say this is that 'once.'"

"Traveling alone?" Abraham asked, continuing to lower his weapon.

"Yes, sir. I'm to deliver some papers in Nacogdoches to a one, Mr. Seabrook. It seems he has a loan that has gone unpaid in Montgomery."

Abraham let out a big laugh. "I'm afraid I'll have to see Hell froze over before I break bread with some lawyer."

The man's face dropped into a deadly serious gaze. "Well, I hope you packed your coat."

Jeremiah jerked as another man came up behind him in the darkness and grabbed him around the neck. He felt the cold steel of a pistol on his temple.

In the same moment, the stranger let off a shot that landed directly in Abraham's thigh. Abraham let out a scream that would likely be heard for miles.

Jeremiah watched his friend drop to the ground, grabbing at the bloody hole in his leg.

The man that had him in his grip shushed him like a crying baby. "We ain't gonna hurt you none, Mr. Cox. Just want to talk is all."

"You better hold on tight, because if you let up I'm gonna kill the both of you," Jeremiah said, his teeth gritted and bared.

The stranger hopped down from his horse and jogged over to Abraham, kicking the repeater away.

"My daddy told me you were pretty tough. He also told me you trusted too easy. Guess he was right on one account, Mr. Monroe."

The man put his foot on the bullet wound, and Abraham let out a loud yelp as he punched at the man's boot. The stranger laughed and bounced away in a half dance.

"We got him didn't we, Quint!" he shouted at his friend holding Jeremiah.

"We sure did! We sure did! Ol' Adam Pepper said they'd be out here!"

"Who is Adam Pepper?" Jeremiah asked, struggling to free himself from the man's grip.

"Adam Pepper is a partner of mine who went into a little spit of a saloon in La Flor. He was roughed up by a man that matched the description of Mr. Monroe here. Quint and I did a little investigating, and it didn't take long before we were on your trail. It must be my lucky day, seein' as I found both of you out here."

"I reckon this is what a half measure gets me. I should have killed him on the spot. Now, what's this all about?" Abraham asked, breathing heavily.

"What's it always about, Mr. Monroe?" The man said turning to face him. "It's about the money." Their captor laughed, as he walked over to their horses and cut them free, sending them running off into the darkness.

Jeremiah wrestled with Quint and looked back to make sure his friend was okay. He could tell by the firelight that the blood was saturating Abraham's pants, but there wasn't much either of them could do about it then. He was struggling to place where they would even know these men from.

"What money?" Abraham shouted.

"The money you and Mr. Cox here owe Samuel Parker for work completed. You robbed a bank in Nacogdoches twenty years ago. It was you, Jeremiah Cox, and Samuel Parker. The papers say you escaped with $25,000 in cash and bonds. Now you and I know that ain't true. You got out with $50,000, and the bank reported half so they could save face. Mr. Parker still wants his."

Jeremiah scoffed. "We didn't give Parker the money, because he didn't have the guts to tough out the whole job. The minute the bullets started flying, he jumped out the back window and ran like his boots were on fire. What he got was what he earned."

"You hush your mouth!" Quint said, pushing the pistol further into Jeremiah's temple.

"Parker's dead," Abraham said calmly. "Whatever claim he thinks he had died with him."

"Sins of the father, Mr. Monroe. My name is Elias Parker. Samuel was my daddy. Now you tell me where the money is, or I'll ride back to La Flor and tell Buford and..." Elias stopped. "What was that whore's name again, Quint?"

"Fiona," he said, dragging it out real slow.

"Right, right. I'll have to tell Buford and the lovely Miss Fiona, that you couldn't give me what I wanted. They'll be real disappointed, Abe."

Jeremiah saw Abraham's eyes grow wide. That rage he only saw every once in a while came hurling toward the surface. At least this time, they'd need it.

"It's gone, Elias. Every last cent," Abraham's voice was gravelly, like he was trying to breathe fire on his captor. "I drank it, ate it, and gambled it all. Wasting every dime of Parker's share might just be the best mistake I ever made."

While Quint's head was turned listening to Abraham burn down Elias's hopes with every word, Jeremiah took advantage of the moment. He slammed his heel down on Quint's foot, causing him to jerk just enough for Jeremiah to pull his head out from in front of the gun barrel.

Quint pulled the trigger, but the bullet missed its mark. The discharge singed Jeremiah's forehead and left his ears ringing painfully, but he was able to wrestle free.

Jeremiah pulled his gun and fired at Elias hitting him directly in the chest.

Abraham let out a warning shout and Jeremiah turned to Quint, but it was too late. The shot rang out and a searing pain moved through Jeremiah's stomach and into his chest. It felt as though hell itself had reached in and pulled at his guts.

Jeremiah heard a shot and opened his eyes to see Abraham holding his captor's pistol. Quint slumped to the ground just a few feet away. Jeremiah was breathing heavily as Abraham dragged himself over to his old friend.

"They dead, Abe?" Jeremiah said, wheezing with every word.

"They're dead," Abraham said. "We did good."

"You dead?"

"Not yet, but maybe by morning. How about you?"

"Yeah. It's been a good ride, Abe." Jeremiah swallowed deeply. "You know, I took all Parker's money. Never told you about it. Should have. You planned that job. You deserved it."

"Oh hell, Jeremiah. Don't go gettin' all sentimental on me now. It wouldn't have done me no good. I'd have found some way to end up out here with a hole in me anyway."

"You're right." Jeremiah laughed and coughed. He felt a wetness in his mouth. "You wouldn't have known what to do with it. You never had no damn imagination." Jeremiah looked at his old friend, and tears welled up in his eyes for the first time in a very long time. "You get yourself to Georgia, Abe. Somehow make up for all this."

Jeremiah closed his eyes and was gone.

The night dragged on as Abraham sat bleeding from his wound. He had seen many men suffer a wound like this one, and in the best case, they never walked again. He dragged himself over to the wagon and pulled some blankets to cover himself up for a long night. The coyotes could be heard echoing over the hills.

Their calls sounded like horrific laughter.

Abraham couldn't help but think the night itself was laughing at him for taking on a journey like this. He was even starting to laugh at himself, but he figured that was probably just the fever settling in. He closed his eyes and did his best to get some sleep.

He awoke the next morning to a strange sensation by his leg. He looked down to see a rattlesnake slithering around his calf. He did his best to stay quiet and still. If the bullet didn't take him, the snakebite certainly would. Neither sounded particularly enjoyable, but he didn't figure it was supposed to be anyway.

"Not a great way to die is it, Abe?" the snake hissed.

"I don't suppose it is, Snake. Why can you talk?" Abraham didn't bother to consider why he would answer a talking snake, but it hadn't exactly been a normal day.

"You have a fever, Abe. I'm not really talking. You're just losing it." The snake rattled and flicked his tongue, staring at Abraham. "Are you just going to sit here, or do you want to try to keep going?"

"I suppose I'll just sit here until I give out. I can't do much with this leg of mine. Can barely move it."

"Well, that's just too bad. I thought you were tough."

"Get on out of here, Snake! I have no interest in speaking with you further."

"You're just going to let Jeremiah die for you and then not keep trying? I thought you owed it to Mabel."

Abraham grimaced at the snake, fuming with anger. "Don't you dare say her name. You don't know her. You don't know what I done to her. She don't need to see me. Least of all in my condition."

"That's not what she wrote, is it? She wrote that she wanted to see you. She wanted to tell you how it is. I'll bet she wants to give you a piece of her mind for leaving her all those years."

"You hush now! I have no need for this conversation. Why do you come to torment me? Am I not already being punished enough? I'll not walk away from here alive. This is the end for me."

The snake began slithering away toward some rocks in the brush. "I suppose if you don't get moving, you'll never know what she really wanted. Nice talk, Abe. Relax a little. It's easier if you don't fight it."

Abraham looked at the bloody wound on his leg. It looked angry, and felt hot to the touch. He knew it was already infected and likely working its way into his system. He closed his eyes to get some rest, knowing he might not get to open them again.

"Well, now. I do believe I've found a helpless cowboy who looks to be in need of some aid."

Abraham heard the voice and opened his eyes slightly. The sun shone behind a silhouette of a black man in a brown felt hat. He had a slight, gray goatee, and was wearing a nice black suit.

Abraham was thirsty and could barely speak. He simply looked at the man for a moment, trying to figure out what he might even say to him.

"Don't you worry none. I have some water here, and I'll see we get you some help. You might think this is a bit crazy," he paused as he pulled his water skin from his side, "but I found you because of this horse."

Abraham looked past the man to see Worthless standing there pulling at some grass and huffing. His saddle still on. Abraham took a drink from the skin the man had offered him.

The cool water felt so refreshing on his throat. "Who are you?" he managed, his voice gruff from being so dry.

"Isaac. Isaac Folson. I was riding east on my way to Baton Rouge when I came across this horse. A saddle with no rider is no good sign, so I told him to take me where he left his rider, and here we are. Now that leg is looking rough, but we might just save it. I'll help you up onto your horse and we'll ride as far as you like. Now, who do I have the pleasure of helping today?"

"Abraham Monroe." He held out his hand allowing Isaac to help him up.

"Well, how about that?" Isaac laughed. "Now you gotta promise me, you won't sacrifice me if you want my help."

Abraham looked confused, before he realized that Isaac was referring to the Bible story that Jeremiah had once shared with him. Abraham had a son named Isaac who God ordered sacrificed to show his faith. At the last moment, God provided a ram so Abraham didn't have to go through with it. It's a story of a powerful faith or a crazed father with delusions, depending on who you asked.

"Well, it just so happens I didn't pack my pyre, so you're safe for now," he said, mustering up a chuckle.

"You're going to make it, Mr. Monroe. Let's get you up on this horse."

A few minutes of work and Abraham was sitting on top of Worthless again. This horse had proven he was anything but worthless.

"Now where were you headed before you got stuck in this mess?" Isaac asked.

"I was traveling to Georgia with my friend Jeremiah..." The thought hit him quickly. "Wait, Jeremiah, we got to bury him."

"I've already done it, Mr. Monroe. Came across the scene and took care of all those fine gentlemen before I stirred you from your slumber."

"One of those 'fine gentlemen' as you say, killed my friend. I do not care for your description."

"My apologies, Mr. Monroe. All souls look the same to me when they're lying face down in the dirt. I don't make a habit of choosing the good from the bad when I was not privy to the altercation. That is simply not my call to make."

Abraham let out a sigh as he looked over his shoulder at the lumps on the ground where his friend lay with his killer. It didn't sit well with him, but it didn't make much difference. Dead men lose their right to complain, and it doesn't do much good for the ones who keep on living either.

The new partners rode off at a decent pace. Abraham looked down at his useless, bloody leg and felt a bit of comfort that it no longer hurt as it had. The numbness had set in. He felt decent enough, but that was no good sign. He was sure the end was coming and he was just facing his second wind. With any luck, he and Isaac would find a town with a good doctor that just might save the leg, or better yet, put a bottle of whiskey in his hand and let him drift off peacefully.

They had been riding for about half an hour when Isaac turned, and said, "Mr. Monroe, I don't think much of riding without conversation. I would like to chat with you if you find it a reasonable request."

"You would join the many who might regret that decision." Abraham chuckled. "I have a tendency to let my mouth run on without me. Or so I've been told." The thought of Fiona drifted through his mind. Her standing behind the bar, smiling with those big blue eyes he so adored.

"I suppose I'll have to take my chances. What did you do before you found yourself in this predicament?"

"A little of this and a little of that, I suppose. Made a living." Abraham was hesitant to talk about the years of thieving and killing that he'd been a part of. He was not ashamed, so to speak, but it was not considered polite conversation for an introduction.

"Well, look at me. Riding along with an outlaw," Isaac said laughing and slapping his knee. "You don't have to tell me, Mr. Monroe. Won't be the first time I've heard that story. Besides, it ain't often I run across a friendly trader with a hole in him surrounded by dead men. Nah, I knew what you were when I found you lying there. I suppose we're a gang now then, aren't we?"

"Those days are behind me, Mr. Folson."

"Not that far behind you. I imagine those boys in the dirt back there would agree."

"That was how I paid for losing my temper. Not nothing to do with stealing or killing."

"The bill does come due, doesn't it?"

Abraham squinted and looked off at the empty horizon. "I suppose it does." He waited a few moments before speaking. The thud of Worthless's hooves filled the air. "Not going to make it, am I, Mr. Folson?"

Isaac looked down at Abraham's wounded leg, "No, sir. I don't believe you will. That won't stop us though, will it?"

"I done a lot of bad, Mr. Folson. An awful lot of bad."

"I'm no preacher, Mr. Monroe. If it's forgiveness you're looking for, you're riding with the wrong man. That being said, I have a couple ears and my mama always said I had a good heart for people. You go on and spill it if it needs spilled. Secrets die in the light."

"Years ago, I left a woman because I was scared. Now, I've never been scared of anything if I could punch at it or shoot it, but she tried to domesticate me. Tried to show me love and care. I've never had that, Mr. Folson. I went off for a spell to work up some money, and I came back to a daughter. Truth be told, I never saw something so beautiful and so terrifying in my life."

Abraham took a moment to wipe a small tear from his eye. "I stuck around for a while, but that life wasn't for me. I got on my horse and rode off. It didn't seem to matter how far I rode, letters would find their way. I even went by once or twice, but couldn't make myself stay. That angel just didn't deserve a daddy like me. Now here I am, at the end, and all I want is to see her one more time. Tell her about my mistakes. My regrets. See that she knows I would have given my all if I'd had any sense. She's sick in Georgia, and I was riding to meet her just to tell her all this before she passed."

"You believe that would make a difference then?" Isaac said. His joyful demeanor seemed to turn a bit more somber upon hearing Abraham's tale.

"Hell, I don't know. Reckon maybe it would be more for me than her."

"Well, maybe you ought to just tell her now then."

"What?" Abraham was confused. He looked in the distance and saw a girl in a beautiful white dress. She was waving at him. Like she was encouraging him to ride faster. "How can this be?"

"Your ride is through, Abe. Go tell her what you told me. Put a bit more good meat in your stew. She's waiting."

Abraham broke down and cried like he never had before, while Worthless carried him to his redemption.

Meet Stephen Adams

Stephen Adams is a software developer and podcaster. He spends the vast majority of his time flipping bits for his day job and yelling into a microphone for the 2Dorks family of podcasts and twitch streams. When not writing or making content on the internet, Stephen is hanging out with his unbelievably supportive family at their home in North Carolina.

The Lion of Saor Grove

Jen Bair

The boy is your son, then?" the local guide asked, nervously wiping his forehead, his hand coming away wet with beads of the condensation that drifted through the mist-filled air.

Distracted, Alexander glanced away from the looming stone walls, smeared with patchwork moss and sprouting lush green ivy like hair from the crenellations. The castle had been abandoned 1500 years before, and he was grateful for that, as it made his task easier. "Yes."

Impatient, he checked his watch, the copper bezel dull in the scattered light. It had been several minutes since they had broken through the last of the tangled vegetation, and Daniel should have made it to them by now.

Lazy child, Alexander thought. *He probably stopped to rest again.* He turned to shout back into the woods, but paused when he saw the distant movement in the trees. He waited until the figure was closer. "Hurry up, Daniel, or we'll lose the light!"

With a shake of his dark head of hair, he waited for the lanky boy to come panting through the trees, wincing with every step. Daniel was slowed by his efforts to keep the four canvas packs from sliding out of their tenuous perch atop one another on his back.

"I can help carry the bags," the guide said tentatively. It wasn't the first time he had offered.

"No!" Alexander snapped, watching the guide shrink back. The man obviously didn't have children of his own. If he did, he would know that you needed strong children if you wanted them to be strong men.

"Sorry, father," Daniel mumbled, staggering to a halt near the men. He stared down at his tennis shoes. "My ribs—"

"Should be mostly healed by now," Alexander said flatly. *Honestly,* he wondered, *would the boy ever be strong?* During their last training session, it had taken only a glancing blow for two of Daniel's ribs to crack. Two! Even his body is weak.

"Your creature is back," the guide said quietly, distracting Alexander from the thoughts that darkened his expression.

Alexander turned to watch as the Golem returned to them through the crumbling entryway of the castle, its head nearly brushing the top of the archway.

"Well, Aryeh?" he asked, impatient.

It stopped in front of him without reply. Alexander sighed. The beast wasn't very good at deciphering the finer points of language.

"Is it safe to continue?" he clarified.

"Yes, Master," the gravelly, monotone voice replied.

"Aryeh is an interesting name," the guide said, eyeing the creature nervously, his gaze following the cracks in its ancient, hardened dirt plating. It had taken quite a bit of money to overcome the guide's reservations about working with such a creature.

"It means Lion," Alexander replied, only half paying attention as he dug through the largest of the packs on Daniel's back.

The child struggled to stay upright as the tugging pulled him off balance. Finding what he wanted, Alexander closed the flap, handing one large flashlight to the guide and keeping another for himself. "My ancestors obviously named it before getting to know it," he said scathingly. "It's rather toothless, as lions go."

He gestured to his two companions and started forward. He had hired the guide from the northern outskirts of Cork after the local historical society insisted the American-born man knew every castle in Ireland, abandoned or occupied. Alexander paused by the entryway, gesturing for the guide to go first. The man gave Aryeh one last, dubious look, before hurrying into the castle.

"Saor Grove Castle was built by Lord Murchado in the fourth century," his voice gained confidence as the facts began to flow. "It was said that he built this castle for his mistress. She objected to the riches that Murchado's wife enjoyed and demanded a castle of her own. He obliged her, but only on the condition that she not make trouble by going public with their affair." They went through a short hallway that led to an open room with stairs on the far side leading up. "The castle has twelve rooms and was built by an architect whose name has been lost, though records indicate the man was well-known at the time for his works. This castle was the inspiration for the layout of four other castles here in Ireland."

As they approached the stairs leading to the second story, Alexander waved a hand at Daniel to stay put on the ground floor. The child's labored breathing was making it difficult to focus. He listened intently as the guide showed him through the castle, giving what few details he had, as well as every bit of gossip he had ever read in dusty records concerning the woman that lived there. She was childless and rumored to have taken a separate lover once Lord Murchado died.

Alexander perked up. "You say her lover was a man of God?"

The guide shrugged. "Either that or he was insane. Some stories say he was devout and that God spoke to him, for what that's worth."

"Tell me, Peter," Alexander began.

"Patrick, sir," the guide corrected.

"Yes, of course," he said, with a dismissive wave of his hand. "Tell me, where is the entrance to the basement?"

"Basement?" Patrick asked, looking bewildered.

"Mmm," Alexander confirmed. "Or cellar, perhaps."

Patrick thought for a long moment before shaking his head. "In all my research, I've never heard of such a thing connected to this castle. Besides, I've been over every inch of this area. I can assure you there is no entryway into any sort of subterranean level."

Alexander blinked, his stride faltering. It wasn't possible. There was an underground room. There had to be. He did not come all this way after all of his years of work to find nothing at all. He had paid the guide good money for nothing, it seemed.

Fuming, he followed as the guide tracked back through the castle. It had to be here. The map had been old and weathered, and the clues required deciphering, but he had done so—masterfully—and it was here that he knew he needed to be. To a subterranean level of *this* castle.

Working hard to keep his anger from boiling over, he followed the guide back into the main hall to see Daniel, sitting in the corner, his head resting against one wall, snoring lightly. Alexander stalked over and kicked him, perhaps more viciously than he would have had his mood not been so foul. Lucky for Daniel, his aim was off, and he managed to land the blow on the boy's forearm instead of his ribs.

Alexander ignored the gasp of pain, reaching down to haul the boy up by his shirt. He whipped him around, away from the cursed wall that gave him the opportunity to get comfortable enough to sleep. He noted the Golem striding towards him from across the room, and he locked eyes with the beast

"Back," he snarled.

Immediately, the Golem paused in mid-stride, his feet backpedaling until he stood against the far wall.

Aryeh's reaction was expected. It nearly always stepped forward when Alexander tried to discipline his son, and he had to, once again, show the creature who was in charge. It amazed Alexander that the beast had absolutely no ability to learn the nuances of common phrases or the appropriate actions in a given situation, but he never failed to step forward in defense of Daniel's precious health. Presumably, it acted out of some form of intuitive command to protect its future owner, for Daniel would inherit the cumbersome thing once Alexander died. *If* Alexander died. Who knew what the treasure he sought contained.

Alexander focused his attention back on the boy writhing in his hands.

"I'm sorry, Father," Daniel gasped pitifully, clutching his arm.

Alexander pulled him close until he could smell the fear seeping from his pores. "What did I tell you before we left home?" he inquired, his voice dripping venom.

"Not to rest," Daniel said, his eyes rolling wildly, seeking anything that might help him.

"Sir, it didn't cause any harm," the guide placated. "He was just taking a bit of a nap while he waited. We all want a nap sometimes," he said with strained joviality.

"Yes," Alexander said, locking eyes on the man, who stood nervously wringing his hands. "And some of us have the strength of will to resist our desires in an attempt at something greater. Some of us have learned to *apply* ourselves, to go after what is important. To be better than those around us. And we learn to be the sort of man others wish they could be, if only they had the fortitude. And we learn these things from the time we are young, or we don't learn them at all," he said pointedly, his derisive glare plainly stating which of the two options fit the guide.

"I'm sorry, Father," Daniel said, his voice now straining to stay even. "It won't happen again."

Alexander turned back to see that the boy's gaze was submissive. Alexander released him, cuffing him on the side of the head. The day was going to go very poorly for Daniel, and their next training session would be moved up. Tomorrow would work nicely. If his ribs really did still hurt, it would be a good opportunity for him to practice working through the pain.

Daniel glanced in Patrick's direction, flashing him a brief look of relief. He bent down to sling the largest pack onto his back, trying to hide his wince as he did so, careful not to anger his father further. Alexander stood, staring at the walls, trying to think as Daniel struggled to get the remaining bags in position, the guide working to covertly assist him.

"Tell me," he finally said, turning to Patrick, whose hand jerked away from the packs on Daniel's back so fast that the 'thwack' of his hand hitting his thigh echoed throughout the chamber. Alexander frowned at him for a long moment, and Daniel surreptitiously took a step away, putting distance between the two.

This placated Alexander somewhat, and he continued, "Have you ever heard reference to the 'Depths of Saor?'"

The guide gave a timid clearing of his throat, then frowned in concentration. Several long heartbeats passed and Alexander opened his mouth to snap at him when a look of surprise crossed the guide's face. "Actually, I believe I have. It was in an obscure text. A story passed down from the servants of the castle. Supposedly, the Depths referred to a cave system nearby. I had forgotten about it. As I recall, it was supposed to be dangerous. If it existed at all. Some stories are just that."

Alexander smiled a Cheshire cat grin. "That sounds *exactly* like what I'm looking for. Where would this cave system be?"

"Let me think," Patrick muttered, tapping his chin. "If I remember correctly, the story said it was near the river. The closest river is to the west of here, nearly a kilometer away, so perhaps that's what they meant."

"Then let us see what we can find," Alexander said, heading for the exit.

As he stepped outside, he glanced up at the sun. Patrick and Daniel came out behind him—the boy already breathing hard, though he had only walked a few steps. The afternoon was wearing on, and the boy would only slow them down.

"Stay here, Daniel. You are to stand there, in that spot, until I return. Do not put down the packs; do not sit; do not rest. You will learn obedience if it kills you," he said, his voice pleasant and silky.

Daniel nodded without objection, standing patiently as Alexander dug through the packs, the pressure almost toppling him over backwards.

With a water bottle in hand, Alexander closed the pack and picked up his flashlight. "West," he said, pointing expectantly at the nearby forest. Reluctantly, Patrick headed for the trees, darting a worried glance at Daniel as he passed him.

"Come, Aryeh," Alexander commanded.

They would need the Golem to explore the cave for danger. Besides, the vibrations of his feet hitting the ground as he walked did an excellent job of clearing the path of lizards and other animals, and his bulk cleared away any spiderwebs strung across their path.

At least he's good for something, Alexander thought.

It took them twenty minutes of stomping through the jungle to find the river that had dried up over the years, leaving behind a damp bed of mud. Much of the underbrush along the way was heavily interspersed with lemongrass, the long, slender leaves causing small scratches all along his forearms. It took them another two hours of searching to finally locate the cave system that was hidden in the side of a hill a third of the way back to the castle. The brush had grown up to cover most of the rocky wall, and the path dipped down into the earth so that the opening didn't protrude more than a handful of feet into the air. If they hadn't been looking so diligently, they would have missed it.

"Finally," Alexander muttered, though the sight renewed his energy. If this was the right cave, his treasure would be inside. He stood at the mouth of the opening, which was more of a hole in the ground than in a rock wall, and felt his pulse quicken. This could be it. This might finally mark the end of his long, arduous search, and his reward would be beyond imagining.

While the cave entrance was well hidden, Alexander had no delusions about how well the treasure was safeguarded. Surely there were other factors protecting such an intriguing and monumental treasure.

Greatness possessed.
Wealth of ages.
Heart's desire.
Perpetual choice.
Monument of the mind.

The translation was rough, but it convinced him that whatever lay at the end of the trail of clues, he wanted it. The phrase "Wealth of Ages" in particular, called to him. "Aryeh, go in. Check for danger in the first room, then return and report."

The Golem was gone for only a few minutes, but Alexander had to fight to keep from fidgeting. He had always been in firm control of the body language he presented to those around him, and he had to call upon that self-control to keep still.

"Amazing," the guide said. "It actually exists. Where did you hear about this place?" he asked with genuine interest. "I've only seen it mentioned in a single text."

Alexander had told him nothing about his true reasons for looking into Saor Grove. He simply stated that he wanted to see it for personal reasons, which was true, but beyond that, the guide hadn't asked, and Alexander hadn't offered.

"An old family book," he muttered vaguely, wishing the Golem would return. It was true. His father had tried to find the treasure to no avail. He hadn't even been on the right continent, spending most of his time in Africa after misconstruing one of the clues. Alexander had gone back to the very beginning of the text, poring over every word, dissecting every reference to find the treasure's true location.

"Well, it looks like we've found it," the guide said slowly. "Were you just wanting to look around?" He had hinted enough times that Alexander knew he was curious about his purposes for looking at the castle, and now the cave, but silence greeted his question and they descended into an awkward, anticipatory stillness.

After a long minute, they heard a slow, rhythmic thudding that marked the return of the Golem, his head emerging from the cave as if being birthed by the earth itself.

"Well?" Alexander asked before catching himself, rephrasing his question. "Is there anything dangerous down there?"

"No," came the dull reply. Alexander pushed past, eager to see what was beyond the entryway, but he soon noticed he was alone in the tunnel. He turned back, impatiently motioning for the others to come along.

The guide stood, hesitantly waiting for the Golem to follow its master, before bringing up the rear at a distance. Alexander's flashlight cut a path of illumination through the dank passageway, moist with gray-green lichen. At the tunnel's end was a short room that led to yet another tunnel, ten feet tall, carved into the back wall. Alexander commanded Aryeh to take the lead, and the men followed behind the Golem, who had no need of light to see through the darkness.

This new tunnel wandered, opening into chambers of various sizes before narrowing once more. Eventually, the path reached a cramped chamber with tunnels branching off into four more directions, and the trio stopped to consider their path. Alexander took up a fist-sized rock and marked the path they had come in through, gouging an aperture in the lichen at head height before taking the next tunnel over.

He led the way down the tunnel to the right, following until it ended in a two-foot drop to an open cavern nearly thirty feet wide. Dozens of small tunnels, ranging from a foot in diameter to mere inches, branched out from down inside the cavern's edge. Snakes of various sizes, shapes, and colors writhed in the patches of light produced by the flashlights, hissing in protest at the disruption of their eternal night.

"Those are snakes," Patrick spoke, his voice quavering. "They shouldn't be here. Ireland doesn't have snakes. We've never had snakes here."

"I suspect Ireland has had snakes for hundreds of years," Alexander said absently, studying the striping on one that was larger than the rest. "You simply didn't know it because they've been restricted to this area by the lemongrass planted all along the path. I suspect it completely circles the hill."

"Snakes don't like lemongrass?" Patrick asked. He stepped back into the tunnel, cringing from the sight. Alexander didn't bother answering him. "Some of those look poisonous."

"Venomous," Alexander corrected. "Though I wonder how many of them are potent enough to kill a man," he mused. Perhaps the snakes masked the treasure hidden somewhere in the pit. Regardless of exactly *how* venomous the snakes were, the sheer quantity of them left no doubt as to the fate of anyone that fell, or was pushed, into the pit.

Alexander sighed.

"Definitely the ones with the flared hoods," Patrick squeaked as one such snake received the full force of a flashlight beam, hissing angrily as its head wove a serpentine pattern through the air. "I've only ever seen them on the tele, but I'm pretty sure those are cobras there." He gulped, taking another step back into the tunnel.

Alexander spent a long minute exploring the entire pit with his flashlight. Though there were hundreds of snakes in total, they weren't thickly layered enough to truly coat the ground. Most were scattered about, though there were small piles of them here and there, slithering themselves into tangled knots. Alexander eventually decided that it was unlikely a treasure could be reliably concealed in the pit.

"We'll try the other tunnels," he announced, turning to head back the way he had come. They could always return, if none of the other paths led to his prize.

The second tunnel led down a wandering trail that narrowed bit by bit until they were wedged in tight enough that Aryeh's hunched shoulders and head scraped on three sides. Eventually, it came to a dead end. The two men turned and headed back to the main room while Aryeh slowly backed his way along until there was enough room for him to turn and walk normally.

They headed down the third tunnel, with Aryeh leading the way, when the path abruptly opened into a long, rectangular room, the walls far too flat to be natural. As they entered, the air shifted from warm to chill in the space of a single step. They ran their flashlight over the room in wonder.

The gray stone walls were pocked with holes—some big and some small—interlaced with cracks that looked remarkably similar to Aryeh's skin. Patrick glanced nervously at the creature who stood, silent and brooding and looking for all the world as if it had finally returned to its home. The ceiling towered twenty-five feet above.

"We've gone farther down than I thought," Patrick muttered, looking back through the tunnel.

Alexander's attention was focused on the floor, which was covered in stone spikes that jutted menacingly upward, each pointing at a slight angle, like jagged teeth. A raised path of obsidian, with glinting bits of mica that shone in the light of their beams, meandered amid the spiked floor to a raised hill of blood red rock at the far end of the room.

This is a fitting place to hide a treasure, he thought.

The room was moist, much like the tunnels but with the lichen strangely absent. Water dripped from several of the cracks in the walls, running in tiny streams downward, making a burbling sound as it went. Despite the water, the air smelled slightly of fumes, almost as if a gas furnace had been run recently.

"Remarkable," Alexander breathed.

Aryeh stood next to him, patiently waiting for instructions while Patrick stepped tentatively forward onto the black path, eyes scanning the room. With his very first step, he stumbled as his foot caught on a raised bit of rock. Alexander's arm shot out, grabbing him, only partly to steady him. He wasn't about to let anyone near his treasure. He would be the first to walk down the path and climb the red hill.

As his hand clamped onto the guide's shoulder, a buzzing noise zipped through the chamber from one wall to another, passing mere inches from Alexander's face, splashing him with tiny droplets of something wet and sticky. Startled, he let go of Patrick, lifting his flashlight to shine it in the direction that the buzzing had gone, but could see nothing of note.

A choking noise gurgled from Patrick's direction, and Alexander swung the flashlight around, stepping back again as shock ran through him. The guide's face was swelling, his mouth gaping open as bloody froth bubbled from his lips. Patrick's flashlight fell from limp hands, flickering once before going out. Aghast, Alexander stared, his flashlight never wavering from Patrick's face, the foam dripping from his chin.

"I knew it would be well protected! The treasure is here!" he shouted. "The Golem. I must use Aryeh."

The adrenaline heightened Alexander's vision, bringing everything into sharper detail, and he noted a small gash that ran along the side of Patrick's neck, a tiny trail of blood trickling down from it. His glee turned to disgust as Patrick's face turned gray, and then green, before he took two stumbling steps and collapsed on the floor, convulsing once before a slow exhale escaped his lips, giving him the impression of a deflating balloon. It seemed to Alexander an unpleasant way to die.

It's a good thing I have protection. Perhaps, the Lion will be useful after all.

Alexander absently reached a hand up to swipe at the stickiness on his face. His hand came away with tiny smears of blood. He turned his flashlight from the gruesome sight before him, tracing it along the stone wall to his left. If some sort of poisonous dart had zipped by, very nearly killing him in the process, he wanted to know where it came from. Thankfully, his dutiful guide had been in the way, but he could only be so lucky once. After diligently searching to no avail, he waved at Aryeh. "You go," he commanded. "Go and see what's at the far end."

Unphased, the Golem stepped forward onto the path. Nothing happened until the third step. Alexander instinctually flinched at the high-pitched whine that once again zipped across the room, too fast to follow. Another dart, this one stopping abruptly with a solid *thunk* as it hit Aryeh's shoulder, tiny blue feathers protruding from the end.

"How is it able to embed itself in stone?" Alexander muttered.

The Golem continued, another dart striking it in the side of the leg. A few steps later, a whistling sound came from somewhere above, abruptly becoming far too loud to be another dart, and a large, flat sheet of rock plummeted from the ceiling, landing on the Golem in an explosion of sound as it splintered into shards that surrounded the path in all directions. Aryeh didn't even pause in his step, plodding forward relentlessly amid the destruction.

Alexander shone his flashlight at the ceiling, noting a shadow that must hide a hole, difficult to make out from his vantage point at the room's edge. A shiver ran through him as he considered what condition he would be in if the sheet of rock had landed on him. He trained his flashlight back on the path, where the Golem continued to the end, a small volley of darts striking him in several places from his ankle to his neck just before he stepped onto the hill of red rock.

He climbed in great, lumbering strides, the grade no match for his strong legs. Soon, he was at the top and he stood, looking down at his feet.

"What is it?" Alexander hissed, as loud as he dared. His voice echoed around the room, bouncing wildly off the walls in a sinister way, like the laughter of a demented clown.

"A hole," came the deep reply, the booming echo making Alexander wince.

He studied the room, making sure that the noise hadn't caused some deadly reaction from the cavern, though any traps triggered by sound would surely have been set off by the crashing rock. He heard only silence but for his breathing and a faint bubbling still coming from Patrick as the foam forced its way out of his mouth, the poison undeterred by the man's death.

"See what's inside," Alexander whispered back across the room.

He watched as the Golem crouched, reaching its hand down to the rock, and then through the hole until its elbow was consumed. A sound, like the hissing of a great snake, bounced wildly around the room, and for a moment Alexander nearly turned to run. Whatever the noise was, it couldn't be good. Only the thought of being so close to the treasure made him hold fast.

A burst of greenish fog flew up from the hole where Aryeh sat. *Likely some form of flesh-eating poison,* Alexander thought sourly. *Or perhaps something that melted organs.* He wasn't sure which of the two he would have preferred but, whatever it was, it caused the Golem no harm.

After a few moments of fumbling around, Aryeh braced his legs and began lifting, the effort obviously more than a human would be able to manage. The Golem was incredibly strong, able to lift the back end of a van with one hand, but whatever it was lifting from the hole must have weighed significantly more, judging by the slow progress. Riveted, Alexander watched as Aryeh's elbow once again revealed itself, then the wrist, then the hand.

Slowly, a square stone pillar was pulled up from the ground, the grating of rock on rock filling the chamber with vibrations. Aryeh's hand gripped a narrowed knob of rock at the top of the pillar and heaved until three feet of it was exposed.

"Aryeh!" Alexander exclaimed, for he had seen a square of shiny, pale material glinting off his beam of light. "What is that square on the side of the pillar?" he asked eagerly, too excited to keep his voice to a whisper. *Am I seeing my treasure? Is this it?* His hands began to shake, and he had to work to focus the beam of the flashlight.

The Golem paused, twisting his torso to study the side of the post. "It is glass," he finally remarked. "Something is inside of it."

The treasure. It must be the treasure. *I've found it!* "Break the glass and retrieve it!" he shouted, no longer worried about whispering. "Bring it back to me."

Aryeh adjusted his footing and swung one large, clublike hand at the glass. The fact that it didn't break proved just how durable it was, likely over an inch in thickness and tempered. The deep reverberations hadn't yet faded when Aryeh struck a second time. Alexander waited impatiently as the third strike landed, but the sound of glass chunks finally hitting the stone floor was beautiful to his ears. This was it.

I have searched for so long, he thought, and he would have it in his hands in mere moments.

Aryeh reached in, knocking glass shards out of the way before closing his fist on something and pulling it out. He let go of the pillar and the roar of grating rock, traveling fast enough to shoot sparks up into the air, blasted through the cavern, forcing Alexander to cover his ears as best he could, while keeping hold of the bulky flashlight.

While the initial noise culminated in a boom that shook the floor, the echoes continued for nearly a full minute.

Alexander watched, hands still over his ears as the Golem picked his way back down the hill.

When the ringing finally faded from his hearing, he asked, "What is it? What did you get?"

"Paper," the Golem answered. "A small scroll." He held the tiny, rolled bit of paper over his head for Alexander to see, though the clublike fingers made it difficult to make out from across the room.

That's it? A tiny piece of paper. *What good will that do me?* Confused, he tried to come up with some great treasure that could be contained on the paper. If it was yet another clue to unravel…

Aryeh reached the bottom of the hill, and stepped onto the black path. Alexander coughed in an effort to expel an irritant he had breathed in, his throat unexpectedly dry in the moist room. It wasn't until a small tendril of gray mist snaked its way across his vision that he realized there was smoke in the air. He coughed again, bringing up his free arm to cover his nose and mouth as a slow burn began in his throat, the acrid stench settling in his lungs. He took a step back towards the tunnel.

Suddenly, the room exploded in light and heat. Stumbling back in a daze, Alexander squinted, staring in horror as the spikes that littered the floor shot fire from their tips in all directions. His mind immediately jumped to the scroll, knowing the paper would be obliterated in the heat and flames. *I can't lose it, whatever it is. I've worked too hard.* He watched as the fire reached Aryeh, so intense that he almost couldn't make out the figure steadily walking forward.

He sucked in a scalding breath through his shirtsleeve. "Protect the scroll!" he yelled hoarsely over the roar of the flames. He couldn't tell if Aryeh heard him, and he couldn't see if the Golem complied. He yelled again, the words cutting off as he hacked, trying to swallow past the sheer dryness of the air, the sudden lack of oxygen, stolen by the flames, causing his vision to swim for a moment.

The heat singed his hair, and tendrils of smoke emanated from his clothing. Thankfully, the flames were mostly pointed towards the path or the walls, the evaporating trickles of water lending the smoke a thick heaviness. The stench of burning meat filled his sinuses, and he glanced down to see flames flickering along Patrick's corpse. His stomach lurched, and he crept back into the mouth of the tunnel, the air fresh in comparison. He turned, focusing his watery eyes on the flame-filled room.

The smoke swirled, an eddy clearing his view to Aryeh for a brief moment. The Golem had stopped, its hand falling away from its mouth. It must have heard Alexander's instructions and placed the scroll where the flames couldn't reach it. He waited as the smoke congregated, once more obscuring his view. Time passed and it felt like eons to Alexander, who stood perched at the tunnel's edge, forcing his lungs to take in slow, shallow breaths through his shirt as he fought the constant and overwhelming urge to cough.

Abruptly, the fires went out, a faint hissing all that remained of the destructive force. The smoke that lingered overcame Alexander, and he gave in to his compulsion to clear his lungs, hacking hard enough that he left specks of blood on his cuff.

When he recovered, he searched the smoke, waiting for a view of Aryeh. "Why isn't it back by now?"

There! Standing on the path, seemingly no farther along than he had been several minutes ago, the Golem stood, staring into space. "Aryeh, come!" Alexander commanded, his voice hoarse. Slowly, the Golem turned its head to look at him and began walking.

Unable to stand the smoke any longer, Alexander turned, stumbling back down the tunnel, his flashlight bobbing wildly, casting erratic shadows down the length of the walls. Once he reached the cramped chamber, he gasped in the stale air, waiting for another coughing fit to pass. He passed the light over his soot-streaked clothing, noticing for the first time the patches where the cloth had been singed. He had been closer to the flames than he realized and looked a mess, but no matter. He listened as Aryeh's footsteps grew near.

"Give it to me," he demanded as Aryeh stepped from the tunnel. He held his hand out for the paper and yelped when the Golem's rocky fist smashed into it. He jerked his arm back, cradling his injured wrist, almost certain bones had been broken.

"Aryeh." He gasped with anger and disbelief.

The Golem reached out, grabbing hold of Alexander's shirt and lifting him from the ground.

"Unhand me!" Alexander demanded, frantic and outraged. Never had his servant disobeyed him. Never, in generations past, had it caused its master harm. It was specifically created to serve and protect. *It can't harm me*, his mind protested.

"You are no longer my master," it said. Gone was the dull, flat tone, replaced with an Irish accent resonating with anger. "I am Aryeh, the Lion of Saor Grove. I am my own master now."

With a casual twist of his arm, the Golem heaved Alexander into the nearest wall, where his head cracked on the uneven stone and blackness engulfed him. He wasn't sure if he lost consciousness or if the flashlight had merely gone out. He thought he heard the Golem's steps as the monster departed, but it could have just been the pounding in his head.

Alexander's thoughts cleared, though whether moments or hours later, he couldn't say. He fumbled around in the dark, the terror of being left to die in the smoky stone tomb surrounding him, making his hands tremble. He worked slowly, cradling his damaged arm as he methodically combed the chamber. He finally managed to find the flashlight a few feet within one of the many tunnels. He shook it, then gave it a few hard slaps against the side of his leg and breathed a sigh of relief when it flickered to life, the light dim, but enough to see by.

Quickly, he worked his way out of the chamber, leaving the treacherous, smoke-filled room behind. His bitterness grew as he walked, the pounding of his head keeping time with his steps. He was supposed to be rich and powerful. It was his destiny. Why else would he have inherited the map his father had left him? *Surely, God had meant for the treasure to be mine.* But now his servant was gone, his guide was dead and burned, and he was injured. Most galling of all, he didn't even know what the treasure had been.

Lost in thought, he stumbled his way out into the moonlight. He picked his way along the trail of flattened foliage he had made merely an hour before, his anger growing along with his frustration. *I will find the Golem and make it give me back the treasure*, he vowed.

When he emerged from the forest, he saw the castle, glowing in the soft moonlight. He stalked forward, noting that Daniel was nowhere to be seen. If he was laying down again, Alexander would teach him a lesson he would never forget. As infuriated as Alexander was with Aryeh, he almost hoped Daniel *was* laying down.

As he approached the castle entryway, he spotted the guide's pack on the ground. Quietly, he eased his way forward, peering through the front entryway. He could make out the remaining packs just inside the doorway, and a figure, hunched on the steps leading to the second floor.

"Daniel," Alexander rasped. His voice was rough and grating from the smoke.

The figure stood hurriedly. "You're back," Daniel said, as if surprised.

He was probably hoping for more time to rest. Perhaps a good night's sleep. The boy will never learn.

"I thought I told you there would be no rest for you," Alexander growled, stepping towards the boy, then stopped short as another figure stepped from the shadows, looming over him.

"You will not hurt him," Aryeh's familiar voice said, though the inflection brought life to the words.

"Aryeh," Alexander said, startled. *At least I won't have to go searching for it.* "There you are," he said, trying to sound confident. "Step back."

The Golem didn't move. "The scroll," it said. "The treasure. It was for me."

Taken aback, Alexander wasn't sure what to say. "What do you mean?" he finally managed.

"I have only ever known obedience. Duty. It is my purpose. My entire existence. Only, when I put the scroll in my mouth, the words were burned into every crevice, every shard of my being, like a brand that gave new birth to my very soul. The scroll had two words on it: Be Free. And I am.

"It was a scroll of freedom. A gift from Saor Grove. I serve you no longer."

The words were simple, yet they made no sense. Golems can't be free. It isn't part of their nature.

"That's ridiculous," Alexander said, as if convincing the creature would make it behave properly again.

"Every second of my life played before my eyes, each experience, each moment taking on new meaning. And I felt...*everything*. Anger at masters past for abusing their wives, for stealing from their fellow man, for kicking a street urchin. So much anger that I wanted to roar my outrage to the world. I felt joy at the birth of a new child, knowing that child had grown up to be a good master. I felt sorrow at the death of good masters and agony over the wrongs I had done and frustration at my lack of choice in doing so. But I have a choice now."

He looked down at Alexander and his eyes held a world of judgment. Alexander shrank back before that gaze. "I no longer serve you," Aryeh repeated.

"Then who *do* you serve?" He had a sneaking suspicion that he knew the answer. His eyes darted to Daniel, his tongue sliding across his cracked lips. If Aryeh's bond to Alexander was somehow broken, then the boy was next in line.

"I serve no man. I am my own master," came the reply.

Alexander gave a snort of derision. Servitude was inherent for Golems. If they didn't serve, they weren't Golems. A thought crept into Alexander's brain. *So, if it's not a Golem... what is it?*

"Oh?" he said, his voice wavering, "If you're free, then why haven't you left yet?"

The Golem's gaze moved to the boy, still hunched by the stairs.

"Because of me," Daniel said in a quiet voice. "It's why he didn't kill you when he had the chance."

The Golem crossed the room to put a hand on one lanky shoulder in a very human gesture.

Alexander's brain refused to process the statement. He turned to Daniel. "So, the child becomes the master?"

"I'm not you, Father," Daniel said softly, "I don't need a servant. I'm happy with a friend."

Meet Jen Bair

Jen Bair is an author with an MBA, living wherever the Air Force dictates. Her short story Judge Not has been published in *Cursed Collectibles: An Anthology*. She spent five years serving her country in the Army as a Korean linguist and over a decade on the front lines of parenting a family consisting of a husband, four kids, and an energetic Malinois. She fills her life with adventure, from feeding a baby tiger a bottle of milk in Thailand to trying her hand at the flying trapeze in the Bahamas. She has been skydiving off the North Shore of Hawaii and logged hundreds of ocean dives in her pursuit for the perfect date with her husband 100 feet under the ocean's surface. Her family is her life. Her writing is her passion.

A Hero's Curse

Citlalin Ossio

From birth, Chi Ran was a fearless camafol, like every Tonayol for the past one hundred years. Rarely had she been so startled that her scales faded uncontrollably, and never had she been frightened to the point of camouflaging completely into hiding against her will. Even now Chi Ran measured her opponent confidently.

The young camafol wore his emotions on every burgundy and violet scale of his body; their pale shade betrayed his fear, as much as his words attempted to prove contrary. "If you don't want your heart at the end of my sword, don't interfere." The glint of his blade reflected onto an emerald jeweled pin on the breast of his shirt, the symbol of the local bandit gang.

Now Chi Ran understood, and her gaze turned sympathetic. "What's your name?"

"That's none of your concern."

"I'll tell you mine first then. I am Chi Ran Tonayol."

This made his eyes widen, revealing light brown irises. His grip on the hilt tightened. "I'm not afraid of you."

"I'm glad. I only wish to help you."

"You'll help by leaving."

Chi Ran sighed. "You shouldn't waste your life serving cowards who hurt others."

"Señor and Señora Soler are no cowards." His right eye glanced to his side, up a brick wall.

Shoot. Chi Ran moved her left eye to scout her surroundings. She simultaneously saw the young camafol where he stood and the moving shadow of another on the roof of the building. *They're camouflaged?*

A smart camafol used their unique ability of camouflage as a strategy, while a panicked one disappeared without thinking. But camouflaging was a useless tactic when facing other camafols since it was easy for them to spot each other when invisible. Their eyes honed on the movement of surfaces that would logically remain still faster than non-camafols, like the family huddled and trembling behind Chi Ran.

She brandished two small throwing knives from her belt hook. "This knife is for you, if you don't stand down. But I promise not to kill you." She raised the second higher, and in a louder voice said, "And this one is for the camafol scampering on the roof, but unless you stop hiding, I can't guarantee I won't hit a vital organ."

The hidden camafol jumped off the roof and landed beside the first where she revealed her navy scales. Chi Ran's left eye moved forward and she blinked so only one image filled her vision.

A cocky, high-pitched laugh escaped the second camafol's lips. "I just wanted to give you a challenge. A Tonayol can certainly handle that."

"Really? I thought you just didn't want others to see you trembling in fear."

The bandit bared her teeth at the insult, and her scales deepened in color.

Chi Ran continued, "Hand over what you stole and turn your lives around before it's too late."

"Worry about your own life, because you're about to lose it."

Chi Ran remained unfazed as five more enemies, camafol and non-camafol, emerged from hiding.

The navy scaled camafol smiled wickedly. "Still think you can win against us alone?"

"Who said she's alone?"

Chi Ran smiled at the familiar voice. Her right eye moved to her side. Xol Tei, a camafol with the same green scales as her own, stood beside her. Her eye kept searching. "Elden?"

"Taking his time as usual."

"Who're you?" asked the first camafol, annoyed.

The newcomer wrapped his arm around Chi Ran's shoulders and flashed a toothy grin. "Can't you tell? I'm her older brother."

His admission made the gang falter.

Xol Tei kept one eye on them and looked down at his sister with the other. "Same deal as always?"

Chi Ran smiled. "Of course."

The siblings charged forward. Xol Tei knocked down two bandits with the rod of his spear, while Chi Ran dodged a blue ball of light that flew past her head and hit the ground with an explosion. She threw knives at the burgundy-violet camafol and a human and fought with both at once. Chi Ran kept her vision focused on one target, until she heard the charge of a magic attack. One eye looked for the source: a mage in the distance. Chi Ran kicked the camafol and tripped her second opponent with her tail before rolling forward as the blue ball hit where she had stood.

She eyed the mage and readied her blades, but the navy camafol grabbed her from behind in a choke hold. Chi Ran's eyes darted around, but not out of fear. Even as the air was leaving her lungs, she wasn't frightened. Her mind raced with solutions. She whipped her tail hard against the camafol's hip. The latter cried out and released Chi Ran, who gasped for air. Chi Ran moved to stand, but her opponent had quickly recovered and yanked her leg. The cold, rough cobblestone scraped Chi Ran's knees and she winced.

Chi Ran reached for a knife but a human guard pulled her enemy away, and bound the bandit's hands behind her back. The prisoner thrashed under his hold.

Chi Ran jumped up and smiled. "Thanks, Elden."

He returned her smile under a bushy beard and helped Xol Tei fight two enemies.

The mage and the burgundy-violet scaled camafol realized they were beaten. Chi Ran chased them, but rays of blue light shielded them, blinding her. When she recovered, the two had escaped.

Xol Tei knocked out the last enemy, and smiling, said to Elden, "Took you long enough."

Elden shrugged, and quipped back, "I prefer to save my energy until you absolutely need me. I'm extra weight until then."

The assailants cursed and hissed as they were loaded into an iron cage cart.

A guard captain saluted the trio and said, "Thanks to you, we can finally connect Soler to the recent attacks. Their gang hit every town east of Vilaru River." She smirked. "They never expected to run into a Tonayol."

Chi Ran said, "Thankfully, we were in the right place at the right time. But, unfortunately, two escaped."

The captain nodded. "We'll catch them in the end. You're going to make an excellent elite guard, Chi Ran."

"I have to pass the trials next month first."

"You're a Tonayol with a courageous spirit. The trials are just a formality for you. We're betting on who'll place second instead of first since you're participating."

Chi Ran smiled. "Thank you for your confidence, Captain."

The prisoners were hauled away and the store owners thanked the trio.

Their oldest daughter spoke in awe, "Oh wow, you're all so cool!"

"But which one of us is the coolest?" asked Xol Tei, wearing a confident, almost cocky, grin on his face.

The young child looked between the trio, then between Xol Tei and Chi Ran. She scratched her head, and pointed to the siblings. "I can't decide between you two."

"Surprise, surprise," joked Elden.

"I wanna be a guard like you and fight enemies too!"

"Your bravery is admirable," Xol Tei said. "But for now, take care of your younger siblings. As the older ones, it's our job to protect them. Got it?"

The girl smiled. "Got it!"

Fading rays of sunlight clung to the mountain tops and cloaked the town in a warm veil. A chill wind sent the last autumn leaves bouncing down the cobblestone street while an orchestra of metal shop signs echoed in the air.

Xol Tei slung his arm around Elden's shoulders. "Since you were late and got the lowest count, you're paying for drinks."

"Ah, but added with Chi Ran's score, we beat you."

Chi Ran laughed. "Sounds good to me."

Xol Tei frowned. "Why are you siding with him? I'm your older brother."

"And as you said earlier, it's your job to take care of us younger ones, which includes buying us drinks." She and Elden high-fived.

He sighed, exasperated, but still agreed. "Fine, let's go."

Chi Ran took only two steps when she was enveloped in swirling yellow lights. The same glowing orbs surrounded her brother, then the world faded together and exploded in a flash of light.

Chi Ran appeared in a lavish white and gold hall, lined with tall marble columns and arched windows. Her brother and father had been transported beside her, mirroring her bewildered expression. Her eyes fell on a young human mage, barely twenty, she guessed, wearing a bright smile, seated in an ornate chair like a throne. In his hand, he spun a short white staff with a topaz orb at the top.

Chi Ran's father asked, "What's going on? Why are we here?"

"Who are you?" asked Xol Tei.

"Bienvenidos, my name is Mikel," he began. "I'm sorry to disrupt your evening, but time is up on your contract. I'm afraid I couldn't wait any longer to summon you."

Chi Ran asked, "What are you talking about? What contract?"

The mage blinked, confused. "The deal Zan Iro Tonayol forged with Calia Grillonova, of course."

Chi Ran gasped.

Her father yelled, "That's ridiculous! My abuelo was a devout camafol. He'd never make any deal with a mage who practiced dark magic."

Mikel was taken aback. "You really don't know he made a deal with her to gain his courage?"

"His courage? What do you mean?" asked Xol Tei.

The mage looked away and rubbed his neck. He took a scroll from a table next to him and rose from his chair. Sighing, he handed the contract to Chi Ran's father. Everyone huddled around the parchment. "Though you don't believe me, Zan Iro did ask Calia for help." He paced in front of them as he continued, "As you see, she granted him and his descendants one hundred years of fearless courage in exchange for two drops of his blood. She agreed to make his courage permanent in return for an ixe stone. Without it, after one hundred years, his living descendants would lose their bravery and be cursed to live in crippling fear."

"Wha—" Chi Ran couldn't look away from her great-grandfather's signature. Faded black ink told the undeniable truth, as much as she wished to wake from this nightmare.

Mikel stopped pacing and faced them. Pity veiled his expression. "So, do you have an ixe?"

Chi Ran looked at her father and brother. They shook their heads.

Mikel sighed. "Then I'm sorry, but I have no choice. A deal's a deal." He raised his staff.

"Wait—"

Pain ripped through Chi Ran's chest as if her ribs crushed into her lungs, and she collapsed onto the white marble floor. The sting left as suddenly as it had come. Chi Ran inhaled sharply as her lungs filled with air again. Her eyes searched the room; her family huffed for air beside her, while the mage studied them. His cold blue eyes caused a foreign uneasiness to fill her body. She rose and instinctively stepped closer to her family.

She asked through deep breaths, "What did you do?"

"I stripped your courage from you."

Her heart raced, and she realized the bubbling in her stomach was fear.

"Wait, wait," faltered her father. "This can't be right. It's a lie." Chi Ran heard an unfamiliar wavering in his voice.

Mikel pointed his staff at him and, to Chi Ran's surprise, her father flinched, and his scales turned a pale green. "It's not a lie. You're afraid."

"But why should we suffer?" protested Xol Tei. "We didn't make this deal."

Mikel sighed. "I understand how you feel. Calia struck the deals. As her great-grandson, I'm the one who has to clean up her mess. My family doesn't even practice dark magic anymore."

"Isn't there a way to undo it?" asked Chi Ran.

"Only the mage who placed the curse can freely break it." He paused. "The only way to regain your courage now is to retrieve an ixe stone. But even when you were fearless—"

"We'll bring it to you," answered Chi Ran, without a second thought.

Mikel's eyes widened. "It's not an easy journey. It's only mined in the extreme frigid summit of Mount Nevos. Even if you make it past the wild predators and monsters that roam the mountains, you'll likely freeze to death."

"Don't, mijita," pleaded Chi Ran's father.

She gulped audibly. "We don't have another choice, Papi."

"Then I'll go too—"

"No, stay with Mami," Xol Tei said. "Chi Ran and I will find it." He nodded to his sister, and she looked at Mikel.

"Erm, if you're really sure, then recite this spell to teleport here once you find it, and your curse will be broken." He handed her a small scroll. "I wish you a safe journey."

He raised his staff and, for the second time, yellow swirls of light enveloped Chi Ran, and she and her family disappeared.

That night Chi Ran was plagued with worries. *What if we get hurt? What if we die? Maybe we should just forget it.* She gasped and bolted up from the cowardly thought.

"No, we're Tonayols," she said aloud. "We can do this."

The darkness of the night sent a chill down her spine, but she ignored it and recited internally, *I'm not afraid.*

Chi Ran, Xol Tei, and Elden, the only person they trusted to reveal the truth to, walked along a dirt road.

Chi Ran kicked a rock into a patch of swaying wildflowers, startling a grazing blue jay into flight. She and Xol Tei jumped at the sudden movement.

He clicked his tongue at her.

"Sorry." She smiled sheepishly.

When a horse drawn cart approached, Chi Ran stepped off the road. She looked back at the calm horse and sighed. It had been a week since her courage was ripped from her. Two days into their journey, Chi Ran's horse was startled and nearly threw her off. Though uninjured, she had been scared to her core and now feared her trusted mount and all horses. Since then, the trio had to make the remainder of the trip on foot.

"Do you think God forgave bisabuelo for making a deal with a dark mage?" Chi Ran asked, worried for the eternal soul of her great-grandfather.

Xol Tei thought. "If bisabuelo was truly sorry, I'm sure God did...I hope."

Elden said, "It's hard to imagine Don Zan Iro as anything but a fearless hero. Just in the week before his death, he led an attack on an outlaw hideout, captured a robber that crossed his path, and raised money to expand the clinic." He paused. "I wonder why he didn't warn you of the curse."

Chi Ran answered, "I expect he would've told us eventually if he hadn't died suddenly." Zan Iro had died twelve years earlier rescuing townspeople from a burning inn when the building collapsed, burying him and others. Even his death had been heroic.

"I'm sure he was just waiting for the right time to tell us," Chi Ran continued. "It couldn't have been easy to admit what he did."

If they didn't succeed, it wouldn't be any easier for her family to admit the truth: the town heroes were nothing but frauds.

She gasped internally. *Would they hate us?* If she and Xol Tei failed, her family would be ruined. *Will we have to leave home?* Her heartbeat quickened. *Why did you do it, bisabuelo? Were you so fearful before you made the deal that you abandoned your principles for bravery?*

A raindrop hit Chi Ran's head, then another. She looked up, and calm blue skies had given way to dark clouds. A sharp wind picked up and light drops coated her paled scales and clothes. "This rain came out of nowhere."

"Maybe we should find somewhere to wait out the storm," suggested Elden.

Xol Tei looked around the open field dotted with a few, dry, leafless trees. "We're in the middle of a field. Where are we going to find shelter?" He shook his head. "It's just a drizzle; we can keep going."

The wind howled around them.

Elden looked doubtfully at his friends. "You sure you two don't want to wait?"

Xol Tei said, offended, "We may not be as brave as before, but we can still handle some rain."

Chi Ran agreed. "It's fine so long as there's no," a rumble of thunder shook the ground, "lightning," she squeaked. Light flashed on the horizon and she huddled close to her companions.

Elden asked, "Still want to keep going?"

"Okay." Xol Tei gulped audibly. "Let's take shelter."

In the haze of rainfall, Chi Ran squinted and spotted a cave. Lightning struck the ground mere feet from Xol Tei, and his scales turned a faded green before he released a panicked scream. He raced toward safety, and Chi Ran and Elden followed. As lightning chased her heels and tail, Chi Ran tripped over her own feet and tumbled down an incline.

Fear pulsed through her body and, without thinking, she hid in plain sight. *What am I doing? Get up! Get up!* she willed, but her body didn't listen. Only when a bolt hit a boulder beside her and sent rubble flying was she released from her trance. She stopped camouflaging, jumped to her feet, and ran up the hill as Elden raced toward her.

They reached the cave where Xol Tei shivered in darkness. Elden switched on a lightning lantern, and the bouncing lights revealed faded scales on Chi Ran's trembling hands.

Elden asked, "Are you okay?"

She inhaled to steady her voice. "Yes." *Did he see what I did?* she wondered. He didn't question her, maybe he hadn't. Or maybe he was ignoring it to save her pride. "Did you see me..."

The sky roared and she and her brother jumped. The handle of the lantern clinked rapidly against the glass globe.

When the shaking passed, Elden asked her, "Did I see what?"

"Nothing." Bitter wind blew in the cave and chilled her bones, reminding her of her soaked clothes. The blankets in her leather bag were thankfully dry and provided a warm comfort.

That wasn't me. It's this curse. She fingered the small silver crucifix and Miraculous Medal around her neck. *God, please help me.*

The smell of damp earth filled Chi Ran's lungs as she hesitantly threw a knife into a tree trunk, showering the ground with drops of dew. Practicing usually cleared her mind, but the glint of her blades and an image of sliced fingers made her queasy. Her knife landed way off the notch made from a previous throw. She sighed, gave up, and took a seat beside Elden, who studied the map. He offered an orange slice. She accepted, and citrus sweetness exploded in her mouth.

Her scales had returned to their usual shade, but the memory of her unwarranted camouflaging troubled her. If lightning made her hide, what would happen when her allies needed her?

A startled yell and the snaps of twigs and brush made her choke on her orange. She jumped up and held her breathe, as her eyes surveyed the woods.

Xol Tei bolted through the trees, tripping over his feet as he ran.

"What's wrong?" asked Elden.

"There's a swarm of pavirils." Panic rang off every word.

Chi Ran and Elden faced the trees and readied their weapons to attack the paralyzing venom spitting, shadowless creatures. Floating lights hovered before them.

She moved to attack, but Elden stopped her. "Wait. They're just forest fairies."

"What?" Xol Tei asked, aghast.

Chi Ran inched closer and saw their shadows, a definitive sign they were harmless. She nodded and Xol Tei's face darkened. Even if it had been pavirils, a brave guard would never run from the easy to beat forest fairy imposters, but the truth stung more.

Chi Ran comforted him. "It's okay, manito."

His scales turned a deep green. "What part of an elite guard running from puny pavirils, or worse forest fairies, is okay?"

His curt tone made Chi Ran flinch.

He noticed and sighed regretfully. "I'm sorry."

"It's okay," she answered. "I know."

He holstered his spear. Fairies of various colors bobbed past him and fed on the nectar of nearby camellia shrubs. "I'm glad the captain can't see how weak I've become."

"You're not weak," Elden countered. "You're just scared, like everyone else. I was afraid of being struck by lightning as much as you two. And you know I can't climb tall trees."

"But we're Tonayols," said Xol Tei. "We don't get scared. We scare others. We protect and defend. We're heroes."

Chi Ran nodded. "Our scales never turned pale before and now..." she trailed. Now, they were ordinary camafols.

"Don't lose hope," encouraged Elden. "You could've stayed safe and let things be after your courage was taken, but you chose to do something. Besides, you've got me. I may not make up for what you've lost but I'll always support you."

The words of their lifelong friend, practically their brother, eased Chi Ran's frantic heart.

Xol Tei voiced her gratitude, "Thanks Elden. And you're right. This is only temporary. If anyone can succeed, it's us." He smiled, rejuvenated with hope. "Let's go."

They traveled through the night to regain the time lost from the storm. The bright moon formed sharp shadows in the woods around them and Chi Ran swore she saw menacing faces in the dense brush; glowing eyes and hungry teeth with vicious claws. The frigid wind carried howls and moans that swirled among canopies. Chi Ran clutched her Miraculous Medal and crucifix so tight she was sure they left an impression in her skin.

They rounded a hill, and, at last, the moon shone on snowy peaks. Chi Ran's eyes trailed the jagged skyline to the tallest point, Mount Nevos. It was beautiful and intimidating all at once, and she thanked God for bringing them safely. But gratitude was soon replaced by the doubt that now lingered close.

Xol Tei evidently shared her worries. "We have to climb all the way up there?"

Elden said, "Don't think about it yet. We'll take it one step at a time." He gestured forward. "Let's cross the bridge for starters."

At the foot of the mountains lied the town of Neviper, named after Mount Nevos. Faintly glowing, pastel blue wood trees with branches full of autumn gold needles lined the curving road to the main entrance. The temperature dropped as the trio neared and soon Chi Ran could see her own breath. She touched the trunk of the first tree she crossed. It was like touching ice. Even the deceivingly warm colored needles were cool to the touch. More icy spruces dotted the town and a forest of the fantastical plants sprawled out toward the mountain range.

They rented a room at an inn and filled their starving bellies with the popular meal of an icy town: hot, spicy broth and roasted fish.

After washing, Chi Ran plopped onto the bed. Living in fear made her exhausted, and the soft caress of the sheets comforted her into a deep sleep.

But nightmares plagued her rest, and she startled awake in a cold sweat multiple times. Once, she heard Xol Tei whine softly, then shift, his mattress creaking, and she wondered if he shared her terrifying dreams.

Chi Ran strained her neck toward the clouds. The height of the mountain shook her resolve, so she focused on counting her steps, but lost count when a strong frigid wind hit her hard. She pulled her coat closer. The coat vendor had clearly overcharged for the tailored garment—guaranteed to withstand the coldest freezes—and when Chi Ran tried to reason, he threw a fit. Lacking a fighting spirit, Chi Ran caved. Now she huffed, frustrated with herself, as another cold blast of air seeped through the fur and made her shiver.

The trio approached the road that slithered up the mountain but Neviper guards stopped them.

"I'm sorry," said the captain. "But there was an avalanche last night, and the road is blocked. You'll have to take the southern road through the canyon pass." He pointed to a curving road. "Just follow the marked path."

Sharp gusts whistled in the canyon, and snow crunched under Chi Ran's boots as she walked. When they turned onto the marked path a woman sitting by a fire, called to them, "Hey there. Mind pointing me towards the town of Neviper?"

Elden answered, "Follow this path to the road, and it'll lead you there."

She brushed away a lock of her short brown hair and smiled. "I'm so fortunate to have met such kind travelers. Now," she unsheathed a long blade, "hand over your belongings."

"Wha..." Chi Ran faltered back.

Elden wielded his sword.

"Get down!" yelled Xol Tei. He pulled his sister to the ground as a strong gust of wind hit the trees behind them, burying them under heavy snow.

Sunlight blinded Chi Ran when she dug herself out. Her eyes spun frantically to grasp reality, but it only made her dizziness worse. She shut her eyes again. When she opened them, the woman who lured them charged toward her with her sword, her eyes mirroring its vicious glint.

Chi Ran scrambled back and froze when her back collided with a rock. The woman yelled as she lunged her sword. Chi Ran shut her eyes tight and camouflaged into hiding and prayed for God's forgiveness. The clash of steel and yells echoed in the canyon. She didn't know how long she trembled helplessly.

Then Xol Tei's voice called her, "Chi Ran. We're safe now. Open your eyes."

She didn't.

"Chi Ran!" His yell made her jump and turn visible.

Her breath was uneven as she asked, "What happened?"

Their attackers were gone, and the Neviper soldiers that had stopped them earlier loaded Elden onto a moose-drawn cart. He groaned and clutched at his side. Blood oozed slowly between his fingers.

"Elden!" She raced to his side.

"It's just a scratch..." He winced.

"How—"

"He saved you," answered Xol Tei.

Guilt crushed her heart. "I'm sorry. I-I'm so sorry."

A guard urged her and Xol Tei to board the cart. "Please, miss, sir, we must hurry and take him to the hospital."

The whole bumpy ride, Chi Ran sobbed. She was afraid. Worse, she was ashamed.

Elden was treated in Neviper, and Chi Ran rarely left his side. Partly to look after him, another because she was afraid to move. Her brother also remained close.

One day, Chi Ran asked him, "Do you think Papi's still brave? Or do you think he's lost his nerve like us?"

Xol Tei didn't answer, and his silence annoyed her.

"What were you doing? You said as the oldest it was your duty to protect us. Where were you?" She regretted the words as soon as they escaped her lips, but it was too late.

Her brother finally looked at her. His sorrowful eyes were like her own sharp knives stabbing her heart. Without speaking, he left.

Chi Ran bit her lip and buried her face in her hands. She hadn't meant to hurt him. She just wanted him to console her, as he always had. But his silence had irritated and frightened her. "I'm horrible."

Xol Tei never asked for an apology, and Chi Ran didn't offer one.

A few days later, Elden was almost fully recovered.

"Don't push yourself," said Chi Ran, supporting his arm as he moved.

"I'm fine now," he insisted. "I think tomorrow we can head up the mountain."

"Don't worry about that. Rest until you're fully healed."

"No, we have to keep moving before the temperature drops too low, and it's harder to reach the summit."

Chi Ran looked away. Truthfully, her resolve was crushed, and she dreaded going back.

"We're not going."

Chi Ran and Elden turned with widened eyes towards Xol Tei.

Elden asked, "What do you mean?"

"Once you're healed, we're going home."

She was ashamed to admit it, but Chi Ran was relieved.

"Why?" asked Elden. "We're so close."

"It's too dangerous," said Xol Tei.

Elden asked Chi Ran, "You can't agree with him?"

She nodded. "I do."

"Wha..." Elden winced and grabbed at his injury. "You're giving up?"

The admission pained her. "I don't want to give up. I don't want to live in fear anymore, but I can't go further."

"Why?"

"I froze. Worse. I hid like a coward, and you were hurt because of me."

"We were ambushed with nowhere to run. We were all scared," said Elden.

"That didn't stop you from saving me."

"You would've done the same for me."

"But I didn't. I can't anymore. Last week, I would've given my life for you. For anyone. But not now."

"She's right," said Xol Tei. "I should've protected you both, but I failed. You were injured saving Chi Ran when, even as her older brother, I couldn't."

Her heart stung. "Manito, I didn't mean—"

"No, even before you said it, it was all I could think." He paused. "I won't put us at risk when I can't protect you or anyone anymore."

Elden frowned. "You're cursed. That's not really who you two are."

"But it is," said Chi Ran. "It is now, and it always was. We were never truly brave. No one with Tonayol blood. Our reputation, our honor, everything we're known for was a lie. We were heroes, but if bisabuelo hadn't made that deal, we'd be nobodies."

Elden opened his mouth to speak when panicked screams sounded outside. From the window, they saw bandits like the ones that ambushed them, pillaging and attacking the town square.

"We have to help them," said Elden.

Xol Tei and Chi Ran exchanged hesitant looks. Chi Ran's heart urged her to fight, but her feet remained firmly planted on the wooden flooring.

She whispered, "We can't."

For the first time, Elden stared at them with disappointment. Xol Tei clenched his fists and lowered his head in shame.

Elden grabbed his sword, but Chi Ran stopped him. "You're injured; you can't."

"Well, you two won't, will you?" he reproached, frowning.

"That's not fair."

His gaze softened. He holstered his weapon, and said, "I told you, everyone's scared. Even heroes. That's why they're heroes."

He left them alone.

Chi Ran looked at her crucifix and Miraculous Medal. "We've been so focused on what we lost, but, really, haven't we gained something? A chance to be true heroes? No magic, just God's grace? Bisabuelo lost all hope and took the easy road. Are we going to do that too?"

Xol Tei closed his eyes until he grabbed his spear and smiled weakly. "Same deal as always?"

Chi Ran nodded. "Mm."

Elden parried a bandit's attack on a helpless family and disarmed her before delivering a fatal blow. "Get to safety," he ordered.

"Watch out!" yelled a child.

Elden turned, and an axe wielding enemy lunged at him, but a knife hit the assailant's heart. His weapon clattered against the stone street as he fell to the ground.

Elden turned back and smiled. "Took you long enough."

Chi Ran tripped an enemy with her tail. "We were saving our energy until you absolutely needed us."

Xol Tei stabbed another with his spear. "We're extra weight until then."

Elden laughed at the familiar words.

While they led the family to a guarded building, Chi Ran split her vision; her companions turned a corner ahead, but behind her, a small group of assailants overpowered some guards. As she raced over to help them, one soldier collapsed on the ground, dead, killed by a woman with short dark brown hair and matching colored vicious eyes.

Chi Ran froze in place as the bandit she hid from in the canyon smiled at her wickedly. "Look who it is. The scared little camafol who went into hiding."

"I-I..." Chi Ran's resolve was shaken as the memory flooded her mind.

The assailant charged at Chi Ran, and she dodged her. Then, Chi Ran turned and threw a knife but missed.

The woman lunged again and Chi Ran jumped back and instinctively camouflaged, causing the former to yell mockingly, "Hiding again?" She searched for Chi Ran. "Why not fight in the open instead of camouflaging like a coward?"

Chi Ran hid behind a wall, listening to her taunting.

A young soldier attacked the woman, but she parried and stabbed him. He fell to his knees, coughing up blood. He was dying and still no fear veiled his expression as he glared at his attacker.

The courageous fire that burned in his eyes lit a spark in Chi Ran's heart. Hero or coward, she was going to die, and heaven didn't welcome cowards.

The woman raised her sword to deliver the fatal blow, but Chi Ran kicked her down and stood between her and the wounded man.

The woman jumped up and smirked. She spit blood and mocked, "Done hiding?"

Chi Ran answered, "I'm done running."

She camouflaged again and attacked her opponent while she was off guard, disarming her then tripping her and knocking her unconscious.

The surviving attackers were chased away or captured, and Nevipei was saved. Chi Ran brought the young man she rescued to the hospital and found Xol Tei and Elden transporting more wounded. Relieved smiles flashed across their faces when they saw her.

Xol Tei hugged her. "Are you hurt?"

She smiled. "No."

The town leader, wearing a few scars of her own, checked in with the injured. Across the hall, Chi Ran saw her hug the soldier she protected. They talked and his eyes searched the room and landed on her. He smiled and gestured her way. Her eyes widened and she rose from the floor as the town leader approached.

The elderly woman's wrinkles deepened, as she smiled. "You saved my grandson." She held Chi Ran's hands. "Thank you."

She was taken aback. "I-I should thank him. His courage inspired me."

The town leader looked gratefully at Chi Ran's companions. "You all helped us. Thank you. If there's any way I can repay you."

Xol Tei held up his hand. "No, you don't owe us anything. Your people saved us from those bandits first."

She insisted. "There must be something I..." Her wise face lit up. "I have it." She invited them to her manor and gave Chi Ran a piece of silver ice that shimmered like crystal under light. It was as cold as snow but didn't melt in Chi Ran's warm hands. "This is an ixe stone, and my gift to you for saving my grandson and defending the town."

"Wait, this is an ixe?" Elden pointed, dumbfounded.

"Yes. They're difficult to mine, so it'll fetch a high price."

Xol Tei laughed, the first Chi Ran had heard in days. "We traveled all this way for this stone, but we no longer need it. We came to retrieve our courage" —he lightly slapped Elden's back— "and we have."

The town leader cocked her head. "Retrieve your courage?"

Xol Tei recounted the truth of the curse and the mission Mikel had given them.

Her eyes widened, alarmed, at the mage's name. "Mikel? But he *is* a dark mage."

"What?" they asked in unison.

"He came here years ago in search of an ixe but was unsuccessful. Since then, he sends others, desperate like you, to find one for him, but it's almost impossible. Most give up, and those that dare venture to Mount Nevo's summit without experience perish on the freezing cliffs."

Chi Ran's heart sank at the realization that they were fooled and had nearly gone to their deaths. Then, her thoughts turned to those who had already lost their lives. The discouraged and frightened people, like her and Xol Tei, Mikel had preyed on. And would continue to hurt if he wasn't stopped.

"We have to arrest him," she said aloud.

"We will," agreed Xol Tei.

Elden smiled. "Count me in."

They thanked the town leader, then gathered their belongings. Chi Ran recited the teleportation spell and glowing orbs circled them. The world blurred, then burst with light.

Mikel slouched in his chair, yawning. He sat up straight as Chi Ran, Xol Tei, and Elden appeared in his pseudo-throne room.

Chi Ran's eyes moved separately as they adjusted and blinked into one vision of amused Mikel.

"Buenos dias," he welcomed. "What brings you here? Have you given up your search for an ixe? I warned you it wouldn't be easy."

Xol Tei answered, "It wasn't, but with God's help we found it."

Mikel's eyes widened as Chi Ran brandished the stone from her satchel. He blinked, unbelieving, then guffawed. "No one I've sent has ever succeeded, and I only asked you on a whim, but you actually found it!" His laughter echoed in the lavish hall.

Chi Ran said, "We also learned you are in fact a dark mage."

Mikel shrugged. "Guilty."

Xol Tei hissed, his scales darkening into a deep green. "You lied. You do practice dark magic."

Mikel waved his finger. "I didn't lie. I said my family no longer practiced dark magic, which is true. I'm the only one who followed in Calia's footsteps. From the way you reacted when you learned the truth, I knew you'd never agree to find the stone or make a deal if you suspected I did."

Chi Ran's scales matched her brother's. "So instead, you fooled us. You gave us hope of retrieving our courage, but it was only to get your hands on this gem."

Mikel answered, nonchalantly, "Mm." Then he smiled thoughtfully. "It must've been unbearable living with newfound fear. I wonder, how many times did you hide?"

His mocking grin made Chi Ran burn with rage and sorrow.

"Perhaps after everything, your principles have softened? I'll be happy to forge a contract to grant you courage in exchange for the ixe."

Elden said, "Xol Tei and Chi Ran are already brave, and they're stronger than this curse."

"Still," Mikel insisted. "Wouldn't it be easier to just strike a new deal? Won't your reputation be ruined otherwise?" He stretched out his hand. "Just hand over the ixe, and everything will return to normal."

Chi Ran considered it. Zan Iro had done it, why couldn't she? Afterall, she didn't want it for praise and admiration, but to help others. It was a noble reason, wasn't it? She couldn't be the hero people expected if she was...

Everyone's afraid, even heroes. She glanced at Elden and he gave her an encouraging smile that washed away her doubts.

She met Mikel's cold blue eyes. "No, only a coward runs from their problems." She looked to Xol Tei and he nodded. "We may not have made this deal, but if this curse is our cross to carry, then God will give us the strength to bear it."

Grinning, Xol Tei said, "Besides, striking a deal first would make arresting you afterward awkward."

Mikel smirked. "Very well.

He raised his hand and unleashed a strong wind, but they all dodged. Then he charged up his magic, and both siblings camouflaged, while Elden kept Mikel busy.

Xol Tei attacked Mikel from behind, but the latter backflipped behind Xol Tei and threw him across the room. Elden lunged next but was hit by a ball of magic.

Chi Ran gulped down the fear raging in her heart and threw a fan of knives at Mikel. One sliced his arm and he winced. He pointed his staff in her direction and blasted her with a powerful attack. Her back slammed hard against a marble column and caused her to stop camouflaging.

The ixe fell out of her satchel, and she watched, horrified, as Mikel picked it up and replaced the topaz stone on his staff with the silver gem. He turned it, admiring its glimmer.

Chi Ran groaned as she sat up. Her eyes locked with Xol Tei's momentarily, before Mikel approached her and she scrambled back.

The mage pointed his staff at her, and she begged, "Wait, please. Please, don't kill me. I don't want to die. I-I'll do anything; just please don't hurt me."

Mikel scoffed. "You spoke so righteously, but look at you now. Afraid and begging for my mercy. You're a coward. You always were, just like your bisa—"

Xol Tei hit Mikel from behind, and with her tail Chi Ran knocked his staff away. It skidded across the tile floor into Elden's waiting hand. Xol Tei bound Mikel's hands.

He glared at Chi Ran. "This doesn't change anything. You will always be afraid, and you will still die cowards."

"We may be afraid, but we are not cowards."

Chi Ran dismounted her black speckled gelding and ran her fingers through his mane. He nickered happily. It had been two months since Mikel's arrest. As she suspected, the town had been devastated to learn the truth of their beloved heroes, but most still supported them. And though it was difficult to adjust to their new normal Chi Ran and her family didn't give up. She recovered from her fear of horses and passed the elite guard trials; victories she wouldn't have given a second thought to before, but now celebrated with gratitude.

Chi Ran's tan hooded cloak rustled as she entered the chapel. Incense clung to the stone walls and filled her lungs, as she lit a prayer intercession candle and kneeled. She spent more time praying, asking for fortitude when she felt discouraged. Warm candlelight bounced off the marble saints Chi Ran hadn't given importance before, but that now inspired her. Like her, they were brave but they weren't fearless. They were afraid but they weren't cowards. Between their fear and courage was their hope and humility, and she admired their heroic hearts.

Meet Citlalin Ossio

Citlalin Ossio is a hungry panda, whose hours of playing video games, especially Legend of Zelda, and watching anime and Korean dramas (which she justifies as "storytelling research") fueled her desire to write fantasies and romantic comedies. Her short stories are featured in two anthologies, *Eclectically Magical* and *Legion of Dorks Presents: Laundered – An Anthology of Monster Messes*. She lives in Houston, Texas and loves eating, being with her family, and creating art. Once in a blue moon she takes a break from raising her panda army to post on Twitter and Instagram @CitlalinOssio.

The Fate of the Prince

Chisto Healy

Queen Azallan stood at the bow of the ship holding her baby to her bosom. The breeze was gentle, and she could smell the salt of the ocean. If they weren't in a life or death situation, she would find it pleasant, even enjoyable. She nodded as Liam, the head of her guard, approached.

"The waters are clear my lady," he said to her. "Still no sign of the Vorcan raiders."

Azallan nodded again. "Good," she said. "Stay vigilant. We must get the prince back to the kingdom safely. Now that his father has been struck down, he is the only future we have. How do we fare on rations?"

"I understand the importance, my queen. We have enough for three or four more days. I believe we'll be able to make it home without having to replenish."

"That is good news, Liam. The waters may be calm now, but we cannot afford any delays. I should have birthed my son in my own chambers instead of in that coward's den." She spat the final words with disgust. Her baby stirred in her arms, and she held him closer, soothing him and stroking his thin hair. "Strength is in heart, not in the size of your army or the wealth of your kingdom. I went looking for allies, and those weak-hearted Clendines may have doomed us all." She punctuated her words with a longing glance at her sleeping child's innocent pink-cheeked face.

Liam nodded. "My lady, if I may…he looks just like you."

Azallan's face softened. He did bear a great resemblance to her. He had his father's eyes—a king's eyes—but, for the most part, he was the spitting image of his mother, and it warmed her heart. Then the thought of him never making it to rule turned it to ice.

The day went on without sight or sign of the enemy that had been pursuing them since the birth of her son. She had known she was in danger when Derrin chose to be born in a kingdom not his own. She had been visiting the Clendines to discuss an alliance, to protect the future of Avaron. Little did she know, it was a fool's errand and a gesture of futility.

Her husband, Barrimon, perished in a battle with Lord Vorcan's dark army, and all the diplomacy and negotiations were left to her in her most pregnant state. She couldn't shirk the political responsibilities, not with Derrin on the way. Her army was weak without their king, despite the fact that their king was only strong due to the woman at his side and in his ear. The people never saw that side. A king was a spokesperson. Image was important, until he was gone.

In order to keep Derrin safe long enough for him to claim his throne, she needed resources. She needed allies, soldiers, weapons, ships. She had the money and the clout and the ability to offer Derrin's hand in marriage once he was old enough to marry. It should have been more than enough to establish fortitude.

The Clendines were the best bet for a starting place. They were only a few days out from their home kingdom of Avaron, and they had an army big enough to conquer the world if they deemed it necessary. The negotiations went well until the baby came screaming into the world right there in Preacher Mallody's meeting room, in the heart of the Clendine Castle.

Somebody in the kingdom must have been a spy. The dark army had many. It was such that ended the life of the king of Avaron. Now, they witnessed the birth of his only son and had gotten word to Lord

Vorcan. Azallan was recovering from the sudden labor and birth that had ambushed her in the Clendine council chamber, when the raiders arrived to claim the boy. She was weak and in pain and furious. Derrin had lived mere moments, and already those demons aimed to take him from her. She demanded Preacher Mallody assemble his forces and protect the child. The coward declined.

Even with their enormous military, the Clendines were afraid of the dark army. Preacher cowered at the mention of Lord Vorcan's name. He shook his head and backed away from her as if she were a poison. She hadn't expected that. It showed her the futility in journeying there. All she did was put herself, her baby, and the future of her kingdom at risk. She looked Preacher Mallody, leader of the Clendines, in the eye as she left his castle and called him a coward. He would not even help them escape and gain safe passage out of his wretched kingdom. It was all for naught.

Holding her baby in one arm, Azallan took sword in her other and led the charge back to their boat. Derrin cried, and his mother issued a cry of her own as she spun and slashed with Head Guard Liam beside her and the rest flanking her. They fought their way back to their ship and set sail for Avaron, leaving the sea surrounding the Clendines full of Vorcan bodies. Her small band had more heart than Preacher's giant army. They had something to fight for. They had Derrin.

Still, they weren't foolish enough to think they were safe. The Vorcans were like insects; they came in swarms. The horde they had bested in their escape was most likely only the scouting party, there to test the reliability of the tip they had been given. Azallan knew how the dark army worked by now. Hundreds more would be on their tail within the sunlight of day. Now that she had shed Vorcan blood, they would only come faster and angrier.

Margot, the lookout, spied a Vorcan raider ship in the far distance with her telescope, and the queen ordered an increase in speed to widen the distance even further. They couldn't maintain that fast of a speed though, so they stayed paranoid and vigilant. She just prayed to the Gods that they could make it back to Avaron before the raiders caught up to them. Barricaded within her castle walls, Derrin would be much safer than he was out in the open waters. She would have to show Avaron where their strength really came from. It was time.

Lord Vorcan took great pride in his navy though, and the Vorcan ships were smaller and faster than hers. They were like hungry sharks compared to her whale of a vessel. It wasn't a question of whether or not they would catch up. It was a question of when.

Azallan held her son close. She told him she loved him and spoke to him of his father and their kingdom. He looked up at her with his father's eyes and cooed his understanding. He grabbed at her auburn curls as she spoke to the ghost of his father and asked him to watch over them both. She made sure that nobody on her ship saw it, but she was terrified. Derrin didn't seem to echo the sentiment. He looked at his mother with such immovable trust. It steeled her heart. A cornered mother was a greater warrior than any man. She held Derrin's tiny hand in her own and stared out at the sea.

When the night came without stars she felt even more frightened. The stars were the watching eyes of the spirits. Seeing the sky as a blank canvas meant that Barrimon wasn't with them. Her prayer had gone unheard. She wondered if the Gods had abandoned her as well on this trip. Maybe even they were afraid of Lord Vorcan's dark army. Could the firm grip of his power stretch that far? She hoped she was wrong.

The baby cried throughout the starless night as if he knew how dire the situation was. She fed him and sang to him and soothed him with stories of his father's triumphs. He seemed to listen, to absorb the tails of the warrior king's virtue. His small fingers reached up to touch her heart. She made sure that it beat steady and calm for him.

Azallan slept when Derrin slept which wasn't often and always for short intervals, so when the sun arose again, she felt exhausted and sore. Should battle come this day, she thought, she would fall asleep and land on her own sword. She feared her exhausted state would endanger her child. It was the fear that woke her and made her alert.

She carried the baby to the deck above, where Margot informed her that the raider ships had closed the distance. They were still a day behind, but there were three that she could see and they were coming fast. Azallan nodded and thanked her. She handed Derrin to his nurse maid and went to meet with Liam so they could formulate a plan should they need to stand their ground and fight, when a screech pierced the sky. She looked around for the source but her eyes could find nothing. When she looked at Liam, she could see that he heard it as well.

"Griffin," he said to her. "Be alert."

Liam drew his sword so the queen drew her own in turn. She held the sword in her left hand, still blackened by Vorcan blood. Azallan knew she needed to be alert and on guard, but her gaze drifted over her shoulder to her son. The nurse maid was nervous. Derrin squirmed in his blanket and tried to grasp for his mother. His caretaker gently shushed him as she rocked and swayed where she stood in an effort to keep him calm. Azallan told the woman to take him below deck. She nodded and started that way.

Margot shouted a warning but the queen couldn't hear what she was saying over the wind and the screeching of the beast. She looked in her direction, and the distraction was enough. She failed to see the giant bird-like creature swooping in towards them. Azallan screamed and Liam spun around, slashing with his sword, but the blade cut through open air. The griffin had taken flight again, soaring high above them into the sky, with baby Derrin clutched in its claws. Azallan looked to the empty-armed nursemaid, who was already crying. She would deal with her later.

A fire blazed in Azallan's eyes. Her heart pounded with fear, anger and adrenaline. She climbed the mast to the lookout tower, and a fearful Margot stepped aside. The queen was radiating fury. She waited on her moment as the creature swung back, soaring for the mountains. Then she dove. She timed the jump well and grasped its leg, but her sword fell from her grip, toppling back to the deck below. Azallan screamed for the beast to release her child as it took them both over the wild sea below.

Azallan swung her body left and right, swerving to avoid the arrows fired by her own people. One arrow sliced past her, inches from her face, and hit home, which sent the bird-like creature into a frenzy. The thrashing monster's tantrum shook loose Azallan's grip and dropped her, still bellowing fury, into the water below. She screamed as she watched from the ocean as the griffin faded into the distance, Derrin still in its grip.

Immediately the queen swam back to the ship, her mind focused on retrieving her sword. She already envisioned her gutting the beast that stole her child. Then Liam was there, helping her back on board the ship. She didn't spare a breath. With Liam on her heels, she raced through the crew to Stefan, the man working the wheel, scooping up her sword mid-stride as she went. He turned to face them when they arrived behind him.

Stefan saw her empty arms, and his face shone with concern. "Where?"

"The griffin," Azallan said. "The griffin has Derrin, and we must follow it. We must."

Margot walked up to them, shaking her head. "My lady, we cannot. If we change course now and take such a detour, the Vorcans will catch us. There is no way we can track the griffin, recover the baby, and make it back to the kingdom without that fight, and I fear we won't come out of it victorious. Forgive me, my queen, but we need to survive today for there to even be a future."

"Allow me to remind you which one of us is in command," Azallan spat back. "If we survive and Derrin does not, then it doesn't even matter. Without Derrin, we have no kingdom. We have no future. You may very well be right, Margot. Maybe this adventure ends with our demise, but that is a chance we have to take. For Avaron, I command it."

"For Avaron," Margot repeated, though her voice trembled with fear.

"For Avaron," Liam said with conviction.

"For Avaron," Stefan echoed.

The words became a chant that worked its way around the

entirety of the ship, ending with the sixty soldiers and crew aboard the vessel shouting in unison, "For Avaron!"

Then the ship changed course, veering away from home and heading in the direction the monster flew when it left with the baby. Margot looked in her telescope. When she found the griffin again, she shouted down coordinates that were passed down the line to Stefan and he set the ship on the appropriate course.

They were forced to leave the open ocean and sail through tight channels, navigating jagged rocks and wild rapids. They slowed and focused on steering as the current propelled them.

"At this pace, the Vorcan will catch us before we even recover the prince," Liam said to his queen.

"We'll make it," she said, but she didn't feel as sure as she sounded. Huge mountain peaks ascended all around them, and they sailed onward into thick fog.

"Visibility is terrible!" Margot shouted. "I can't see a thing!"

Azallan ran to Stefan. "Margot has lost visibility in this fog. Keep your ears open. Listen for the screech and the flap of those damned wings and follow the sound. We cannot lose that thing out here, or we're all doomed."

"Yes, my queen."

She hurried back to Liam then. "Prepare your soldiers for battle," she said. "We have no idea what we're going to face out here."

"Yes, my lady." Liam placed a comforting hand on her arm. "We'll get him back Queen Azallan. We will."

The queen nodded. "I know we will," she answered, "for there is no other option."

With that, Liam ran off to do as she asked. Azallan's heart pounded. She was already feeling the pull of her baby being gone, the connection they had. She not only feared for all of them and the future of the kingdom, but she also just wanted to hold him again, to feel his skin against hers, to hear the high-pitched sound of his voice and his gleeful laugh, to see the way he looked at her with the same blind devotion that she felt. Her heart was breaking and also blossoming with new found rage.

She felt like her instinct had been on point, and the Gods had abandoned them on this journey. She angered at them for sending her and her sweet child into such peril. She angered at Preacher Mallody and his giant kingdom of cowards. She angered at Lord Vorcan and his soulless minions that never relented. They already took her husband from her, and now they aimed to take her child, her future, and her kingdom. To the Underworld with all of them!

And most of all, she felt furious with that flying monster. How dare it think it could take the crown prince of Avaron and just fly away! Once she had her son back safely, she would make sure the damned thing knew well of its mistake. Her sword would find its heart, a turn well deserved, she thought, as she clutched at her own.

She hoped the Gods returned in time to see her wrath bestowed upon that foul beast. Let them see her triumph and see the error of their own ways. She was not the type of woman anyone should ever doubt. Preacher Mallody would learn that lesson in due time, if she could help it. Her blood boiled like the lava that surrounded the Vorcan homeland.

Then with a sudden shock, the queen lost her footing and slid across the deck. Either they had hit something or something had hit them. The Vorcan couldn't have found them already. It wasn't possible. "What in the Underworld was that?!" she shouted.

"Something hit us," a crew member shouted. "Something under the water."

"Was it a rock?" Liam questioned.

"I don't know."

Azallan waited as Liam growled and rushed below deck, barreling down the stairs to the lowest level of the big ship. Her patience wavered as the ship rocked under a second impact. All she could think about was Derrin. What was the creature doing with him? What if it had taken him to feed its young?

She didn't have this time to waste. Azallan called down to Liam for a report.

"Oh my Gods," she heard him say from below, as he took sight of the enormous sea creature batting them with its giant tentacles.

Azallan felt equal panic and relief when she saw him run up the steps twice as fast as he had gone down them. "It's a beast," he shouted as he emerged. "Fire arrows into the water. It will destroy our hull if we don't act fast!"

The archers fired off of all sides of the ship, unsure if they were hitting their target or not. Azallan stared angrily into the dark water. A sea monster now. Her resolve was truly being tested.

"I will not fail," she said. "I will not fail." She saw her child's face in her mind and could almost hear the sand running from the hourglass that controlled his fate. "I will not fail."

The rocking of the boat ceased, and everyone looked at each other wondering if they had won. "How do we know?" one of Liam's soldiers questioned.

Liam stared thoughtfully at the water. "I don't see any blood," he said.

"By the Gods, just get us moving!" Azallan cried out. "Now!"

No sooner had the ship begun to follow the current once more, then the enormous beast emerged from the water, tentacles wrapping around the ship.

"May the Gods be with us," Liam said at the sight of the monster.

"I wouldn't count on that," the queen said quietly, but bitterly.

Archers fired. The arrows stuck in the monster with a wet thud. Its tentacles lashed out to return the favor and sent the screaming soldiers flying into the rocks nearby. Swordsmen charged and slashed at the whipping tentacles. Liam dodged and ran between them only to have his sword taken in the sea beast's huge jaws. Azallan screamed. It was guttural and primal.

"My son is waiting!" she shouted. "I will do this myself!" Then she bounded over the lashing tentacles and the warriors in combat with them. When she landed before the beast and the struggling Liam fighting to get his blade free, she said, "For Derrin. For Avaron." And she drove her blade into the monster's enormous eye.

There was a shrill scream. Then the creature released its grip and disappeared back into the depths. The crowd aboard the ship pumped their arms and cheered.

"Do not celebrate," the queen told them. "We lost some of our valued soldiers. We are being pursued by the enemy, and our army is now that much weaker. Let us keep moving. That delay could have cost my son his life."

Quietly, the crew got back to navigating the twisting channels until they broke through the fog and were once again in the bright light of day. It felt like a victory and that felt like a trick to Azallan. It was the Gods wanting her to let her guard down. She would leave them unsatisfied.

"Stay vigilant!" she called to her crew.

"I spotted the griffin!" Margot shouted from above.

She gave the coordinates, and Stefan took the ship in that direction. Azallan looked at where they were headed. It was a towering behemoth of a mountain on a small island. They were going to have to make land and ascend the mountain on foot. Their odds of success were feeling dimmer by the moment. By the time they got up there, slayed the griffin and took back the prince, came back down and traveled the maze of channels back out of here, the Vorcan would probably be waiting on them. If only there was another choice, but the Fates would not have it that way. Destiny was theirs to command.

"So be it," Azallan said darkly, her eyes on the mountain.

When they made landfall, Azallan took only Liam and a handful of her soldiers with her. She commanded the rest to remain with the ship, ready to move in a hurry or defend should they get ambushed. Leaving the ship undefended would have been foolish. If the Vorcan were to show, they would seize that opportunity and take the ship to pieces knowing that they would have no other way off that island. The soldiers of the dark army were devilishly clever and matched that attribute with equal ruthlessness.

Margot told them there was a cave at the pinnacle of the mountain, and the griffin was perched on top of it. She said she would keep eyes on it, and if she saw them in trouble, she would send reinforcements. The queen nodded thanks to her. Then they set off, six in total, for the mountain.

"I hope it's not too steep to climb," one of the soldiers, a woman named Marista, said worriedly.

"If it is, we'll climb it anyway," the queen said back, all strength and determination.

"There's a clear walking path that spirals the mountain," Liam stated.

"Which means more than flying beasts take residence here," the queen brought to their attention. "Be swift but alert."

They began their ascent, moving quickly. They stayed close together and ran up the winding path that wrapped around the towering mountain. They passed by many deep holes, avoiding them to keep from falling in. They weren't even a third of the way up when something came out of one of the holes in the mountain, took one of the soldiers, and carried them into another hole, disappearing. The other five stopped in their tracks and looked around. They saw nothing but they couldn't shake the feeling that something saw them.

"Alright. Take it slow, and everybody stay close," Liam said. "Something is here with us. Watch the holes."

They started moving up the mountain again. Then they heard chittering. They stopped and turned to look. Out from one of the holes in the mountain poured man-sized beetles. Another soldier was grabbed by them and dragged over the side of the mountain.

"Damn it to the Underworld!" Azallan griped. "We're losing everyone."

"Take the queen to her son," Marista said to Liam. "We'll hold off the bugs."

Liam nodded at her. "Stay close to me," he said to his queen.

Then he started running up the mountain again. Azallan followed him. The two remaining soldiers drew their swords and stood their ground. Their metal blades clanged off of the hard shells of the giant beetles.

"Slice for the underbelly, or jab at the openings in their shells!" Marista told her partner.

As the queen followed Liam up the mountain she could hear the fighting carrying on below them. She felt so proud of her loyal soldiers and all they had been willing to take on, on behalf of their kingdom. She had lost so many and she grieved for each and every one, as she knew them all by name. So many good lives had been lost on this journey. She heard a scream from below and flinched like she had been physically struck.

"We are almost there," Liam told her. "Stay focused. Press forward. Derrin needs you."

Azallan nodded and continued her climb. Getting back down was going to be another feat but she couldn't think about it until she held Derrin in her arms once more. The path got steeper as she neared the top and could no longer run. They had to hike and be careful not to lose her balance and topple over the side.

Finally, the end was in sight, and she could view the cave that Margot had described, and the humongous beast was perched on top of it. The sight of the monster that stole her son made her want to scream and charge at it with haste, but she reeled her feelings in to keep from making a foolish error. She had to keep her wits about her.

When she and Liam finally reached the top, they bent to catch their breath, but only for a moment, because they feared an ambush. She and her guard had suffered too many of those already. Then they both drew their swords and approached the giant beast slowly and cautiously.

She wasn't just afraid for herself or the loyal man beside her. She was afraid of spooking the griffin and making it fly away. She couldn't see Derrin anywhere. Had the beast dropped him somewhere? If he was already gone, then this was another fruitless adventure and all was already lost. She refused to believe such a thing.

The griffin didn't move. It looked directly at them, and then looked away. Either it was confident they weren't a real threat, or it was purposely giving off the impression of being uninterested in order to get them to lower their guard, something a mother would never do with her son in harm's way. Maybe it knew that the infant was already lost.

Azallan's heart sank at the thought. She willed it to be untrue. Her hand tightened on the pommel of her sword. They continued to close in, step by step.

When they got close enough that they were only a couple of sword lengths away, something else emerged from the cave below the monster. The queen and the leader of her guard raised their weapons. Azallan's chest tightened as she ached for it to be a sign of her child's whereabouts. She clung to hope that he was alive and safe.

Azallan realized a hunched over elderly woman in a dusty brown cloak with a third eye blazing in her forehead had stepped forth from the mouth of the cave. When the cloak shifted, Azallan saw that the strange woman held Derrin in her arms. She finally recovered the ability to breathe at the sight of her precious boy. He was moving. He was alive.

She could hear his little voice, even with the distance between them. He knew that his mother was there, and he spoke to her in his own way. Tears welled in her eyes.

Then her grip tightened on her sword. "Give me my son," she commanded, stepping forward.

The old woman shook her head and approached them.

"I think she's an oracle," Liam said fearfully, touching his queen's arm with a protective hand. "I don't like magic. I don't trust it."

Azallan pulled away from him and held up a hand to silence him. The woman met her eyes, and Azallan saw a knowing in them like nothing she had experienced in her years. The woman shifted so she was holding Derrin snugly in her right arm. She reached out with her left hand and touched the queen's forehead.

Azallan was on her ship with her crew in the open water, and they fought a fierce battle against the Vorcan raiders. They were losing. All of her people were dying before her eyes as those demons in armor came by the dozens over the sides of her ship. An invisible hand gripped her heart.

"Alright. Enough," Azallan said, stepping back and breaking contact with the oracle. "What are you trying to show me? If that happens, you made it happen by delaying us, redirecting us. You have created that future."

The old woman shook her head and stepped forward, touching the queen again. She saw herself injured on the deck of her ship. She was screaming at a Vorcan soldier that was carrying her baby away from her. She tried to get to her feet and fell, and she screamed louder and harder. She was forced to watch as the soldier handed the screaming, struggling, Derrin over to Lord Vorcan, and watch still as he drove a dagger into her son's tiny heart. She watched as the wriggling baby stilled.

Azallan fell to her knees, breaking contact with the oracle, a silent scream on her lips. Tears flowed freely from her eyes as she gazed up at the woman. "You saw it. You knew. But why do you care? Why did you save him?"

The old woman bent over and touched her forehead one more time. This time Azallan saw a ruggedly handsome man around thirty years old. She recognized Barrimon's eyes and knew it was her son, grown up. He was beautiful. The crown on his head proclaimed him king. He stepped out onto the balcony she knew so well, and the people of Avaron cheered like nothing she had ever heard. Her heart swelled with pride.

She understood. This would be her end, but not the end of Avaron. The oracle had taken him so that he could be safe and grow to manhood where he would take his place as king and make their nation great again.

She also knew that the Vorcans were most likely almost upon them, and if she took him from this mountain, she would be taking him to his death, the vision of which still lingered behind her eyes. She sighed with a grief that only a parent could understand, and then she stood on weak legs.

With her heart crumbling in her chest, she asked, "May I hold him one last time?"

The old woman nodded and held the child out to her. Liam watched with confusion and concern as his queen took her son and hugged him to her. Derrin smiled up at her, and his eyes shone with delight at the sight of her which caused her own to spill tears.

She told him that she loved him and to never forget her, and then she quickly gave him back to the oracle before she lost her nerve and made a perilous error in judgment. He grabbed for her as she passed him away, and her heart screamed in agony. Then the old woman nodded to her and walked backwards until she disappeared into the darkness of the cave.

"Queen Azallan, what is happening?" Liam asked her, his voice filled with dripping tension.

"The future is safe. Now we go down fighting," Azallan said sullenly. She started back down the mountain.

"What did she show you?" Liam wanted to know.

"The end, Liam. He will be a great king someday. It is a shame we won't see it."

Liam felt taken aback by this, as he followed her down the mountain. "Maybe the Vorcans won't find us here. They were far back. Maybe they didn't see us turn off. Maybe we can all hide here and leave when it's safe."

"No," Azallan said firmly. "We cannot afford to take that chance. We need to leave here and make them follow. We need to lead them as far from this place as we can before we perish. Our duty is to protect the future and protect our kingdom. Our duty is to protect Derrin. For Avaron."

Liam nodded. "For Avaron," he said.

When they got further down the mountain they found that Marista had survived, and many giant bugs had not. It was a shame, Azallan thought, that she fought so hard and now her queen was going to lead her to her death anyway.

"I want you to stay," Azallan told a shocked Marista. "Protect my child with your life. Kill anything not from Avaron that steps foot on this mountain."

"I fight for you," Marista said. "I fight for the good of my kingdom. For Avaron. I will give my life for the future."

Azallan nodded. She took off her necklace and let it twirl into Marista's open hand. "When he is old enough, give him this. It will tell the people of Avaron who he is. Tell him who his father was. Tell him who I was. Lead him home."

"For Avaron," Marista responded and Liam echoed.

When Azallan and Liam re-boarded the ship they told Stefan to take them back to the open waters and head for home once more. Many people had questions but the queen wasn't ready to answer them. She was heartbroken and proud all the same. Victorious and grieving.

Not until they hit the open waters and Margot spotted more than a dozen Vorcan ships that would be on them by nightfall, did Azallan tell her crew that they were going to have to trust her. She explained that they wouldn't win, and they wouldn't survive. That was how it was always going to go, but now their deaths were going to have purpose. They were fighting for the future. Their sacrifices would be noble and virtuous, and she couldn't tell them any more than that.

It was enough.

"For Avaron!" they shouted in unison.

They kept sailing as the hours passed, leading the dark army away from the future king. Azallan stood at the back of the ship, hand on her hilt, and stared into the distance. She was numb, resigned to her fate. She touched her chest and remembered the feeling of her child's warmth pressed against her, the sound of his small voice still resonating in her ears. His loving gaze lingered behind her eyes.

This was for him, she reminded herself, all for him. "Be a noble king," she said quietly, her eyes watering as she kept his face clear in her mind. She wanted to see it until the end. "Make your mother proud."

As Margot predicted, night fell and the Vorcan ships appeared, flying towards the ship at a charge. This was it. The raiders were death, here to claim them all. Azallan wouldn't make it easy for them.

"For Avaron!" the queen shouted, tears streamed down her cheeks and her raised hand balled into a fist.

"For Avaron!" the crew shouted back from all around her.

Then Azallan screamed and drew her sword.

Meet Chisto Healy

Chisto Healy has been writing since his brother handed him Dean Koontz's *Servants of Twilight* at age nine. His hero and favorite author is Simon Clark, so go read him right now. Chisto's got a lot of great stuff of his own coming out and you can find all the details at https:// chistohealy.blogspot.com which he does his best to keep updated. There are almost 20 books coming out with his work in them. He lives in North Carolina with his beautiful and wacky fiancée, her chill mom, three of the most creative and awesome kids the world has to offer, and a plethora of kickass pets. Please reach out. He would love to hear from you. You can also follow him on Amazon.

Floating Castle

Kelly Lynn Colby

Dear Gift,

Of all the gifts I could have received on my birthday, I don't know why my grandmother thought *you* were better than one of her flying horses. She came to me all excited with a package behind her back. I just *knew* it was a halter for Uluiria, the gleaming white mare with rainbow wings I'd been eyeing since she foaled four years ago.

Grandmother made me swear by the Gods of Good that every day I would use the gift she hid behind her back. Then she made me swear by the Gods of Evil, just in case the Gods of Good forgave me for my transgressions or something. I didn't hesitate to swear whatever she asked of me. I wouldn't face any consequences. Who wouldn't want to fly around the kingdom on Uluiria with her glowing white tail flowing behind me like a daytime comet?

A tear dropped down Grandmother's face as she pulled you from behind her back. "I knew you were ready."

Now, don't get me wrong. Your shimmering purple cover with silver embossed filigree would catch my eye in any papier shop. But I'm sixteen now. I'm ready for the next level of gift. I flipped you open as I'm sure you remember. I'm a bit embarrassed to inform you, I was hoping you were hollow inside and held a halter, because you're much thicker than any book I'd ever held. No such luck. Nothing but blank page after blank page.

Then it hit me.

I promised to use you every day. My face must have done that thing it does where my inner thoughts show up in ugly wrinkles and pinched lips, for Mother loudly cleared her throat from up on her throne. Father smiled and nodded indulgently.

I managed to say, "Thank you, Grandmother," and leaned in for a hug to give me time to straighten out my face in fake gratitude. I mean, I *am* grateful for Grandmother, but her gift buying needs some improvement. I'll never give my granddaughter a present that makes more work for her for no reason. Mother gives me enough princessy things to do already.

When I tried to pull away, Grandmother squeezed me firmly and whispered in my ear, "This book has been in my family for generations and given to the youngest girl when the pages are full. It is your turn, child. Guard her well. Tell her your nightmares and dreams and failures and triumphs. She will know your heart and see you through it all. But take care to think of more than yourself, or she will be most unforgiving."

Dramatic much? Plus, I have no idea what she was talking about with that completed pages bit, because your pages are blank. ALL of them.

My hand hurts. I'm going to bed.

Princess Grenoir Trundel of Lilopura of the Nine Kingdoms

Dear Gift,

Zoey said you feel weird, but in a good way. I don't know what she means. You feel normal to me, nowhere near as amazing as a flying horse mane running through my fingers, if I might add.

Do you have another name? Grandmother seemed to think you were a she. Should I *give* you a name? How about Not-Uluiria? You would tell me if you minded, right?

Can we make it short and sweet today? I said I'd use you every day. I never said I'd write an entire diatribe with each entry.

Princess Grenoir Trundel of Lilopura of the Nine Kingdoms

Dear Not-Uluiria,

Father wants to do a tour of the wheat fields. It's been a bit dry and he's sent a courier to summon the weather wizard to request rain from Silus, the Sky God. You don't happen to have a connection, do you?

I remember two years ago when we had a drought so bad, Hanta Village was completely abandoned after many starved to death. It was horrible. It's not right that I'm never hungry while so many of our people have to struggle to find enough food. Mother tells me it's my privilege for bearing the burdens of my position. The only burden I feel on a regular basis is her rules.

Anyway, I'll be too tired when I get home. So, this is it for today.

Princess Grenoir Trundel of Lilopura of the Nine Kingdoms

Dear Not-Uluiria,

The weather wizard must have gotten word even though he never showed up. Silus answered enthusiastically. The storms have ripped through the valley, soaking the fields. I hope the wheat is happy now.

Sadly, archery practice was canceled due to the rain. Zoey and I couldn't stand to be cooped up all day, so we opened the windows in the ballroom. The rain slicked the shiny floors just enough so we could slide around like we were ice skating. I've always wanted to ice skate on real ice. Maybe Father will allow me to accompany him when he visits frosty Coldspine of the Nine Kingdoms. Of course, he might think it's too dangerous and only allow me to watch from a safe distance.

Archery's the only physical exertion Father allows for his precious princess. I begged and pleaded with him to let me try swordsman-ship, but he vetoed the idea immediately. Though, if I'm remembering Mother's face at my request, it might have been her stern, wordless admonishment that convinced Father to say no. I wish she would let me do more than stand beside her throne looking presentable. I will marry soon enough.

Speaking of which, Prince Waincott of Hildern, Duke of Sunset Castle is set to visit in a week. He is much too old for me. Plus, his elongated face with nose to match makes me think our children will look like donkeys.

Sorry about the ink stain. My shiver was uncontrollable.

Why can't I have a bit of fun before I'm weighed down with all the responsibility my title demands? Shouldn't I tour the Nine Kingdoms extensively so I'll truly know what each requires? I mean, I don't know which one I'm to marry into. I need to be prepared.

If only I'd gotten Uluiria as a gift, I could be off on my adventure in the skies now.

Princess Grenoir, flying horse rider wanna be

Dear Not-Uluiria,

How do you like the new quill Zoey found? I think it was an "I'm sorry" gift since she refused to do my entry for me. Something about godly retribution. She's just looking out for me, but still. I did ask her about naming you. She was quite upset with me being so disrespectful. And she's probably right. Zoe recommended I call you Amethyst because of your gorgeous cover. I think it's pretty fitting. What do you think?

Zoey always has good ideas. I can't imagine functioning without her. I'm hopeful she'll go with me when I have to relocate to a new kingdom. I haven't asked her yet, because I'm so afraid she'll say no. I could order her, of course, but somehow that doesn't feel right. Not to Zoey.

Oh, I almost forgot to tell you. I think I might be in such a good mood, because Father agreed to allow me to take fencing lessons with Head Guard Joules. I get fitted for my protective gear tomorrow. I *even* get to wear pants. I guess Father realized I could handle it.

Or he might have been frustrated with the flooded ballroom and wanted to keep me busy during rainy days.

Either way, I win!

Another odd thing? That courier sent to the weather wizard came back today and said he never made it to the conclave. Something about the rain making the road impassable before he could drop off his message. It seems Silus decided to save our fields without any magic intervention. I should make an offering to him first thing in the morning.

Princess Grenoir, soon-to-be master swordswoman

Dear Amethyst,

Today was not fun. That's all I have to say.

Even a princess's life gets mundane, you know. Lessons with Mother on table manners and etiquette. Tutoring with Mistress Numar in the nine native languages of the Nine Kingdoms. (I really don't understand the point. We all speak Common.) Walks with Father around the castle grounds.

I seriously need some adventure. If only Grandmother had gifted me Uluiria. I wish I was flying over the countryside from kingdom to kingdom. Now *that* would be something to write about.

At least I have you to share my frustrations with. Thank you for being here for me, Amethyst. Yes, I think that name fits perfectly.

Grenoir, bored princess of Lilopura

Dear Amethyst,

Um, I don't know how to say this so I'll just come right out with it.

The castle's flying.

At first, I thought the entire structure was sliding down the muddy hill after all the rain. I crouched on my bed and waited for the ceiling to come crashing down.

Zoey rushed to my chamber. "You must see this, Princess," she said.

I couldn't even talk. Afraid of death and destruction and who knows what horrors, I kept my eyes on her feet and scrambled after her. Between the panic and the physical exertion, my breathing came in raspy gulps until we reached the parapets over the gates.

Then I stopped breathing altogether, because over the castle walls was nothing but sky.

"Isn't it glorious?" Zoey's voice broke the spell and I inhaled to ease my burning lungs.

Straight below yawned the visitors' garden, planted to greet all who came to the castle. The rose bushes looked as small as seeds spotting a green landscape. The giant oaks planted before my grandfather was born looked like twigs stuck in the ground. In the sea of mud below, a gaping hole of jail cells and cheering prisoners was all that was left of the ground where the castle used to sit. We were high above it all.

As dizziness threatened to send me tumbling over the side, I crouched with my back against the parapet. A cry escaped my lips as the tower off center of the main complex pushed through a cloud. The cloud flowed around the tower—like the brick building was a stone in a stream. The liquid air barreled its icy tendrils toward me and poked its freezing fingers through my nightgown. Tiny water droplets blossomed across my exposed skin.

After it rushed past, the sky cleared to the deepest blue I'd ever seen.

Still gazing over the parapet, Zoey yelped next to me. "We're moving."

I couldn't let the servant show more bravery than her charge. What would Father say? With a mighty push of will, I stood. My fear faded as the beauty of everything in front of me overwhelmed my senses. I wish you could see it, Amethyst. The deep blue of the sky, the luscious green of the ground, even the sludgy brown where the castle used to sit has its own kind of beauty. My mind flooded with color and texture, as I took in the natural quilt displayed below.

My euphoria melted as Cook screamed from the courtyard that has no stone floor but somehow came with us anyway—magic is weird. "We've been cursed! Some evil witch or wizard has targeted our precious Princess Grenoir. What are we going to do?"

Cursed? I didn't understand. Why would someone curse me? I don't have a jealous stepmother or a witch who wants my father's power. There was that one princess who stoked the ire of a witch when she refused to buy apples from her because of her appearance. After the whole Snow White thing, the princess might have been justified. The witch, however, thought she was stereotyping and turned her into a toad.

Is it weird that I'm kind of happy I'm cursed? I get to travel now. I mean, I've been to all Nine Kingdoms at one time or another, but I only get to see the palaces. I want to visit the historical sites and shop freely at the bazaars and roam the countryside with just me and Zoey and a walking stick like a ranger taking stock of the land. I like being a princess, don't get me wrong. But sometimes, I'd like to shrug off my responsibilities and hit the road for a time.

Grenoir, Roamer of the Skies

Dear Amethyst,

You will *not* believe what happened today. After drifting more or less straight east, we crossed the border into Renetton. On little more than basic civil terms with them, Father became anxious King Torik would fire all his cannons at us.

The entire castle knelt in the courtyard and prayed to the Gods of Good to see through to King Torik's hidden, tiny heart to let us pass through in peace. It might even have worked if, for no apparent reason, the castle hadn't decided to settle on the ground crushing a mill and its surrounding town. Luckily, we descended slowly enough that everyone was able to get out of the way, but I can't imagine King Torik will interpret this in any other way than the start to war.

Father ordered everyone to abandon the castle, for we didn't know why the castle landed and we didn't know for how long. Servants and guardsmen and groomsmen with horses rushed through the castle gate. Even Mother, who usually insists on her carriage lest she touch the ground outside, took mine and Father's hand and headed for the escape. We were surrounded by the Elite Guard, whose Captain was certain the entire enchantment might be a trick pulled by King Torik to claim invasion and make the Nine Kingdoms Eight.

Now here's why I know for sure that I'm the one cursed.

As I rushed with Mother and Father—Zoey by my side—I rammed straight into an invisible wall. My head, knee, and forward swinging arm slammed into something so hard that it threw me backwards. When I was able to focus again, Zoey was holding my head in her lap and Father leaned over my face, gently slapping my cheeks.

The temblor in his voice made *me* shake in fear. "Are you okay, my sweet girl?"

"I don't know." I tried to stop it—because a princess must be stoic in public as Mother had drilled into me since I attempted my first temper tantrum at three—but there was no use. A tear slipped down my cheek, followed by another.

When I noticed Mother over Father's shoulder looking more concerned than annoyed at me lying on the ground in front of the royal court crying, I knew I was in real trouble.

Father helped me stand, as he waved over the Captain of the Guard. "Joules, carry her for now. We must make haste lest the castle decide to shift on top of us or act in any other uncastle-like manner."

Those tears flashed to steam as my cheeks heated up in embarrassment as the strong man—old enough to be my uncle—slung me into his arms like a maiden in distress. I mean, I suppose that's what I looked like at the moment, but that was certainly *not* who I am.

With much effort, I struggled from his grasp. "I'll be fine, Father. I must have tripped in our frantic escape."

To prove that I really was fine, I casually walked ahead of my worried family. Though I felt a little dizzy, my balance was perfect and my legs obeyed my commands.

When I hit the same spot, I paused and watched Zoey and Mother continue unheeded. A sigh relaxed my limbs. It must have just been a clumsy moment. Maybe I should pay better attention to dance lessons.

Relief quickly morphed to puzzlement though, because pain ripped through my foot as I stubbed my toe on nothing. As I hopped in place thinking of how horrified Mother would be if she could read the curses running through my mind, my forehead slammed into the barrier.

Joules bent to pick me up again as Father's face scowled at my seeming inability to walk.

"Wait." I ordered him. Slowly, I put my hands out as if searching for the wall in a night-darkened room. A barrier as smooth as the polished altar in the Gods of Good Sanctuary vibrated gently against my hands. It was not exactly unpleasant, but it didn't give even a little when I pushed on it.

My mother walked right through and turned to me. "What are you doing? We don't have time to dawdle." Her voice dropped to a whisper as she came within a centimeter of my nose. "The court is watching."

The strangest thing of all? I could feel her breath on the hairs of my eyebrow. I could smell the herbs from her breakfast tea. Yet, when I pointed my finger to touch her nose, it wouldn't go passed the wall that no one could see and—at least it seemed so far—only I could feel.

Father grabbed my hand and tried to guide me forward. My fingertips bounced on the barrier as Father's hand slipped right through. "What is happening?"

I couldn't help but stare back at the castle. "I don't think it wants me to go."

Mother gasped dramatically. With both hands over her mouth, she mumbled, "It *is* a curse."

I walked the perimeter of the castle, hoping for a hole somewhere. I found no hole.

Anyway, most of us came back inside the castle walls. We did get fresh supplies of food and a few other perishables we'd run short on.

And now as we float through the sky with the servants who chose to return, we know for sure that I am cursed. I guess I *am* a maiden in distress and have to wait for my prince to save me.

I wish he'd hurry up.

Grenoir, Distressed Maiden

Dear Amethyst,

Some men on horseback are following us. They have a flag, but they're still too far away to tell from which kingdom. I hope it's not Renetton. I'm already cursed which has caused the literal upheaval of everything and everyone I care about. I'm not sure my conscience could handle the weight—or the guilt—of war. I wish I knew someone who could help me solve this issue and free the royal court. Would it be too much to ask to return the castle to Lilopura? I just don't know.

I'm going to pray to the Gods of Good in Their Sanctuary before heading to bed. I'm not sure I could sleep anyway.

Grenoir, feeling guilty even though none of this is her fault

Amethyst,

You are not going to believe what happened today. I do seem to say that a lot, don't I? Anyway, those men following us *were* there to save me. They're from Bronter just like Grandmother. I suppose that means it's *your* prince who came to rescue me. How fitting.

The men got within shouting distance at night. I wanted to rush out and ask them who they were and what they wanted, but Mother said it was very unlady-like to shout at men on horseback in the middle of the night. A princess must wait for a formal gathering to address royal guests. The men must handle business first.

Plus, it was raining and I *knew* she shuddered at my maybe-future husband seeing me like a wet dog shivering in the storm. Zoey said it would make me look more in need of saving and would work to bolster the horsemen's desire to rescue me. Poor Zoey hasn't seen her family for weeks, because she chose to stick with me instead of abandoning us like so many other servants had. I owed it to her to swallow my pride and find out if the men from Bronter had answers.

Even if they couldn't counter this curse, maybe they could run to the market and get us some fresh greens. I wish I could spend an entire day picking spinach out of my teeth. It would be a welcome change from dried meats, fruits, and flat bread.

Oran save me, I've gotten off topic again. Long story short, I ignored my mother, and me and Zoey snuck out.

When I breached the outer wall around the gate, I didn't see the horsemen. I mean, it was dark and we had no moonlight with the clouds dropping rain. Yet, the torchlight that burned from the covered awnings should have given me some glimpse. I wondered if they'd stopped to camp for the night even though it was still early. Surely, it's a nightmare to ride in the rain for hours following a floating castle that has no discernible destination in mind. Anyway, I'm going to try to get the conversations right, but give me some leeway because my memory isn't exactly exact.

I shouted into the empty night. "Are you there?"

Zoey rung her hands. "Oh, I hope they haven't left."

The distinct sound of horses' hooves slogging through mud made me sigh in relief. I'm not sure what I would have done if they'd given up. "I can hear them. Just can't see them."

A blue light flashed to life, emanating from beneath us.

Zoey gasped and turned her wide eyes to me. "They're under the castle."

The image of the flattened village still haunts my dreams. My breath caught in my throat and I fell to my knees and leaned over the side where the moat would be if we were sedentary like any proper royal residence.

I'm pretty proud of how calm my voice sounded even though my mind swirled with panic. "Excuse me, kind sirs, but would you mind not riding under the castle?"

Glowing figures appeared from directly below me.

Now, look, the light might have been dim, but a blind girl could see his chiseled chin and slightly sloping eyes that begged you to follow. The rain only helped his appeal, because it made his tunic stick to his carved chest and thick arm muscles. "I must know who speaks from the grounds of the enchanted castle?"

A welcome warmth flooded my insides even though I shivered from the freezing rain. "Um, I'm Princess Grenoir of Lilopura of the Nine Kingdoms. And this castle is pretty unpredictable, and we'd rather you not be under it if it decides to settle."

"We only wished for a respite from the rain." He wove his words together like poetry. I didn't know people could even talk like that. "If I may be so bold, are you the daughter to King Trundel of Lilopura and Queen Amalial from Bronter?"

It was then I realized how much my own dress stuck to my body and was grateful that I laid flat on the ground and he could only see my hair. My mother would be horrified. "Um, yes?"

The rider's face lit up with a huge smile displaying the whitest, straightest teeth I'd ever seen. "I'm Prince Kapina, son to King Rousch of Bronter and Queen Kopilli from Renetton. I have come to save you."

"Yes, we recognized the flag. Did my grandmother send you?"

A wizened old man in a darkened cape that looked heavy on his thin shoulders maneuvered his horse beside the prince's. "The Lady Troil of Bronter Estates asked me to check in on you, Princess Grenoir."

"She did?" I cleared my throat. I remember that because my voice got all squeaky when I thought about my grandmother. "And you are?"

The prince interrupted, which I thought rather rude. But then again, I don't know the rules of polite society in Bronter. Not yet, anyway. "Wizard Horngill is our court mage."

I whistled in appreciation. If Bronter could afford a court mage, they were much richer than my father's kingdom, especially after we go to war with Renetton.

Apparently unsatisfied with his introduction, the wizard added, "I search for arcane knowledge throughout the Nine Kingdoms, and I believe I can counter the curse laid upon you."

I could be mistaken, but I'm pretty sure Kapina pushed his horse into Horngill's. "My father, King Rousch, is a great intellectual who wishes to gather all knowledge of magic and alchemy into one grand collection."

I might have been seeing things in the dim light, but I swear the wizard rolled his eyes.

"This is the task he's assigned our court mage." Kapina smiled, and for once I was grateful the sun wasn't out. The reflection from his teeth would have blinded me. "I am here to rescue you. Wizard Horngill has found a way to free you from this curse, and return your home back to the soil upon which it originated."

Seriously? Where did he learn to talk like that?

I kind of liked it.

Zoey tugged on my sleeves, trying to pull me back from the edge. "I have to go. I'll tell my father what I've learned. In the meantime, please come out from under the castle. I wouldn't want my would-be savior to be squished like a roach under Cook's foot."

Kapina pulled a leather hood over his head and spurred his horse forward. "As you wish, Princess."

Zoey yanked more insistently on my collar, causing me to push up to my feet. "Okay, okay, we can go now."

It wasn't Zoey pulling me up, because she was against the wall. She mouthed, "I'm sorry."

Instead, Mother glared at me. Standing in front of her with my dripping wet dress and tangled hair, I spurted out the first thing I thought would distract her from my unprincess-like behavior. "That's Prince Kapina and Wizard Horngill of Bronter. And they're here to save us."

Amethyst, you should have seen my mother's face change from fury to utter relief. Then it morphed into true horror. "And you greeted him looking like that?"

I can't win, I'm telling you.

I wish she had someone else to groom for her level of greatness so I could get a little peace.

Princess Grenoir

. . .

Dear Amethyst,

The last few days have been a whirlwind. The castle landed in a swamp. The smell was absolutely unforgettable. I feel so sorry for the citizens of Murlanirous, especially since from now on I'm going to call it "Malodorous." Ha! Yes, I do amuse myself. Thank you for asking. But seriously, there has to be something that can be done about that horrible odor.

I know. I'm hiding the big story. That's because I can't quite wrap my head around it. Prince Kapina and his entourage waltzed right into the castle today, completely unafraid of being stuck in the air for weeks. It's madness if you ask me. I mean, sure it's one adventure after another, but it's also a trap when you have no control. He sure is confident. As annoying as his speech is, I have to admit that his good looks are intoxicating. Zoey couldn't stop talking about his forearms. Who the heck looks at a man's forearms?

This time I met him perfectly coifed thanks to Mother's forcing all of the servants—even the kitchen wenches—to get me ready. I did kind of feel like a trussed-up roast, so it kind of made sense. Plus, he brought baskets of greens from the local market. The freshness of the food was gods-blessed.

Even though I had to pick spinach from my teeth for hours afterward, Kapina never made me feel awkward. I know what he wants now. He wants to marry me. Of all the people I could have been paired with, I could do much worse than Kapina.

My only hesitation is that creepy wizard. He said he must search our archives to find the relic that has caused this castle to float. Father was so desperate that he gave Horngill free reign. The wizard keeps asking if Grandmother gave me a piece of jewelry or a special box. There's a gleam in his eye that scares me and I don't know why.

Princess Grenoir

Oh, Honored Wisdom,

Blessed Fandrare, I have found you at last. The incessant buzzing of magic hovered around the princess's chambers. "Gift?" "Not Uluiria?" "Amethyst?" I apologize for the disrespect the ignorant child has shown. I see why she wanders lost through the skies, instead of having her every desire fulfilled by your pristine pages. My words shall always address the utmost respect to your superior power and knowledge.

Currently, the one known as Grenoir—who gives a princess such an inelegant name?—promenades with Prince Kapina along the walls of this fortress. The prince is as foolish as the princess. He truly believes we've been sent here to break the curse, earning him the hand of the fair Grenoir.

Naturally, I have told him I could easily remove the curse once the king agrees to the marriage. I had to buy time, and it worked! I have successfully rescued you, Honored Wisdom, from the whims of a witless royal.

Fret not, I have no intention of using your power for vanity, but only as a means to ensure the resurrection of the great wizards who created you and the other relics of your era. For now, I wish only for a peaceful spot to rest my head while I contemplate how best to move forward.

I await your advice with you tucked safely under my pillow. Bring me the dreams of the wise, and I will restore the glory of sorcerers everywhere.

Horngill, Wizard of the Bronter Court

Oh, Honored Wisdom,

My exhaustion must have been great last night. We were, after all, many weeks on the road in search of you. I did not rise until the prince tossed a pillow at me from his adjacent room. The giggling buffoon apparently had an entertaining night with the princess and couldn't wait to tell me the good news, as if I cared about his love life. He's going to ask for her hand in marriage tonight. That gave me the entire day to study and meditate.

Kapina waltzed from my chamber like a trained dog at the Spring Festival. This is why it is imperative that I revive the power of the wizards of old and save the Nine Kingdoms from the rule of the moronic royalty.

To that end, I spent the day studying all I could find on the magic of the written word and enchanted books. Of all I read, I discovered nothing to help me decipher your unique soul or how to call to you and get you to answer.

You are not my first relic. Since the sight first came to me, when I reached my fourteenth year, I have used the ability to sense magic to recover twenty-two items of varying usage. For a reason I cannot discern, a wizard of old enchanted a pair of socks to hiccup whenever they became separated by more than a body length. Regardless of the practicality of the artifact, I am well on my way to acquiring the twenty-five pieces necessary to attract the attention of Fandrarc in his Mountain Top Fortress. Once He sees how dedicated I am to the Resurrection, the God of all Wizards will reinstate our true place as rulers of man.

But I get ahead of myself. With the easy travel of a floating castle, I must learn how to ask you to take us to the next relic. By all accounts, you should be able to amplify my ability to search every area we pass over so I can find those last two elusive pieces. Yet, the written records are vague on how I get my request granted. The guide I am compiling for each relic will act as a record so no wizard will ever have to...

I'm afraid I managed to bend the corner of a page in my haste to put you away at a frantic knock on my door. Please forgive my innocent abuse. Princess Grenoir—with that ever-present handmaiden of hers—practically broke the wood from the hinges in her desperate insistence that I open the door immediately. I must say your pull, oh Honored One, is great. The girl's eyes were red from crying, and she begged me to use magic to find her lost book. She couldn't imagine where she'd left it, but she had a promise to keep and had to have it back.

The inside of my cheek is sore from the bite I gave myself to stifle a smile of triumph. She thought she lost it. Never even suggested someone stole it. That child knows nothing of the world and does not deserve to hold your power within her grasp. After offering her platitudes of cooperation, I sent her away. Nevertheless, I must discover your secrets quickly before she orders a complete search of the castle.

Horngill, Wizard of the Bronter Court, soon-to-be ruler of Bronter

Oh, Honored Wisdom,

In desperation, I read the entries by the child. First, I offer my gratitude to the Great God Fandrare for giving me the gift of magic so I never experience such moronic desires. She is so self-absorbed she didn't realize her power rested within her grasp the whole time. But I saw it, and I see how the magic works now.

She wished for rain to fall and it did, in great torrents. She wished to fly through the sky on an adventure, so you gave her a floating castle. She wished for a green salad, so you influenced Kapina to purchase the entire market's worth of greens. You truly are powerful.

I wish to discover the last three relics so I can awaken the sleeping power and stand at the head of the new Age of Wizardry.

Wizard Horngill, soon-to-be Grand Wizard of the Nine Kingdoms

Hello,

I feel as if I am somehow trespassing, and yet, I cannot refrain from scribing my innermost thoughts onto your pristine pages. Such an odd thing to find in Horngill's quarters. I knew at once this book of some girth was the very item my dear Princess Grenoir had been searching for frantically for two days and nights.

I cannot believe Horngill has sacrificed himself in some sort of quest to obtain mythical items of ancient magic. I cannot clear my mind of the image of the old mage atop the highest tower, standing tall with arms stretched into the clouds. He beseeched a god whose name I had never encountered at the same moment that we drifted over the Blackened Volcano in the Unnamed Land to the north of the Nine Kingdoms. Spouting off nonsense about a magical circlet deep below the magma chambers, Horngill dived off the tower into the volcano. The entire way down, he laughed like a madman who sniffed far too much of an apothecary's wares.

I should be sad for his loss, but his disappearance as soon as I needed him to enchant the princess to adore me forced me to discount him as useful in any way. Luckily, my natural charm and incredible good looks won Princess Grenoir over.

I still, however, needed a way to break the curse on my future queen so we could ride off to our life. As soon as I found you tucked into Wizard Horngill's bag—where he routinely endeavors to hide his delectable sweet treats from me—I knew at once I had to bring you to my beloved. It is true I only met her a couple days ago, and yet, I am attached to her like a duck to its bill. The thought of her going one more evening without your comfort brought me endless sorrow. Yet, I found no indication of Horngill's method for dispelling the curse.

This is why I opened your cover. Something told me the answer was inside.

Still, I cannot help but be a tad jealous that all of the attention Grenoir showed me, when I first arrived, evaporated as soon as you disappeared from her life. Do I need to be rid of you to ensure I am her top priority? What must happen when we are married and she must accompany me to the throne dais and look upon me adoringly as I rule the people in the righteous way only I can? The then-Queen Grenoir must not dwell internally on what she will tell her secret paper lover when she should spend each thought on her husband, the king. I cannot tolerate another underling disobeying my wishes.

Hence, I have decided. I must destroy you. For my future queen must not practice fidelity to an inanimate object. Let us determine if Wizard Horngill was correct in his interpretation on your inner workings.

I wish for you to disappear from my life and may we never cross paths again.

Prince Kapina, heir to the throne of Bronter, the most illustrious kingdom of the Nine

. . .

Dear Amethyst,

Please forgive my absence. But then, you have, haven't you? You knew full well that it wasn't my fault I wasn't writing in you every day. As I scoured the castle looking for you, I was so afraid the Gods of Good or the Gods of Evil—maybe even both—were going to destroy us for breaking my oath with Grandmother. It turns out I needed to be more worried about you being upset than them, didn't I?

For, I read what that horrible wizard and handsome, but deeply arrogant, prince wrote in you. Horngill was right, wasn't he? You *are* one of the ancient magical artifacts. Grandmother must have known. I think I understand her warning to me now. Let me clarify.

The prince told you what happened to Wizard Horngill. Apparently, we must be careful what we wish for. I bet there *is* a magical circlet under the lava pit.

As for Kapina, the man I thought I was going to marry, well, that's an interesting tale. I wonder if you set these things up precisely or if the magic designs its own path? I read his words wishing to be far apart from you. He climbed to the same tower as the wizard.

Mother almost had a heart attack. You know she had already planned what she would do with my chambers when I was married off. Though, I might be judging my mother unfairly. After watching Horngill dive from the same spot, maybe she was a bit sensitive to death at the moment.

Father paced the ramparts shouting orders to anyone who got too near. He kept mumbling about war with Renetton *and* Bronter. And he wasn't wrong. How would we convince the king of Bronter that his son threw himself off the floating castle, a day after his wizard, all on his own?

Sometimes made up stories are easier to believe than the real-life things that happen.

Instead of jumping, Prince Kapina threw *you* over the side. My scream reverberated off the stone walls of the castle like the call of some sort of desperate mother bird who watched her baby fall from its nest. The silver in your lettering and spine sparkled—looking back, it could have been the sun—but I *swear* it wasn't a natural glow.

Then the miraculous happened. A gust of wind—strong enough to lift you from freefall—blew you back over the wall and right into my arms. You felt warm and secure, and I never felt more of a connection in my life. I owe Grandmother an apology for thinking she was a bad gift giver. She's the best.

Right now the prince paces in the courtyard awaiting the opening of the gates when we touch ground. He can't get anywhere near me, because I refuse to put you down. I guess he *is* getting what he wished for.

I'm not as disappointed as I thought I would be if he rejected me. After reading his entry, I know we would have been a horrible match. I care for way more than my own ego, even if it's not so much the princessy things my mother wishes I focused on.

We've got a lot to do, Amethyst. I promise to keep my wishes to a bare minimum. I promise to think of others before myself. And I promise to do a lot of research before making any decisions.

I think we should first get those magical artifacts from Wizard Horngill's private collection and hide them wherever you think is appropriate. What do you say?

By the Gods of Good, you just flashed your spine at me! I *knew* it was on purpose. We're going to make the perfect pair, Amethyst.

Let's head to Bronter. We can drop off Prince Pretty Teeth, find those magical items, and give Grandmother a big kiss. I have to write it though, don't I? Okay, here goes.

I wish to travel to Bronter.

Grenoir, Keeper of Amethyst and Protector of the Nine Kingdoms

Meet Kelly Lynn Colby

Kelly Lynn Colby is a writer of all things fantasy. Whenever she tries to create a mundane story, a dragon pops in to take over. She eventually stopped fighting and caved to the magic. The dragons must have known something she didn't, because her debut novel, *Tarbin's True*

Heir, won a bronze medal in the IPPYs for fantasy. You can find her work in the Recharging series as well as numerous short stories in various anthologies. Look for her new paranormal thriller series Emergence, with first book *The Collector* set to release in February 2021. Her BS in biology hangs above her desk looking important while she writes about other worlds. To learn more about Kelly, follow her on Facebook.com/kcolbywrites or Twitter @kcolbywrites. If you really want to stalk her, check out her website at https://kellylynncolby.com.

Only the Dead

John D. Payne

They say only the dead know no fear, but I know that's a lie. I've been dead for thirty years, and I'm still scared as hell.

Bugs used to freak me out. For a while I just couldn't stop thinking about all those bugs eating my body. I would just be sitting there, trying to fade out, and all of a sudden in the darkness I would think I was in my coffin, and I could feel the bugs burrowing into my blind eyes. I would scream and scream, and the more I screamed the more I believed I could feel them wriggling around inside my squishy rotten head. It's not true, though. I can't feel my body.

But when you're deprived of your senses, you start to imagine that you can still sense things. Your mind works overtime and starts seeing patterns in the static. That's why it's so hard to tell what's real and what's not. Mostly, it's what's not. Mostly, it's just me, just me and my regrets, stumbling around in the blackness, shouting at people who think I'm a hallucination, telling them to leave me alone when all I really want is someone to talk to, but I'm afraid. I'm afraid of everybody. I'm afraid they're really not there, and all there is is me.

The scariest thing is the not-knowing. I don't just mean not knowing what comes next. I'm used to that, although somehow I thought that would change when I kicked it.

But you also don't know what's going on now. Again, not new. But it's worse here. Not even sure where *here* is. Sometimes, I think I haven't gone anywhere at all. It's the same crummy planet I've known and loved, just dead and decayed now. Like me.

But sometimes everything seems different. Alien landscapes, impossible and incomprehensible. Have I gone somewhere? Or have things just fallen apart? I don't know. I can't even decide which possibility is more frightening.

A certain woman I know says that this is all there ever was, and all my memories are fake. When she was alive she went to a shrink for years and years until she became convinced that her father had molested her when she was a little girl. And then after years of going to another shrink, she realized that those memories were false, and her father never molested her at all. She cried about that a lot when she was alive, because she had slandered her father, and he had gone to the grave with bitter words between them.

Then she died, too, and she couldn't wait to find him. But she couldn't find him, couldn't find anything, couldn't find herself, and she was left alone with her regrets and her false memories. Now she believes that all her memories are false, that she never lived, that she's always been dead, that this is all there is. And now she cries because she can never apologize to the imaginary father she falsely remembers slandering in an insane hallucination that never was a life. But she loves that father she never had, and she keeps trying to imagine him back, except he won't come, and she's left here alone again, which is why she says that it's not real, that it never was real, that nothing is real and it's all in her head. But she cries because that's a lie. She used to be alive and she used to have a father who loved her, but now she's just dead, and nobody loves anybody here.

Back when I was alive, I was in the television business. Mostly, I produced a lot of crappy shows. I think the best thing I ever did was this made-for-television, war movie called "The Ten Commandos." See, it was one of those allegorical kind of things. Each of the commandos represented one of the ten commandments. You remember that, right? Came out about twenty years ago. More, maybe. I mean, I've been dead for twelve or thirteen years now. After you're dead, you sort of lose track of time.

That movie worked on a lot of different levels. I mean, Joe Six-pack just watches for the action. Like the scene where Pappy rides the motorcycle into the pillbox and takes out a whole nest of Nazis before one of them shoots him in the back. Or when Steele and Daltrey have that huge shootout with a bunch of SS guys in the brothel. Great scene. Bullets and black bustiers. I mean, that's entertainment.

On the other hand, your churchy crowd likes the fact that Sgt. Sunday is the one who is always telling the lieutenant to stop and give the boys a rest. Keep the Sabbath day holy. Fourth command-ment or whatever. "These boys have been working hard, Graven. Let's give 'em a rest. Let 'em stop and say a prayer and thank God they're still alive. Let 'em rest, lieutenant." Or how nobody ever says the name of the third commando, even in the credits. He's just the third commando, and you can't take his name in vain. That kind of thing. Lot of symbolism. Pretty deep for a TV movie.

Doesn't matter, though. It's all gone, now. The TV, the comman-dos, the commandments, all gone. Just me and my memories. And I sit back and think about my life if it was a life and not just wishful thinking, a hallucination—and the best thing I ever did was a stupid made-for-television movie. The best thing I ever did, and it didn't mean a thing, even when I was alive, and things mattered and made sense.

I have nothing now. Nothing. It's all gone. I used to be scared of being alone, and so I always made sure I was surrounded by people, always in a crowd. Three marriages, two lousy kids, and a bunch of friends, and none of them care enough to come find me and get me out of here. Leave me here with a bunch of dead people and I'm all alone, all alone. Does everybody feel this empty? Has it always been this way? Am I just noticing this now because I'm dead?

I can't see too good now, and that scares me. That doesn't make any sense, because my eyes worked just fine when I was alive. Up until the last few years, anyway, and even then I could see. Funny story about that. When I first died, I thought I was a vegetable. Apparently, I was having a stroke or something. I don't know, I'm not a doctor. And then I couldn't see. Not a thing.

And for the longest time, I thought I had gone blind and I sat there crying and crying because I couldn't see anything and there were all these horrible sounds and nothing made sense, so I figured that I had become a paraplegic or something and I was hallucinating. And then it came to me that I was dead, and I remember thinking, "Thank God! I'm not blind after all!"

Cracks me up.

There's a lot of things you got to watch out for when you're dead. Other people, for instance. Whole lot of crazies, mostly. Go around moaning and screaming. Sometimes, I think I can feel them touching me, feel them biting me.

I read the Bible a few times before I croaked, and I remember bits and pieces. I keep thinking of this bit where it talks about "weeping and wailing and gnashing of teeth," and now a lot of times when I start to space out, all of a sudden there are these teeth gnashing on me and I start screaming, but then I realize it's just me. Just me imagining those damn teeth. Nobody here has a mouth to gnash me with, except me and the mouth in my head.

That's why I went up North. Quieter. Not that it's deserted or anything. I mean, if you thought that the world was crowded when you were alive, just wait until you're dead. There's just people all over the place. Sometimes, it seems like everybody in the world who ever lived is here, but that can't be right. Somebody must have got out; somebody must have got away.

I went to Canada to get away—from the war, I mean. Back in the day. But it's not really Canada anymore. Canada's dead. So I came back.

One of those horse-shit, holy roller evangelists on a show I produced told me once that this world is a prison. He said, we spend all our time sprucing up our cell, trying to get it nice. What we should really be doing is trying to escape. Get out of Dodge, get up and get out of here, that's what we should be trying to do. He was drunk when he said it, and so was I so maybe I didn't get it all right, but I still thought he was trying to say something preachy. Year and a half later he was dead. Shot himself.

Maybe that evangelist thought he was going to escape, but I guess he found out that this prison's a lot better built than you might think.

That scares me, too, because it makes me wonder who built this jail cell, and why they hate me so much. Think about it. No escape. No getting out. Stay here, like this, forever. That's some serious hate. It's crazy. Nobody deserves that. I know I wasn't much of a man, but I never would have thought I deserved this. I never used to pray when I was alive, but I've tried it a few times since being dead. I can't tell if there's anyone there listening besides all the crazy people. I wish there were.

Sometimes I wonder what God knows about me that I don't, why he did this to me. And then I remember—I remember everything—and I think maybe this is what I deserve, to be left here all alone with the imaginary bugs and the gnashing teeth and all the crazy people who won't shut up and leave me alone and sit down and talk to me. I know I wasn't much of a man, but I still just want to get out of here.

But everybody misses sleep. It's hard to be awake all the time, to always be on. People get edgy. They go nuts. That's why there's no more politeness. Everyone screams at each other all day long and all night. Everybody hates everybody. I hate everybody, and everybody hates me. Even you.

That's okay. I don't take it personal. Hate's all we got left, so we hang on to it. I'm no different. I hate me; I hate everybody. I don't know who you are but I hate you—because if you really loved me you would get me out of here. But you won't. You're going to get out of here yourself and leave me alone with my false memories to die and die and die and die all by myself and never be dead. So get out, go away, what do I care, I hate you.

I didn't mean that. Come back.

No, leave me alone. Don't talk to me. I can't hear you, anyway. I'm dead. And I'm trying to sleep. So shut up, already.

I just want to sleep, just want to blank out and shut down and be nothing. The blackness came and swallowed me up but I'm still here and I can't get out and I'm scared and I can't sleep. I'm so tired, but I just can't sleep.

Once I was with this bunch of people who were talking about one of my old shows, and they had everything wrong, and I was trying to correct them but they couldn't hear what I was saying and that made me angry, even though nobody can ever hear anybody anymore because everybody is dead.

But these people all heard each other; they all saw each other. They had found the secret, they had figured it out, and they had someone to talk to who wasn't a crazy old dead person, and they wouldn't tell me what it was. They were sitting around talking about me, about my shows, and they won't talk to me even though I was right there.

I got so angry, got so frightened that I tried to kill them all, but I couldn't, of course, because I got no hands or teeth or anything to kill them with. So I left. Sometimes, I think maybe they were alive, but maybe it's just another false memory.

Sometimes when I was alive people would say things like, if you could sit down and talk with anyone who ever lived, who would it be? Or people would say, when I get to the other side, I can't wait to talk to so and so.

Well, guess what? They're not here. Nobody is. There's no God, no angels, no saints, no happy people singing on clouds. There's no people at all, no people anywhere. Only the dead.

All those people you wanted to talk to? They're dead, and they're gone. Even if you find them, they're still gone. Everybody's gone. All those beautiful interesting funny people who were alive once, they left. And nobody is here but us hateful old dead people.

You know what scares me most? That this is all there is. When I was alive, I was scared that there was no afterlife. Now I'm scared because there is.

And I'm afraid it won't ever stop.

Meet John D. Payne

John D. Payne grew up on the prairie, where the tornadoes and electrical storms play. Watching the lightning flash outside his window, he imagined himself as everything from a leaf on the wind to the god of thunder. Today, he lives with his wife and family at the foot of the Organ Mountains in New Mexico, where he focuses his weather-god powers on rustling up enough cloud cover for a little shade. John's debut novel, *The Crown and the Dragon*, is an epic fantasy published by WordFire Press. You can find his stories on podcasts like The Overcast, magazines like StoryHack, and books like *X Marks the Spot: An Anthology of Treasure and Theft*. Stalk him on Twitter @jdp_writes. Patronize him at https://www.patreon.com/johndpayne.

Across the Unknown

L.T. Adams

Sweat rolled down the back of Köga'ra's neck, sliding between her shoulder blades and along her spine before soaking into the leather of her breechcloth. Every muscle in her body quivered under the strain of her climb, fingers and toes tucked deeply into the cracks and crevices between the crumbling stones of the tower. With a grunt, she pushed upward, the strength of her brawny thighs propelling her upward to the lip of the window. A strong hand reached out and grasped hers, pulling her up and over the ledge and into the shadows within the tower.

She accepted the canteen offered to her and drank deeply, then handed it back and wiped her mouth, leaning out of the window and looking down the side of the tower. Below, another pair of Bloodfire orcs labored up the same climb. They had already surpassed the point where the vines and other vegetation stopped, leaving them nothing but the crumbling cracks between stones as handholds. The faded white stone had weakened with time, and more than once she had been forced to shift her grip before the stone disintegrated beneath her hand—a fact that made her fear for those that were still climbing.

"They will make it." A hand fell on her shoulder as reassurance.

She shrugged it off. "Easy enough for you to say. Dükog could barely stand when he woke this morning, and Grotug is twice your size. Not all of us are scrawny enough to make the climb without trouble," she snarled.

Skrôl said nothing, but his body stiffened. Scrawny really was the wrong word for him. He had broad shoulders with long arms, in addition to being taller and smaller through the hips than most of his kinsmen. He moved up to the window next to her, staring out across the bog below, his fierce yellow eyes fixed beyond the horizon. Black mud and verdant, scrubby vegetation stretched for leagues to the east. Steep, rocky slopes lined the sides of the valley to the north and south, affording someone at the top of the tower—situated as it was at the west end of the valley—a commanding view of the land below.

Far beyond the mouth of the valley, Köga'ra knew, was a plain so wide and vast that it had taken them months to traverse it. Waist high grass, the color of fresh blood rolling as far as the eye could see, had hidden terrifying threats that even their years in this new world had not prepared them for. The months before that, they had wandered through a labyrinth of rocky hills so covered in mist that even their sharpened senses and heightened skill at wildcraft gave them no advantage. And within that mist, the dead, awakened by some malevolent force. Their ancient tombs, relics of a civilization long lost, had disguised their dangers under the elegance of skilled stone carving. So many had died there.

"How have we discovered no other beings here?" Skrôl asked, staring down at his tribesmen as they struggled to make the rest of the journey.

"We have discovered many living things," Köga'ra responded.

Skrôl snorted. "But no cultures. No humans or elves. No dwarves or half-people. The signs of their being are everywhere. Tombs in the Mistlands, the abandoned fortresses in the Frostclaws, even this tower. People of some kind lived here once. Where have they gone?"

"Does it matter? They are not here now." Sometimes the rangy orc let himself think too much. "At least we did not have to kill them to take this place. It is simply ours."

"No." A voice, almost completely breathless, came from below them.

They extended their hands and with little effort pulled Dükog through the tower window. Skrôl passed the waterskin, and the lanky shaman on the floor drank deeply. He breathed heavily for several moments, then drank again before handing the skin back. After a moment, he stood with some help from Köga'ra.

Sweat beaded on his bald head, playing along the lines of the intricate black tattoos that snaked across his gray-green skin from his unruly black eyebrows to the base of his skull. "No. This place is not ours. It is the place we live, not where we belong."

Neither Köga'ra nor Skrôl said anything. They knew what he meant, but even after three years in this abandoned world, it was difficult to say aloud.

The discovery had not taken them long after they arrived. Perhaps some had even felt it the moment their feet touched the grass of this strange new place. If they had, they would have attributed their troubled hearts to their tremendous loss and the sudden change in their circumstance. The Night of Blood—that single night when they stepped through the World Door and all of their tribe's warriors sacrificed themselves to save their children from slavery—could explain all of their unease. But the next day, when they performed their sacred ritual to summon the spirits of their ancestors and thank them for their protection, they learned the terrible truth about this place.

Their spirits could not see them here.

Fear had never reigned so completely among them. Even Köga'ra, whose bravery and fortitude were given high praise among her people and whose father had led their warriors to victory and slaughter at the Blood Pass, had not been able to comfort or console the Bloodfire orcs on that day. Only time and the wild young orc shaman before them had been able to do it.

With his herbs and fungi, Dükog had planted himself firmly between the worlds of the physical and the spiritual, seeking a source for answers. For days, he drank his tonics and danced madly around bonfires made of wood from trees that had no name in orc-tongue. Screaming at the heavens one moment and weeping in the dirt the next, he prayed and sang until his voice was hoarse. Dark spirits came and the rest of them hid in their newly made huts while Dükog conversed with them in tongues no sane orc could know. What was said was a mystery, but after days in stupor and madness, the young shaman—no more than fifteen summers out of his mother's womb—had come back to them. With clear eyes, he shared his good news; he had a plan, and he knew where to go.

A heavy hand planted itself in the window. Skrôl offered help, but Grotug pulled himself through on his own, his massive body crashing onto the floor like a felled tree. With an effort, the three of them managed to get him to his feet. The gargantuan warrior was sweating profusely, his thick ebony braid soaked in perspiration that ran in rivulets down his broad shoulders and thick chest. Without asking, he swiped the waterskin from Skrôl's hand and drank heavily until it was exhausted. Wiping his lips with a heavy hand, he tossed the empty bag back at his tall companion.

Skrôl growled.

"So, where do we go next?" Grotug was glancing around the interior of the tower. The room was large and empty but for a single door that stood opposite the window. He raised an eyebrow and looked at Dükog.

The wiry shaman pointed a single, heavy nail at the floor. "I can feel the pull, brother. I have for years now. We go down."

"Back to the bottom? We were just there," Grotug huffed.

"No. Farther." Dükog looked certain.

Grotug nodded. "Then let's go." He moved toward the door.

"Easy, Grotug." Skrôl laid a hand on the larger warrior's arm. "We've already lost many. A little caution might be good."

Grotug looked into the thinner warrior's eyes and laughed. He shrugged off the hand and moved as if he meant to kick the door in.

"Stop, idiot." Köga'ra grabbed Grotug by his thick braid and pulled him backwards. While the action did not move him, it did cause him to stop. "Too many have died already. Stop being foolish and slow down."

Her people often suffered from a lack of caution, and none more so than Grotug. It was tiring having to be his milk mother. She moved past him into the dimly lit interior, the light from the window dissipating into the large space.

Skrôl produced a torch and lit it quickly, then the four of them moved toward the interior. Köga'ra drew her father's bone-bladed axe from her back. Each of the others drew their weapons as well: Skrôl one of the short spears from the leather casing on his back, Grotug the massive bronze maul he had found in one of the fortresses in the Frostclaws, and Dükog a long bone dagger decorated with the feathers of a large native bird. Köga'ra pushed cautiously at the door with her axe and to her surprise, it swung quietly on its hinges.

The four of them moved silently with Köga'ra in the lead. Wide steps led straight down to a shadowed landing, with more disappearing into the darkness. They were broad enough for them to spread out and they did so. Though it was full daylight outside, the black inside the tower was complete. Only the light of the torch allowed them to see at all, and what they could see was very plain. Cut stones fit closely together, no windows, with plain dressing on the stairs and railing.

Their steps carried them down one landing at a time. After a half-dozen or so, they noticed a door. A simple look at Dükog was all it took. He pointed down, and they continued descending.

Dükog had shown them the way since the beginning. After his visions and rituals, he had slept for days while the rest of the tribe adjusted to their new world. When he awoke, he was insistent that they leave immediately. But the tribe had to be settled—hunting grounds established and herbs and vegetables found. It had taken them almost a year just to get the tribe on its feet. At the end of that time, the young shaman stood up at a council meeting and declared that he was leaving to search for the "pull," as he called it. It was something between an urge and a voice, and he often described it in both terms or as being between the two. Many of the tribe's warriors had volunteered to come, and it was decided that Köga'ra would lead them. She had swelled with pride on that night, so sure that her father would approve and that she would be the one to get them all home safely. It had been a sorely misplaced confidence.

The whole lot of them, more than a dozen in total, had almost turned back after being poisoned by water from a seemingly harmless spring. It was not long until Ulog died of a single bite from a tiny lizard the length of his hand with a snake's neck and head. Only a few weeks later, Gara succumbed to a sickness that caused her to vomit a thick yellow slime for days. One by one, they fell to wildlife or disease. Îka was swallowed up by a creature the size of a dragon that looked just like a boulder at the foot of the Frostclaws. Rùtog was buried by an avalanche in those same mountains. Gopü, Dug'gâ, and Drügô had died in the Mistlands at the hands of the ghouls that lurked in that sunless place. And Gûnlog, Ülg, and Hag'gâ simply disappeared from camp one night in the Silk Forest without a sound or trace.

Of course, the journey had not been all evil and adversity. She had seen wonderful and amazing things as they trekked across this strange new world. Herds of creatures that looked like aurochs stretched from horizon to horizon as they migrated across the ruby grass of the Blood Prairie. There was a river so wide that at first they believed it to be a lake—and a pair of creatures battling in its waters that resembled wingless, legless dragons of immense size. Îka aptly dubbed it Running Lake, to Köga'ra's amusement. There were other marvels as well: an entire month when the sun was a beautiful, deep purple, swarms of colorful moths that nearly blocked out the moon, and—perhaps the most amazing of all—pods of creatures larger than a dragon that seemed to *swim* through the sky.

Through it all, Dükog pushed them relentlessly forward. Just as they honed their skills as hunters and warriors, he drove himself to learn about this new world. When Skrôl discovered a new wood from which to make his spears, Dükog discovered the leaves of the same tree could be boiled to make a potent salve for burns. As Köga'ra learned to hunt new and bizarre creatures, the dark spirits that spoke to Dükog showed him rites and rituals that could freeze waters, tame the wind, and summon a dark and forbidding flame that could be manipulated with his mind. All the while, they pushed forward, guided only by the young shaman's connection to the "pull."

The four of them passed several more doors on the way down, leaving them behind, untouched, as they followed Dükog's direction. The last landing, wider than the rest, led to stairs that broadened before touching down to a room that must have been as large around as the tower itself. "This is the ground floor," Köga'ra said quietly. Skrôl nodded his agreement, his spearpoint indicating a large double door to one side of the room. From the outside, the door had been covered with vines and roots so thick it would have taken weeks to work through them.

"Well, now what?" Grotug grunted irritably, his yellow eyes roving the shadows of the massive room. He was unsettled and rightly so. The place was unnerving. There had been no furniture, no broken chests or decayed bodies. Other than mild aging, everything in the tower showed no damage or habitation at all.

Dükog huffed. "We must keep going down. Whatever is calling to me, it's beneath us."

"Get to looking. Yell if you find anything." Köga'ra shoved her own torch into Skrôl's hand as she spoke. Her steps carried her into the darkness as her keen senses bent to the task of searching for a way down.

The others wandered off, tiny orbs of orange glow in the vast expanse of the room. Not for the first time, she looked around and felt a mild revulsion for this place. It was so empty, yet completely intact. The combination felt unnatural and she mused that something terrible must have happened to the people who had lived here once. Did the power that they now searched for destroy them? She tried to shake away the thought, but it nagged her.

Her thoughts were interrupted when Grotug shouted and they made their way over to him. He waved his torch at the ground. At his feet was a large metal grate, inlaid in the stone with a rusty lock securing it.

"Grotug, open it."

The massive orc's eyes lit up with undisguised joy. He tossed his torch to the side, gripped his bronze maul in two gargantuan hands and swung. The muscles of his shoulders bunched and flexed, and the lock flew across the floor, narrowly missing Skrôl's foot.

"Watch it!" Skrôl growled.

Grotug laughed, then reached down and opened the grate with one arm. There was only a slight creak of the hinges, then a deafening boom as it slammed into the stone. Again, stairs were visible in the flickering light of the torch, and again they led downward. These stairs, however, were hewn from the living rock and far too narrow to descend more than one at a time.

"Skrôl, you're in the lead with the torch, then me, then Dükog. Grotug, you watch our backs. If anything comes from behind us, you don't let us get stuck down here." Köga'ra readied her axe and motioned to the stairs.

"We should slow down. What is down here that needed to be locked in?" Skrôl said. He squatted next to the entrance, eyes focused on its invisible depths. "This feels... off."

"We didn't come all this way for nothing," Köga'ra snapped, irritated by his caution. "Do you see any sign up here of what might be down there?"

Skrôl shook his head.

"Then no matter how it feels, we go in or we go back. And we didn't survive fire and ice and beast to be defeated by nagging doubt."

Skrôl growled, but did as he was bid. Köga'ra fell in behind him, with the others gathering behind her. Going through the entry felt like entering another unfamiliar world. Stone transitioned abruptly from well-cut white to rough-hewn brown in a matter of moments. The smell of moisture and mold wafted up to them from below, and shortly after they began to hear sounds of water dripping. The going was slow—the stones being slick underfoot—and they strained their eyes and ears for any trace of sound.

The stairway wound downward for what seemed an eternity. Every step brought with it a new anxiety about the step after it, and soon they could not bear the thought of another moment in the cramped space. Just when Köga'ra began to wonder if they should go back, she noticed Skrôl's saffron ponytail stopped moving.

"We're here," he whispered.

Köga'ra prodded him with the top of her axe, and he moved forward slowly, eyes scanning the room. She had thought the room at the bottom of the tower to be large, but it was paltry in size compared to the cavern they now found themselves in. The light of their torches disappeared into endless darkness above them, barely illuminating the tips of stalactites throughout the space. Small puddles were everywhere, and the sound of running water seemed to come from all directions at once. Step by careful step they moved into the cavern, around the huge stalagmites that haphazardly dotted the floor.

Dükog knelt suddenly, motioning for them to look. A trench, clearly not a natural part of the cavern, ran into the darkness. It was filled nearly to the brim with a fine powder that seemed unaffected by the moisture of the cave. Without hesitation, the shaman shoved his torch into the powder.

Köga'ra jumped back as the powder caught fire. Hissing loudly, it leapt into the darkness, running up ledges and around the vast space, splitting every so often to create another branch in the fiery tree spreading through the cave. In moments, the entire cavern was illuminated with a soft, off-white light. The flame seemed to produce almost no heat and cast no smoke. A spicy scent filled the air, something akin to dried peppers.

"What kind of magic is this?" Grotug snarled, his maul readied as if an enemy would jump from behind a nearby rock.

Perhaps they would.

"Some kind of herb-work, brother." Dükog was holding his hand over the flame, his eyes focused. "The people who were here before must have been sorcerers."

Skrôl motioned ahead. "They must have been great builders as well."

Now that the cavern was fully illuminated, Köga'ra could see a broad bridge of cut stone that matched the tower above in color. It appeared well constructed but had no rails or walls of any kind. Below it, a wide underground river rushed through the cave, running from a wall to their left and disappearing into the wall to their far right. She could also see a large natural opening in the wall opposite them and the only way to reach it appeared to be the bridge.

"Watch your step," Köga'ra said quietly. Or perhaps she was loud. It was difficult to hear anything over the sound of the water.

They made their way to the bridge. Grotug wasted no time before he was up the steps and on the bridge itself. In a blink, he slipped and fell to one knee, cursing loudly as his torch went flying into the water and was carried off.

"Watch out; it's slick," Skrôl offered.

Grotug cursed again, this time not at the wet stone, if the words he used were any indication.

"Be careful, Grotug. If you fall in, we cannot save you. This water is too fa... " she began, but never finished the sentence.

A beast leaped from the water, as long as an orc from hair to heel and as large around as Grotug's forearm. It was as white as a pearl and had no arms or legs, only a fin that ran the length of its body on top and bottom. The sound of its jaws snapping together could be heard above the rush of the river, and it seemed it only missed because Grotug fell. It touched the left side of the bridge just barely before slipping back into the water below.

"What the hell!?" Grotug roared.

"Brother, stay low!" Dükog shouted from the foot of the bridge.

His words had no sooner left his mouth than another beast leapt from the water at him, its jaws wide. The wiry shaman had little time to move before the beast was upon him, and he dove just below the water creature. It sailed over him and landed on the unworked stone. Though it seemed like an eel when she first glimpsed it, Köga'ra saw now it was just as much a snake as anything, hissing loudly with its toothy maw wide open while its body coiled beneath it. Two vertical fans stuck straight out from behind its powerful jaws and rattled quickly back and forth as it hissed.

Köga'ra growled back at it and closed quickly, bringing her axe down in a deadly arc. It was a killing blow, but the beast did something unexpected—it leaped again, straight at her. She was too off-balance to dodge the blow, but brought her torch down just in time to knock it off its path. Instead of biting her in the face or throat, the beast closed its jaws too early and sailed into her shoulder with its mouth closed. It had some weight to it and plenty of momentum, enough to knock her backward. With its path to the water clear again, it slithered back in, hissing at Dükog as it moved past him. He roared back from his hands and knees.

"Skrôl—" Köga'ra began.

"I see them!" he shouted back, as another finsnake erupted from the water, this one targeting him.

His spear darted forward, catching the beast along the side, behind its jaw fan. It hissed, squirming wildly as it hit the floor with a meaty thud. The tall orc moved quickly and speared it through the bottom of its head before it had a chance to recover.

He stepped back toward Köga'ra. "We need to go back or get across the bridge. If we wait long enough, they'll get through and I don't want to know what those fangs have on them!"

Köga'ra grunted in agreement. Tossing her torch down, she helped Dükog stand and started across the bridge. Ahead of them, Grotug was crouched and trying to see in every direction at once. "Get across the bridge, idiot! You're a sitting duck out here."

Despite Köga'ra's warning, he waited for the rest of them. Another finsnake burst from the water, aiming for the big orc. He ducked, and it sailed over the top of him, landing with a splash on the other side of him. Another erupted from the water, then another. The first he dodged, the second he knocked away with a powerful fist. Both finsnakes fell off the bridge with a hiss.

Köga'ra finally reached Grotug, Dükog in tow with Skrôl in step to her left. Their weapons darted and slashed as finsnakes flew back and forth through the air. Milky green blood leaked across the white stones, making them even more slippery. Despite the fighting he was doing, Grotug's maul hung snugly from the harness on his back, undoubtedly because he realized it was too heavy to use against these creatures. As they approached, he ushered them forward, turning to watch their backs as they moved across.

A pair of finsnakes burst from the water together, aiming for Skrôl's exposed back. The rangy orc was already fending off an opponent to his left. Even if he were to see them coming, there was nothing he could do. Köga'ra only saw them, because she was looking backward to check on Grotug. They moved so quickly she did not have time to warn him.

With a speed that belied his great size, Grotug's meaty hands shot out, each of them wrapping themselves around a finsnake in midair. There was a moment when Köga'ra was simply impressed that he was strong enough to hold one in each hand while they squirmed madly. But the moment soon passed. She realized he had grabbed them too low. Twin tails wrapped themselves around his arms and their heads darted in, their fearsome teeth sinking into his bicep on one side and his shoulder on the other.

Grotug cried out and the other two turned. Skrôl reacted quickly, turning his spear in his hand and striking the creature hard just behind the head with the heavy wooden shaft. The creature reacted, letting go for a brief moment.

It was all the time Köga'ra needed.

Her bone axe lashed out, lopping the beast's head off. Its body writhed uncontrollably and Grotug released it, bringing his hand over to the other side and pulling on the beast with its teeth in his shoulder. Before he had a chance to force it free, another finsnake pounced from the water and bit deeply in the back of his thigh while wrapping its tail around his leg. The big warrior fell to one knee with a roar. Köga'ra, Skrôl, and Dükog jumped to work, stabbing and clubbing the beasts. Just when they had them all off, another creature jumped from the water, latching itself in Skrôl's shoulder.

Köga'ra cursed loudly and looked to the end of the bridge. They were very nearly to the other side. Thinking quickly, she grabbed Dükog by the shoulders and kicked his feet from underneath him, throwing him toward the steps on the far side. Just as she suspected, he slid across the slick stones without pause, rolling awkwardly down the steps. Skrôl, grunting loudly, was able to dislodge his attacker and saw her logic. He dove feet-first, sliding on his hip to the end of the bridge and rolling down the steps. There was a flash of bone axe, and half of the beast attached to Grotug fell away. The rest of it let go and hissed unsettlingly.

Köga'ra grabbed Grotug by his fur shoulder cover and pulled, dragging him along the bridge on his behind. She heard a meaty smack behind her and turned to see the massive warrior had picked up one of Skrôl's discarded spears as he was being dragged and swatted a finsnake away with the broken shaft. The two of them stumbled down the steps and she released him to fall on his back. Her heart was racing and her eyes burned as sweat dripped into them. She closed her eyes and wiped her face with the back of her hand.

The finsnake that hit her came out of nowhere. It must have been sitting atop one of the stalagmites. She caught it in midair with both hands, dropping her axe in the process. But the momentum carried her backward, and she tripped, falling into the water behind her.

To say that it was freezing would not do the water justice, and all coherent thought escaped her mind as she was enveloped. The beast escaped her grasp as she fell, and she scrambled to see anything. Before she could think, the bridge had passed above her, and she was headed toward the hole in the wall where the water disappeared.

Fear gripped her in a dread far colder than the water could ever be. No doubt this river ran for miles through pitch-black corridors, past unspeakable horrors much worse than the finsnakes, before, hopefully, depositing itself somewhere under the sun. But how long would it be until there was more air to breathe? Before the next cavern?

Instinctively, she began to paddle her legs and feet in an attempt to slow herself, but her efforts did nothing. Even as it occurred to her, she rolled to try and reach the rocky edge, only to have a finsnake bite deeply into her forearm. Her mouth opened to roar and immediately filled with water. She pulled her arm close, grabbing the beast behind the fans on its head and squeezing. It might be that she would die today in the dark and lonely tunnels through which the river ran. Or it might be that she would be eaten by some terrifying creature in the depths of the earth, unable to see the thing that devoured her. One thing was certain, though, she would choke this squirmy white bastard to death before she died.

Even as the thought occurred to her, she felt herself lifted from the water. The finsnake fell from her hand and back into the water below. With a painful thud, she slammed into the cavern floor, soaked and hacking up water. It took her a couple moments to catch her breath, but Skrôl was right there, hauling her up by her wounded arm and telling her to get moving. She acted by instinct, following her warrior's lead. Her legs worked of their own accord, propelling her forward toward a waiting Dükog. The shaman was breathing heavily, she noticed, and his eyes were the color of a summer sky from edge to edge.

Skrôl led her through the opening in the far wall, where it seemed the white fire ran down both sides of a long, wide corridor. Grotug sat just inside the opening, tending his wounds with bandages of tightly woven peddleroot and a bitter-smelling green salve of his brother's making. Skrôl sat in front of Köga'ra and started dressing his own wounds.

Köga'ra tried to catch her breath. Fear still coursed through her veins, and her chest felt as if Grotug were sitting on it. "What in the hell just happened? How did I not drown?"

Grotug motioned to Dükog. "Turns out this one is good for something besides picking flowers and turning them into drugs. He pulled you from the water with his magic."

Köga'ra looked up at Dükog, who was now kneeling and dressing the wound on her arm. She had seen magic before and had even seen him perform it. But never had she seen him perform anything like that. For the first time, she saw how this journey across the new world had changed him. He had gone from a scrawny pup, that she used to chase with snakes, to a capable shaman. But power was never free, and she wondered how much he had sacrificed to claim it. It was a dark thought, and not one that she could shake from her mind easily.

"Does it sting?" he asked her, as he wrapped the bleeding punctures, completely oblivious to her thoughts. His eyes had returned to their normal color, and they searched her wound, pushing and prodding.

"No, just hurts," she snarled as she searched his eyes for some hint that the power he wielded affected his mind.

But nothing in him indicated he had changed. Satisfied by her answer, he patched her arm.

It did not take long to cover their wounds, and Dükog mixed a concoction he said would dull their pain. It was the color of a misty sky and tasted terrible, but it did not take long for him to be proven mostly correct. In less than an hour, she was standing, axe in hand as they walked steadily down the long hallway.

Dükog's intensity increased the longer they walked. Köga'ra could see just by watching him that they were closing in on their prize. "So you really believe that whatever this is, it can help us speak to the ancestors again?"

Even as the words came from her mouth, she felt stupid. If she did not believe his vision, then why did she spend the last two years following him across the most dangerous place any of her people had ever seen? But she knew the answer—if she was being honest with herself—she was afraid that Skrôl was right. A people long before them had secured whatever was down here so well it was hard to believe that it was anything good.

Dükog paid no mind to the absurdity of the question. He only nodded. "It can help us; I am sure of it. The spirits of the world showed me. Whatever is at the end of this, it can help us."

They finally reached the end of the hallway. A large double door stood closed before them, a massive wooden beam set in brackets against it. Köga'ra and Grotug stepped up to the beam, taking positions at either end. Skrôl stood ready before the door, a spear raised to throw at whatever should come rushing out. With a heave, they threw the brace onto the floor—the loud slam of it echoing down the long corridor—and pushed the doors open.

Beyond was an unfinished stone tunnel a half dozen paces in

length with an opening at the far end. Nothing could be seen beyond the portal because of the intense darkness. Köga'ra motioned to them, and they moved forward together, Grotug in the lead with his bronze maul at the ready. The moment the large orc's foot passed into the opening, a light flickered deep in the darkness. They froze, then stared in amazement as the light grew in size and brightness. She could now see a large room, thirty paces across in each direction and at least twenty paces high.

In its midst a large ball floated in midair, seemingly made of glass, and within it swirled a whirlwind of fire. Brighter and brighter it grew until its light filled the space, illuminating every corner and crevice. Green runes swirled within the sphere, flashing too quickly to study closely.

It appeared they were standing in an ancient temple. Black marble columns lined the edges of the space while gray and white marble covered everything else. The room was roughly cubical. In the middle of the room, below the ball of swirling flame, rose a dais of white marble. Broad steps leading to the summit rose from all four sides. At the top, bronze chains rattled as a creature stirred, its features indiscernible from where they stood.

Dükog was the first to mount the stairs, and Köga'ra hurried to keep up. A few quick steps and they neared the top. Even in his anticipation, the wiry shaman slowed as he approached the bound creature. When Köga'ra caught her first glimpse of it, she also paused in mute fascination.

Before them sat a being the likes of which none of them had ever seen. Deep purple skin covered every part of the body visible through a tattered, dirty robe. The body itself was orc-like, if very thin. Its legs were crossed beneath it, arms out to each side, and its round, elongated head was tilted back. But all resemblance to orcs ended at its jaw. In place of a mouth, it possessed writhing, wet tentacles that extended down to its chest, like squid from the old world. The creature did not seem to have a nose and its eyes harbored white, cat-like pupils amidst a sea of deepest black.

Heavy bronze chains ran from each corner of the dais and

attached to thick golden cuffs that fit snugly around its wrists, two chains to each arm. Glowing green runes were etched into the links of chain and cuffs, and Köga'ra could only guess their meaning. She also noticed a golden band around the forehead of the creature, like a crown, etched with runes that glowed a soft, pale blue. Bones of small animals were piled around the creature in heaps, and ran down the dais opposite their approach.

When Dükog's foot finally touched the top step, the creature's eyes focused, and it seemingly noticed them for the first time. Köga'ra saw Skrôl tighten his grip on the spear in his hand out of the corner of her eye, and she reflexively did the same on her axe. Something was wrong with this being, something more than its tentacles or its eyes or the glowing chains.

Hello.

The voice, soft and melodic, neither male nor female in tone, entered her head. She gasped in surprise, then noticed the others do the same.

Do not be startled. This is how my people communicate, as we do not have mouths like you do.

It was an unnatural feeling to hear a voice without using ears and Köga'ra disliked it.

"Who are you?" she demanded. Her voice was harder than she meant it to be, but she did not apologize.

My name is Zi'xi'quall-Iz'tox'ix, the creature answered. *But you may call me Zi, if that is your preference.*

Köga'ra shuddered. The creature's voice was too smooth and too rough. It felt like the sound of a snake's belly slithering through leaves.

"Are you the pull? Are you what I've been searching for?" Dükog asked, voice quavering. He did not reach for his knife, but his body language made him seem agitated.

Yes. I am the "pull," as you say. I have been calling to you all these long years. And now you have come to learn my secrets. Free me, and I will gladly share all that I know.

"Dükog, you know more of these things than we can ever hope to.

We have trusted you this far. What do we do?" Köga'ra asked, walking up next to the shaman. He was running his hand over his bald head, using a long index nail to unconsciously trace the tattoos on his head.

"All knowledge of our people and all of my experience fails me here. I have never met a being such as this, and I have no idea how to reach our ancestors. What other choice do we have?" Dükog might have sounded hopeless or frustrated in this situation. Instead, he seemed resigned. "How do we free you, Zi?"

The squid-mouthed creature sat straighter. *In your communion with the ethereal beings of this world, have you learned the art of dark fire?* Its voice was more energized, though it felt as if it was trying to restrain itself.

"Yes."

Then simply use it to destroy these chains, and I will be freed.

Dükog nodded. "Step back, Köga'ra."

She took two steps back down the stairs, and he held his hands out to his sides, palms up. Tilting his head back toward the ceiling, he began a guttural hum deep in his chest. Her eyes widened as fire, entirely shades of gray with a heart of black, began to burn in his palms. It spread up his forearms all the way to his elbows, seeming to consume part of him. A dark mist settled around his head, swirling around his eyes and temples. With a roar, he aimed his hands at the chains and the fire poured off him.

Köga'ra had never seen anything like it and imagined she never would again. The chains, though they were bronze and thick, burned like leaves beneath the black fire. Bits curled up, turned into tiny embers, and floated upward as if carried by heat from the flames. Dükog's breathing came in short gasps now, but he continued, holding his hands forward until the chains were completely disintegrated. As the last of the bronze floated away, the young shaman fell to his knees and vomited a thin, black mucus.

Oh, what an impressive race you are. And now, this crown. It indicated the gold band on its head. *I cannot remove it myself. Please.*

Skrôl laid his hand on Grotug's arm as he stepped forward. "No. The crown stays on for now."

The big warrior pulled his arm from the taller orc's grip and moved to step forward again.

"No!" Skrôl shouted, jumping in front of Grotug. "It stays on," he growled.

Grotug reached for his maul, and Skrôl brought his spear up.

"Stop, idiots!" Köga'ra roared. Her body ached, her arm hurt, and the stale air within the temple made it difficult for her to breathe. On top of it all, she had to deal with these two thick-headed half-wits who could not agree on the color of the sky. It was more than she asked for and more than she wanted to deal with. But if they could not agree, she would make the decision.

Both warriors paused, but neither backed away. She stepped up to the pair of them and growled, scraping her tusks against theirs with a turn of her head. Their posture slackened.

"Move," she said, as she grabbed Skrôl by the arm and pushed him back.

When Grotug made to step forward, she stopped him with the end of her axe. "No. The crown stays on for now."

For how long? The creature asked, as it unfolded its long legs and stood.

"Until we know what it does."

Now that the creature was on its feet, she could see how incredibly tall it was—a full half head or more than Skrôl. It stepped forward, bringing itself face to face with her, its tentacles hanging down, leaking what looked like spittle onto her cheek.

She did not flinch.

Her warriors growled deep in their chests, but did as they were bade and did not move.

The creature seemed pleased. *Very well. It stays on. For now.*

Dükog managed to pull himself together and wiped black mucus from his mouth as he found his feet. Köga'ra reached down and helped him up with her empty hand, her yellow eyes never once leaving the creature. She wondered absently what it would take to kill the thing. If experience was any indication, her warriors were wondering the same. The silence stretched on for several more heart-beats until it took a step back.

I see that trust will be hard to earn from you. You have freed me. Perhaps an act of goodwill to show I mean you no evil? You, young sorcerer, concentrate on your village. An open location near it will suffice. It steepled its long, skinny fingers before its purple face with its black eyes. It was a posture that made Köga'ra's stomach sink. Deep in her soul, she suspected they had made a mistake. But if this creature could connect them with their ancestors again, what choice did they have but to help him? Zi's hands began moving, slowly at first and picking up speed as his spindly fingers traced arcane symbols in the air. She blinked, then narrowed her eyes as a faint green afterburn began to follow the tips of his fingers.

Köga'ra started and jumped back, grabbing Dükog by his bone necklace and pulling him with her. To her amazement, a dark purple haze formed to the side of the creature. It began as a mist, coalescing and writhing as if pestered by an unseen breeze. Moments passed and the mist grew from fist size to the length of a spear in height and width and yet no thicker than her hand from the thumb to the last finger. She heard Skrôl gasp and tightened her hand on Dükog.

An image began to appear in the mist, swirling at first and gaining increasing clarity with each breath. In what seemed the briefest of moments, she could see within the swirling violet a perfect vision of a broad meadow west of the village. Smoke from the cookfires floated above a line of trees just before the horizon. From that meadow, it was less than half a day back to their huts and the kin they had left behind.

Zi let his hands fall, but the mist and the image within it remained. His tentacles pulled into what Köga'ra imagined must pass for a smile to his strange race. She did not like it. *A gift for my freedom, my new friends. There are many ways for me to help you. This is only the beginning.* He motioned to the portal before them, his large eyes pools of unreadable obsidian.

Köga'ra looked at each of her warriors in turn. Dükog seemed skeptical for the first time since they began their journey, his face twisted in uncertainty. Skrôl, predictably, narrowed his yellow eyes warily at the creature. Even Grotug—brave and short-sighted as he was—seemed to carry the tightness of apprehension in his massive jaws. And, even as she examined each of them, they turned their faces to her, expectant.

She closed her eyes and breathed deeply, the mustiness of this underground temple filling her nose and lungs. As she exhaled, she opened her eyes and straightened her shoulders. Whether the creature could help them, time would tell. It certainly had its own goals and she sensed that it would use her tribe to get what it wanted. But that did not matter. They would use its abilities for the tribe's gain, and if it tried to harm any of them she would cut off its head and spike it to her hut.

Refusing to give the creature any more satisfaction by continuing to marvel at its power, Köga'ra motioned toward the portal with her axe. "Come," she grunted, and her warriors moved to obey. She stared into the creature's calculating eyes as her thick legs carried her past, then turned her face forward as she stepped through the portal and back across the unknown.

Meet L.T. Adams

L.T. Adams currently lives in northern Missouri where he spends most of his time with his children, wife, and three dogs. He finds his greatest peace outdoors and enjoys camping, kayaking, and making fire. As a professional amateur, he satisfies his diverse interests with hobbies that include archery, mead-making, crafting, and tabletop game design. L.T. studied history at the University of Missouri and education at Saint Louis University for his latest graduate degree, where he hopes to finally complete his doctorate someday. You can follow him on Twitter (@ltadamswriting or email him at ltadamswriting@gmail.com.

Sea-foam

A.F. Hartsell

Walk across the burning sands of the Hurab; have a good time; become a full member of the tribe," Avery mumbled to herself moodily.

Sunlight slanted its way down into the girl's eyes, causing her to curl her lip in annoyance. Avery supposed she shouldn't be bothered by the blaring orb of irritation, as he was just doing his job, but still.

She looked around to make sure no one was watching, and then made a rude gesture at the bright ball.

"How would you like it if I were to blaze into *your* eye sockets?" the teen snarled.

Taking a kerchief fit with a thin slit of amber glass, she tied it across her eyes to help dim the sun's attempt to blind her.

Shrugging her shoulders under the weight of her pack, she walked forward again.

Seven of them were venturing out this year, but they all started at different times of the day because the elders were particularly evil on occasion. Lots were drawn to keep the timing fair, but Avery figured starting out at midday to cross a desert didn't seem promising.

Kenn was starting two hours behind her.

Kenn and Avery had been best friends since birth. Their mothers

"

had delivered the same day, so the two had been Tied by the doctor, which was just a fancy way of saying they were destined to be in each other's lives for a long time. The cord they were tied together with was cut a week later and used to make two thong necklaces that Kenn and Avery wore to show they were Tied, as was custom.

The Molichai tribe was big on destiny and customs, which was why she was currently hiking through the blasted desert.

Elder Zola had given her a small pouch she was to open upon her first night away. It contained her trial description, a luck stone, and something particular to each individual.

Staring out across the vast expanse of desert, Avery considered opening the pouch, but thought better of it this close to the city. What if someone saw her and decided she was unworthy of becoming a full member?

If she wasn't able to cross the sands and complete her task— whatever it happened to be—she was to be set aside in a neighboring village that was reserved for those that could not work harmoniously with the Molichai.

The villages were forbidden to interact.

Avery would be placed away from her family, friends, and home.

It was rare for one to fail the Test of Sand or to be otherwise removed to the sister village, but it wasn't unheard of.

Three years ago, a venturling called Richet had confessed that he did not intend to come back from his trek, but to venture through the forest at the far end of the Hurab and find his fate there. Avery hoped he had found what he was searching for and not been eaten by a sand worm.

He probably got eaten by a sand worm.

Avery was able to take one bag with her, under the condition that she packed it by herself. It was understood that a worthwhile member of the Molichai tribe would have paid enough attention in the last sixteen years that preparing for a one-moon trek across the desert would be manageable.

As luck would have it, Avery did not possess the ability to pay attention.

Just last week, she had been talking to her mother about what to purchase from the market when a pretty bit of sea-foam had skipped its way across the sand. Avery's mind had drifted along with the foam for just long enough that she came back from market with only half of what her mother had requested—and several things she had not mentioned at all.

"Avery Lynn, what in all the world am I going to do with this lovely bunch of coconuts and a ball of twine?"

Avery had shrugged. "You could bang the coconuts together and pretend to ride a horse?"

Occasionally, her lax memory caused more than an added trip to market. She had burnt down their hut twice, the neighbor's kitchen once, and even forgot to feed a friend's goat until the animal had eaten its way through the local bakery. The poor beast had gotten so fat on sweets that it was unable to fit back out the loose board it had sneaked its way through.

Now, Avery slid her way down a dune, feeling the weight in her pack settle.

She had thought to bring a tool for gathering water from plant roots, hard tack, a brush for her hair, a stick for her teeth, a powder to keep her skin from burning, and a fluffy blanket for the cold nights.

She vaguely recalled throwing rope, a spoon, and a half-finished bracelet she was making for Kenn in at the last minute. She had started the project a year ago when they had found a particularly pretty chunk of sea-glass, but she kept forgetting to finish.

Just like she had forgotten to bring a knife.

Avery sighed and shrugged.

She supposed she could bite a lizard's head off before cooking it.

Had she brought supplies to make a fire? She was sure she had. That would have been a stupid thing to forget.

Much like a knife was a stupid thing to forget.

After slowly plodding for hours, Avery decided it was as good a time as any to stop and fill her canteen. She had drained it, and there were plants at her feet that collected water at their roots. She dug in her rucksack and pulled out a long tool used for digging through sand and cutting away root. She also removed a bit of dried lizard and chomped into the salted meat.

Avery had inadvertently left behind the siphon tubing that went along with her digging tool, so her canteen now contained a bit of sand along with the water.

"I suppose sand is edible enough," she reasoned aloud, while masticating the grit between her teeth.

By the time the sun had lowered beyond the flat plains of sand ahead of her, Avery was quite ready to have a sit down. She wasn't mentally tired so much as her legs were bored of walking in one direction all day.

Sitting, Avery crossed her legs and pulled the pouch Elder Zola had given her out from the front of her shirt.

There was a letter, a smooth rock inscribed with a prayer and shaped like a seashell, and a small carving of a fish. The carving was so realistic, Avery patted it a few times to make sure it wasn't real. Shrugging, she looped the small charm around the leather thong always at her neck. She wasn't sure how this was meant to help her, but it was awfully cute.

There was also a sweet and bitter pastry made from cocoa beans, ground coconut, and dates. It was her favorite, and she was pleased the Elder had thought of her.

She tossed the pastry into her mouth and chewed happily while unfolding the letter.

In large, bold writing, Elder Zola had scrawled, "The cookie is not for you, Avery!"

"Should have said that before I ate it, eh?" She mumbled aloud, annoyed at why anyone would give a pastry to someone and then take it away in a letter.

Now, she couldn't even enjoy the aftertaste of coconut and cocoa.

"You are to venture to the far-side of the Hurab and deliver the sweet to your spirit guide."

Avery took a swig of her sandy, root-water and sniffed. She supposed she could turn back and grab another sweet from the village. She *had* only been walking half a day.

Avery balked at the thought of having to retrace her steps. The desert was boring.

The village seer had told Avery's parents that she was too full of water and needed more earth in her diet to balance her.

"Avery flows whichever way the riverbed takes her. She will slowly carve out her path, if she has to, but is more apt to go around impediments," the Seer had said in a most grandiose manner.

If she just kept going forward, Avery was sure a way would present itself. The spirit guide would probably take any offering, really. If not, Avery was decently skilled at talking her way out of things.

That's what spirit guides were there for, right? If it wasn't going to guide her, then it was just a spirit.

What good was just a spirit?

Fluffing her sack of goodies under her head, Avery decided she would keep on heading toward the forest when she woke in the morning. How hard would it be to convince a guide to do some guiding anyway?

"Didn't you leave hours before me?"

Avery scrunched her eyes and rolled over, her face falling from her pack and into the sand.

She sat up, spitting, and stared at the person who had addressed her.

"Huh?" She mumbled around the grit sticking to her lips.

"I said, didn't you leave at mid-sun yesterday?"

Recognizing Kenn, Avery grinned before standing and dusting herself off.

"I did." She looked around for a moment before settling her eyes back on him. "How did you catch up with me?"

The boy shrugged as if it should have been obvious. "The sun has been up for hours. I woke with him."

Avery twitched sand from her nose, more convinced than ever that the sun should be abolished.

"Not sure how you slept so long while facing the rising light."

Avery sniffed. "It's a gift. Are we allowed to travel together?"

Kenn chuckled. "You don't listen to anything, do you?"

"I do!" Avery protested. "Sometimes I just misplace the message."

"We can travel together as far as our paths align, but we may not discuss our quests until they are finished or seek the same guide together."

Gathering her pack and knocking the sand off her rear, Avery started walking. "How do we know if we are seeking the same guide if we cannot talk about it?"

Kenn frowned, his dark brows drawing over light eyes. "I guess we wouldn't be, really... if we didn't know we were."

"Are you this way?" Avery asked while nodding in the direction she was headed.

"Sure am."

"Good luck for me, then!"

Kenn moaned dramatically. "Bad for me and my poor ears."

Avery knew herself to be a fairly chatty person. She hoped it wasn't in an unpleasant way, but she did enjoy sharing her thoughts aloud.

Sometimes those thoughts coincided with the conversation, and sometimes they were far away indeed.

If someone happened to mention the annual snowfall and their excitement for the white, fluffy bits that descended from the heavens, Avery would follow patiently for a time. However, her thoughts would inevitably turn course and meander down a grown-over path. The snow would make her think of the blinding white it turned their coast, which would make her think of the occasional white rabbit her cousin would catch and sell for a nice fee. And that, of course, would lead to why her people considered rodent feet a lucky item.

It made little sense.

If a rabbit were unlucky enough to be caught, then how could his feet be considered fortunate for someone that carried them?

Surely, a caught rabbit was an unlucky rabbit.

"Considering most venturlings make it back inside of one moon, I guesstimate it should take us a little under two weeks both ways," Kenn stated, interrupting Avery from her thoughts. "That gives us time for the ritual—whatever it is. It will be nice to have a traveling companion," Kenn said cheerfully, as if the sun were not trying his best to blind all of humanity.

Avery pulled a tooth-stick from her pack and chewed on it, vigorously gnawing away the scummy film that coated her mouth each morning.

"So, you're going to the forest as well?" Avery asked Kenn as they plodded along.

Kenn frowned, and then widened his eyes. "We must not discuss this!"

"Why not?" Avery questioned. "If we can speak on it when we return, then it makes no sense that we can't speak on it while we are away."

"It is part of the rules, Avery. We do not discuss rituals until all venturlings have returned."

"Well, I didn't ask about your ritual, did I? I just figured, if you were going this way and *I* was going this way, then you were going to the desert edge as well. You could be going to chop a tree down and drag it back, for all I know."

Avery stopped walking. "Heavens, you don't think they would ask anyone to do that, do you? I think that might be a bit much."

Kenn shook his head before gently pushing Avery. "The elders have asked for a few ridiculous things, when the venturling was of the ridiculous sort."

"Like what?"

"Well," started Kenn, "Mortimer Quickstep was asked to walk to the dead center of the desert, dig a hole three times his height, and then collect what he found at the bottom."

Avery frowned. She vaguely recalled the name, but couldn't place him in their tribe. "What did he find?" she asked.

Kenn shrugged. "Death, I suppose. He never returned. Some

think he dug straight down with no way to crawl back up and thereby trapped himself."

"Ugh. What a horrible way to die," said Avery pragmatically.

"I don't imagine there are many good ways, Avery."

She chewed on her stick for a moment before responding, "Sure, there are."

Kenn raised his dark brows and stared down at Avery like she were not just as old as he was.

"Quickly, for one," she shot back. "Or doing something you enjoy."

"I enjoy sailing, but I wouldn't want to die at sea," Kenn retorted.

"What if a mermaid lured you down and you drown without knowing it? That would be better than buried in a hole!"

"Your head is so full of air, I don't know how you keep from floating," teased Kenn. "There are no such things as mermaids. It's a tale to keep younglings and venturlings from drowning out of stupidity."

Avery shrugged. "The story had to come from somewhere. And just because we haven't seen them, doesn't mean they aren't real."

Kenn ticked his tongue at Avery.

"You believe in the forest at the edge of the desert, don't you?" Avery said.

"Of course."

"You've never seen *that*," she replied with a smug smile.

"Others have, Fluff-head."

"Well, *others* say there are mermaids."

"That is completely different, and you know it!" Kenn shouted while pulling down a blue kerchief over his face. "Only full members of the tribe tell us about mermaids, and it's always in warning."

"Perhaps they were venturlings that had to cross the sea and not the desert?" Avery said, feeling as if she were winning the conversation.

Kenn rolled his eyes. "Arguing with you is like bashing my head against a tree."

"Pointless?" asked Avery with a hopeful grin.

"Painful," he responded.

A pleasant week went by as Kenn and Avery trod across the varying sands. They gathered water at the base of desert plants, munched on a few flowers that grew on thorny vines, and managed to hunt down several lizards of goodly size to keep their bellies full.

A day into their second week, they came along another venturling. Avery groaned, but Kenn seemed to stand up straighter, adjusting his hair before shouting a greeting.

"Oi! Daisy!"

Avery hated daisies. They were ugly, useless flowers with tiny petals and idiotic pops of yellow. What a despicable color, yellow. The sun was yellow.

"Kenn!" shouted Daisy, her hair fluttering prettily around her face. "Oh, and hello, Avery."

Avery puffed her cheeks out and waved listlessly.

She knew Kenn would be more interested in the color of Daisy's stupid eyes than any conversation from now on.

"Are you headed to the forest too?" Kenn asked.

Avery tossed her hands up in exasperation, her face screwing up into a tight frown. "So, you've recovered from your abject horror when I asked you the same thing a week ago?" she whisper-yelled at her friend.

Kenn frowned down at her in a dismissive manner. It stung Avery more than she cared to admit, but she knew Kenn valued her friendship as much as she his. Even if he was a bit of a toad on occasion.

Daisy smiled impishly. "Does that mean we will be traveling together?" she cried.

Avery stared at the sun for a beat too long. Maybe the bright rays would melt her face, and she wouldn't have to spend the next few weeks listening to Kenn attempt to court Daisy.

She didn't like Kenn in any particularly romantic way herself, but she enjoyed their closeness. With Daisy around, she would be the tag-along pet at best and a full-on annoyance at worst.

Besides, Daisy had no sense of humor to speak of. Maybe the

elders would have her digging a hole somewhere in the forest. With any luck, Daisy would become stuck and go the way of Mortimer Quickstep.

The following few days trudged by a bit less quickly than the preceding week. Kenn periodically stopped to address his compass and eye the sun, and neither him nor Daisy seemed interested in Avery's thoughts on anything—not that it really stopped her from offering them.

One evening, as they sat around a small fire made from the increasingly wooded area, Avery asked of Kenn, "Did you tell Daisy about Mortimer?"

"Is that the venturling that died?" Daisy asked, her face paling in the moonlight. "What a thing to bring up," she chastised, as if scandalized.

"I mean, we assume he died," said Avery with a shrug. "Perhaps he didn't come back of his own volition."

"Why would anyone not come back?" snapped Daisy.

Avery rubbed her chin. "Lots of reasons, I suppose. Have you never thought about it?"

"The tribe is my *home*, Avery; why would I think of leaving that?"

"Adventure?" Avery tossed with a shrug. She didn't necessarily want to leave her family or home either, but she could think of reasons why some people would stay away. Only an imagination-stunted fungus couldn't see the allure of the unknown.

Avery widened her eyes at Kenn, who was staring at Daisy with a frown.

"Never been even the littlest bit curious?" Kenn asked gently.

"Oh, not you too!" Daisy huffed, grabbing her cloak and walking away from the fire to throw it over herself dramatically. "You always think you're so much better," she called back as if in afterthought.

Avery snickered at Daisy's pique. She quite enjoyed prodding people into throwing tantrums. It just meant that Avery was most assuredly correct, and the other party could not convincingly rebuff her thoughts.

"You should probably go after her," Avery said to Kenn.

He sniffed. "Has she always been like that?"

Avery raised a knowing eyebrow and nodded.

Kenn huffed a sigh through his lips. "If Daisy looked like Daisy, but talked like you, I would be a happy man."

Avery blinked twice and then tossed a handful of sand at her obnoxious friend. "You are the biggest toad-brained idiot the sun ever plopped down on the earth."

He shrugged. "Maybe, but I doubt you'd have made it across the desert without me."

"I would have made it," Avery said with conviction. "It would have just been boring, is all."

"How can someone have too much water *and* too much air in their personality?" he said with a puff. "Anyway, let's get some rest. We will reach the forest around high-sun tomorrow; then we must split up until our rituals have been performed."

Avery stretched and nodded. "Oh! You wouldn't happen to have a cookie in your pack? I ate mine, but I suppose I wasn't meant to just yet."

"I do, actually. I was saving it as a treat, but if you need it—"

"Sorry. I'll have my aunt make you a bunch when we return home," Avery said with a yawn.

Morning came as a shock to Avery, as both Kenn and Daisy were missing. She glanced around, noting twin footprints that lead off toward the wooded horizon.

Kenn had scrawled a note and set a cookie upon it.

"Daisy insisted on leaving. I know you'll get to the forest just fine, but she's still in a huff. See you soon, Kenn."

He had drawn a little lizard in the corner of the paper.

"You had enough time to draw a lizard, but not enough time to wake me up?" Avery grouched to herself, as she shoved her blanket and the borrowed cookie into her pack.

The cookie looked appetizing, but she knew she had to save it for her spirit guide.

Just like the rest of the tribe, Avery had been taught about spirit guides from an early age. The guides were important to her people, as they assigned life tasks and helped lead through difficult situations.

Avery's mother had been sent on a spirit quest when Avery's father had requested a marriage match. Many chose to consult their guides on important matters such as marriage, child birth, and annoying relatives that came with both of the former.

Some guides came in human form, some in animal, and some were as mundane as shrubbery. Avery's uncle swore his guide was a kitchen table. He *had* stubbed his toe on the thing on many occasions, so perhaps it wasn't an outright joke.

Sighing, Avery plodded one foot in front of the other and headed toward the woods. With any luck, she would make it before dark. Kenn had thought it would only take half a day, but Avery knew she would probably get distracted without him prodding her along.

Time was a concept that tended to elude her totally. It was a vague mist that had no *real* value or weight, and was therefore wholly stupid. It served only to thwart her in her everyday life and to cause strife between her and those that had a firm grasp on the slimy thing.

As the day stretched on, she realized she had no idea where to go once she reached the start of the woods.

The vast expanse of forest stretched as far as she could see from either side, and who knew how far forward.

The elders had—most helpfully—provided no guidance whatsoever.

Avery shrugged. No use worrying about it now.

Perhaps it was a magical forest, and once she entered, she would be teleported to where she needed to go.

As she munched on a stick of dried meat, Avery noticed a little tuft of smoke to her right. It was an odd shade of turquoise.

"Hmm," she grunted to herself before altering her footsteps to head in that direction.

As she came closer, she saw a bright, pink hut set a few yards back from the mouth of the woods. She supposed she could ask the color-blind resident if they had any information on spirit guides.

Knocking politely at the door, Avery shouted out a greeting.

"Oi! I come from the shores in search of a guide."

"Don't you have guides where you're from?" came a reply.

Avery frowned. Did that mean she could come in?

"Er, could I come in?"

"I suppose you could if you opened the door," replied the voice inside the hut.

Looking around in confusion, Avery's hand hovered over the door handle. She did not want to seem rude, but she was also a bit flummoxed on what was expected of her.

She licked her lips, and said, "Would it be an inconvenience if I came in?"

"To whom?"

Avery's mouth popped open in exasperation.

"May I come inside your hut?" she said, thinking herself clever for finding a direct question.

"How do you know it's my hut?"

"*Is* it your hut?"

"I'm inside it, aren't I?"

Avery fought the urge to rip down the door and throw it at the person inside.

"Then, may I come in?"

"Well, of course you can. It's quite odd that you've been talking through the door the entire time."

"For the love of..." muttered Avery quietly as she walked through the pink door. She sniffed twice and then sneezed.

"Cinnamon," said the voice.

Avery's eyes were taking their time acclimating to the darker interior of the hut, but flickering lanterns and a large fireplace helped shed light around the room.

"I'm not normally one to sneeze at cinnamon," Avery responded.

"No, no, my *name*. My name is Cinnamon."

"I see," said Avery, not seeing at all, in fact. She couldn't find anyone in the room.

A pot of something blue simmered softly over the fireplace and a myriad of books littered every corner of the big, circular room.

"This is where you introduce yourself."

"Ah, I'm Avery."

"Just Avery?"

"Avery Lynn from the family of Hill," she responded, still looking around, trying to find the voice that beckoned her.

"And you go by 'Avery?' Why not something prettier."

"Like what?" She asked, picking up a small book written in a language she didn't recognize.

"Like 'Lynn?'" replied Cinnamon. "I'm down here," she said, huffing as if annoyed.

Avery glanced down to a long table that ran the length of the kitchen area. A few vials of this and that sat in neat rows. At the end of one particular row of purple liquid was a turquoise snail staring up at a book four times its size.

"You're a snail?" asked Avery, unable to keep the shock out of her voice.

"*Under* the table, girl. Where are your senses?"

At this, a woman crawled out from under the table, holding a silver ring. "I dropped this," she said by way of explanation.

Cinnamon dipped the ring into one of her seven purple vials and then handed it to Avery. "This is yours."

Avery held her hand out, accepting the ring. It was a small band of silver etched with carefully painted blue waves.

"Are you my guide, then?"

"Bah. Do I look like a guide to you?"

Avery shrugged. "Well, I've never seen one, so I'm not quite sure."

"I'm not," said Cinnamon, holding her chin up as if this was an insulting charge.

"Do you know where I can find my guide?"

Cinnamon gestured to the ring. "Put that on and it will lead you.

You're a bit dafter than the other two that came by. Are you sure you're the same age?"

"You saw Daisy and Kenn, then?"

Cinnamon shrugged. "They were boring."

Avery frowned. "They left me this morning."

"Well, that is quite rude, I should think."

Avery nodded in agreement.

"I suppose I should get going?" Avery asked, unsure of what to do now.

Cinnamon shrugged. "Up to you. If you're ready to speak to your guide, leave and then place the ring on your finger."

Avery waved a good bye and walked from the eyesore of a hut. She slid the silver band over her finger and waited.

Nothing of note happened.

Twisting her mouth sideways, Avery knocked on the door again and entered without waiting for Cinnamon to respond.

Only now, inside the hut was a cave, which was particularly irregular. A shaft of light shone down on the center of a pool of water that took up most of the cavern.

"Uh," said Avery, her confusion transforming her face into an expression of wonderment.

"Hullo, there!" shouted someone swimming in the pool.

Avery waved and walked over, her feet sinking softly into the sandy ground surrounding the water.

"I am Coco," said the girl in the water.

"Avery." Her brain still struggled to take in everything.

Coco swam to the edge of the pool and rested her arms on the rocky edge surrounding it. A soft radiance reflected from her skin, almost like fish scales.

"Oh! Well, you should have something for me? I do so like coconut. Passing difficult to get when you're water bound, though."

Avery sniffed and peered deeper into the pale blue of the water. Coco had a tail where her legs should have been.

"Aha! You exist!" Avery cried, pumping her fist into the air as if she had won a tournament purse. She couldn't wait to tell Kenn about this development.

Coco looked affronted. "Obviously. Who said I didn't?" The sea creature held her hand out. "Cookie?"

Avery dug around in her pack. "I ate the first one, you know? A friend let me borrow his."

The mermaid snatched the coconut cookie and gobbled it down like a stray dog after fallen food. "I do hope he doesn't want it back."

Stretching, Avery sat down at the edge of the water and put her feet in. "So, what am I meant to be doing, anyway?"

"Nothing, really."

Frowning, Avery looked around the cave. "But, I came all this way to meet with my spirit guide."

Coco gestured grandly. "And you have! Tada!"

"This was it? Just trek across the desert to give you a cookie?"

"Well, they are quite good, aren't they?"

Avery looked around the cavern and furrowed her brows together. "This all seems rather pointless. I can't imagine Elder Zola being happy with me for not accomplishing anything."

"You got here, didn't you?"

Avery shrugged and twisted her mouth into a thoughtful grimace.

The teen struggled to fit in with her people. Not because she was rebellious or contrary, but because her thoughts tended to run amok like a ferret that had gotten into spin-weed.

She wanted to aid the tribe, but she knew herself to be unreliable. She found that fiercely wanting something and being able to do that something were oceans apart from one another.

It was as if her mind were made of the shifting sand she had just traveled across. Each grain a thought that constantly blew and fluctuated until it was impossible to find it amongst other myriad of grains.

Many people had given her advice; some of it good natured and some coming from a lack of understanding.

Brie, who owned the bakery, thought Avery needed a schedule.

Hannah told Avery that standing on her head would make her memory better.

Someone had even suggested that Avery tie a rope around her wrist to help remind her she had a task to do. Avery had tried for a solid month, but would often stare at the rope around her wrist, wondering why she had tied it to begin with.

She was given juice to calm her, milk to steady her, and crushed herbs to help her memory.

She was punished when she failed, rewarded when she succeeded, and still, nothing could keep her mind from straying to areas it was not meant to go.

Recently, an elderly gentleman insisted that she was simply lazy, which made her feel even worse than usual.

Coco flicked her tail like an aquatic cat and smiled slightly. "Life can seem pointless, Avery."

"That's optimistic; thank you," Avery responded with the full force of her teenage-eye-roll directed at the mermaid.

"Did you enjoy your trek?"

Avery thought back on the time spent with Kenn and even Daisy. She shrugged and added, "I guess I did. It wasn't always pleasant, but satisfying overall."

"And you did bring me a cookie, so that was helpful," added Coco.

"So, I'm simply here to enjoy?" asked Avery, her brows furrowing.

Stretching, Coco said, "No, of course not, but it helps. What matters is we do our best and help people when we can. I think you already know that, though. Seems silly they sent you all that way for me to tell you."

"I think the Elders just want a week to be rid of everyone my age," said Avery with a twist of her lips. "Do I go back now?"

Coco nodded. "You could take the waterways back, if you want."

"The waterways?"

Slapping the water around her, Coco said, "This. It connects to the ocean. You would need a temporary tail, of course. Your kind wouldn't survive elsewise."

"Where would I get a tail?"

"You could borrow mine. I would take the desert back, and you could take the ocean back."

Avery puzzled over the strange offer. "Do you exchange your tail for legs often?"

"No, but my ex-boyfriend has been clingy lately, and I would love to escape the ocean for a week or two. Besides, you have too much water in your blood, and the sea is equalizing."

"So I keep hearing," muttered Avery.

Avery slipped into the water beside Coco and flinched when the mermaid flicked her between the brows.

Avery opened her mouth to fuss at the girl, but was shocked out of her annoyance when she realized her legs had been fused together into a bright, purple tail.

Floundering in an attempt to swim, Avery found herself feeling both a fool and slightly terrified of dying. She doubted there was anything so ignoble as drowning while in the form of a mermaid.

Coco pulled herself out of the pool and shook like a wet dog. "You're awfully tall," she complained while slipping on Avery's pants.

Avery reached out toward Coco and sputtered, "I'm dying!"

The previously tailed woman took her stab at an eye roll. "So dramatic," she chastised.

"Dying should be dramatic!" argued Avery, realizing she didn't so much need to operate her new tail as her new tail needed to operate her.

She dove under the layer of undulating water and gasped at the life teaming around her. The floor was rife with vivid colors she lacked the vocabulary to explain. Underwater scents tickled their way up her nose. It was a curious sensation. Sea urchins had a definitive musty smell she was heretofore unaware of.

"How will I know where to go?" Avery asked, realizing she probably should have cleared that minor detail up beforehand.

Coco gestured to the water. "You can read the sea floor now. It's a giant map. You just head out of the cave and then take a tunnel straight south to the open sea. The ring you were given allows you to travel through water at a faster than normal rate."

"And you'll be fine in the desert?"

The girl nodded her head, her skin still oddly shimmery. "I plan on following your traveling companions back."

"I can't wait to see the look on Kenn's face when he realizes you're a mermaid!" cried Avery.

"Well, I'm not technically one at the moment," Coco replied, while adjusting Avery's pack across her shoulders.

Flipping her tail in a decidedly annoyed manner, Avery huffed in resignation. She supposed her friend would just have to admit she was right at a later date.

The duo parted ways with Avery dunking her head under the water. She had gills on her hips that flapped open and closed like any other fish. Much to her surprise, Avery realized she *could* read the bottom of the sea floor as if it were a map.

A short tunnel lead from the mouth of the cave into the bluest ocean she had ever seen. Granted, she supposed all the ocean was the same ocean, so this was the bluest *part* of the ocean she had ever seen.

Avery wasn't certain she was swimming any faster than a normal merperson would swim—as she had never previously been a merperson—but she was surprised to find ocean this close to the desert.

On her way, she met a grumpy octopus, a curious lion fish, and an eel that offered her some advice on what was tasty and what could make her sick.

Mussels were quite good, she discovered, and sea cucumbers were vile and to be avoided at all costs. A pod of dolphins had a lark with convincing Avery she was headed in the wrong direction, but it only cost her about half a day before she realized she had been duped.

Dolphins were jerks.

She figured they were slightly less vexing than the sun, but not by much. On several occasions she attempted to swim deep enough that the sun's rays did not penetrate the water, but to no avail. She would need to swim much farther out to sea for that; and the darker water freaked her out a bit, if she was honest with herself.

All in all, the adventure back was fairly diverting, but did nothing for Avery's ability to focus for more than a few moments on her drifting thoughts.

If anything, she figured she could be more diligent about taking the herbs the seer had prescribed and perhaps make more reminders versus trying to recall all the tiny, shifting details of life on her own.

It irked her that everyone else seemed to function without a book of scribbled notes, but such is life, she supposed.

If it helped her, what did it matter what other people did?

She knew when she was trying her best, and that was all she could do, really. If she didn't do it quite like everyone else, then so be it. The end of the world would not be summoned, because she forgot to buy beets at the market.

She also figured the next person who wanted to give her friendly advice about how to overcome her laziness could suck on a goat's teat.

"Avery Lynn!"

Avery's mind registered the voice, as if through a long tunnel.

"What are you doing?" shouted the voice, louder this time.

Avery spun around to stare at her mother, her mouth opening with a soft pop of surprise. Her brain was a bit foggy with imagined details of her made-up society. How long had she been standing there? Kenn and Daisy were with her a split-second ago, right?

Time was such a fiddly thing.

"Huh? Sorry, Mom. I just heard you."

"I've been calling you for the last minute straight. What were you staring at?"

Avery turned her head to glance back over the dune she had been staring at. "Kenn asked me what I thought was past that big dune there and I guess my brain wandered a bit. Was I gone long?"

Avery's mother shook her head and chuckled. "Long enough. Probably longer in your head than outside it. Anyway, we just got lunch unpacked onto a beach towel. Dad said we need to hustle or the tide will get us."

"Shouldn't he have unpacked the food farther away from the waves, then?" Avery asked with a smirk.

Her mother sighed patiently and nodded. "One would think," she muttered good-naturedly.

The duo walked back toward the rest of their group. The Hill family often took day trips to the beach with Kenn's family. She and Kenn had been friends since she could remember. They were born in the same hospital on the same day and lived on the same street.

Avery always enjoyed their beach trips together until Kenn began inviting Daisy to go with them.

"What did you decide about Kenn's question?"

"Huh? Oh! What's across the dune? I actually came up with a fun story about a tribe of people called the Molichai and a mermaid named Coco."

"Your mind really is a special place," her mother teased. "You can tell us the whole story over lunch, then."

Avery rolled her eyes. "Daisy will interrupt me."

Her mother laughed. "She is a bit full of herself, isn't she?"

"She's got a crush on Kenn," Avery said with an annoyed snarl.

"She does. I think he likes her a bit too." Avery's mother laid her hand on the girl's back, "It's rough losing your best friend to a relationship, but give him time. He will come around and realize he has room for you both."

"I guess," Avery said with a huff. "He could have waited for me before running off with Daisy, though."

Avery's mom grinned. "Honey, you have been standing in the same spot for almost ten minutes. I would say Kenn and Daisy grew bored waiting for your brain to join them back in the real world."

"I can't help it that they lack imagination."

Avery's mother snorted. "Go on then; everyone is waiting on us."

Avery looked up to see Kenn waving at her, gesturing to a plate of coconut cookies and patting the towel to his right.

She ran up to him, eager to tell him what she had envisioned was past the dune.

Meet A.F. Hartsell

While not keeping a tiny human alive, Ashley can be found co-hosting her podcast Horseshoes and Hand Grenades, hitting the keys on her next writing adventure, rolling around in glitter, or dreaming of sleep. To hear more from Ashley, join her on Twitter @Phatekills.

The Misadventures of the Twin Moon

Ben Collins

Rain softly plinked off the roof of the Soggy Figurehead tavern. It was named for the tropical region's year round rainfall, and sat on the edge of a cliff just like a figurehead sits on the prow of a boat. Inside were twenty sailors from various walks of life. Some were reputable sailors; some were devious pirates; and others were outright murderers. None of that mattered inside, though. Inside, everyone just wanted three things: warm food, a cold drink, and shelter from the rain. The wind that accompanied most storms in the area would occasionally blow open the door, and when it did, nearly everyone would glance to see if another water-logged soul had stumbled in before returning to their conversation or meal.

This time, however, someone did walk through the tavern doors. Captain Sheepbeard was his name, because instead of the traditional mess of hairs haphazardly attached to a chin, he had a pair of mutton chops framing his face. Because every self-respecting captain is named after their beard, he was just glad that he wasn't one of the poor saps that had not a single hair below their eyes. He had no idea how they led a crew if they didn't even have a beard to show seniority.

Questions like that could wait as he came here for a reason, not a meal like the other patrons. He was here for the patrons themselves.

As he walked through the door, everyone looked up in some level of drink-induced haze.

"Listen up. Listen well. I've got a story to tell, and it starts not here, but two steps from Hell," he bellowed. "I have a large expedition planned, charted, and supplied. All I need now is a few more luke-warm bodies to keep the *Twin Moon* running smooth. You'll, of course, be paid for your work, plus an extra share of anything you carry onboard. I don't care what you did before, or what you'll do after, but you will listen to my orders while on my ship. We are tied up on the west dock for anyone who intends on joining."

He reached into his pocket and pulled out a golden coin. "First person to sign on doesn't have a bill tonight," he said, as he flicked the coin to the man behind the bar. "Don't be late. We ship off in two days," he said, walking out of the tavern and back to the *Twin Moon*.

Sheepbeard and one of his veteran crew members, Mr. Williams, stood on the dock.

"Have you got the contracts ready, Mr. Williams?" Sheepbeard asked. After half an hour of waiting, the first potential recruit walked up to the two pirates. He was a scrawny boy, no older than twenty-two. He fidgeted in place before them, unsure if he should talk first or stay quiet.

"I did say lukewarm bodies," Sheepbeard said with his hand on his chin. "What's your name boy, or should I just keep calling you boy until you have some hair on your face?"

"John, sir," the boy said barely above a whisper.

"At least you know some respect, John. I might be able to make a pirate out of you yet. Ever held a gun before? Ever fired a cannon? Can you fish? What makes you think you are cut out for a pirate's life?" Sheepbeard asked in rapid succession. "I ain't gonna lie and say this will be easy. It will probably be a two or three month voyage. You will only be on land maybe four days of that time. Think you're up for that, John?"

"Well, sir, I grew up on a farm, so I am well accustomed to both guns and fishing. I could hit a fox from fifty yards with a pistol by twelve and could reel in a fish the size of me by nine. I want to join your crew because I am looking for adventu—"

"Let me stop you there, boy." The captain took a dark tone. "You don't join a pirate crew for some fanciful sense of adventure. What we do is illegal, and there are a fair few cities in eyesight of here that would drop you from the rooftops for talkin' to me. I'll read you the articles if you can come up with some other reason besides some diluted dream of adventure. If ye can't do that, I suggest you head on back to the tavern, and wait for the next admiralty ship to take you back to a big city 'cause the pirate life ain't like the stories." Sheepbeard growled, while glaring at the man in front of him.

"You want a better reason? Try this one then. I. Want. Money. I grew up on a farm. If the sun rose ten minutes late, we lost half our money for the next year. I am done with that life, and I ain't going back. If I join you for a voyage, I can have enough money to live off of for a while. Anything else would be a bonus. How is that for a reason, my capitan?" John spat back.

"BWAHAHA, I thought I saw a fire in your eyes, John! Just took the right spark to bring it to the surface. That is an answer I can be happy with. I'd be glad to have you aboard if you keep that fire lit the entire voyage," Sheepbeard said with a wide grin on his face. "Let's get down to proper business then. First article if you'd please, Mr. Williams."

Williams read off a long and tattered paper. "Aye, Captain. First article: Captain's orders are to be followed to the letter. Second article: If a man tries to desert or mutiny, he will be the new figurehead for no less than two days and dropped on the next ground that sticks o'er the water. Third article: Any man caught stealing will have a hand cut off. Fourth article: Any infighting will be met with twenty lashes for each blow dealt during a fight. Fifth article: Any who neglect their duty to ship, arms, and role will be stripped of their share. Sixth article: Any parts lost, not part as a punishment, shall receive a payment in accordance to the part lost. Seventh article: Insubordination shall be met with brig time determined by the captain."

"I'm going to add one more for you, John. You can never lose that fire, or you will be dropped on the next inhabited island," Sheepbeard said, offering his hand to John. "Do we have an agreement?"

"We do, Captain," John replied with a smile on his face and shook Sheepbeard's hand.

"Then climb aboard and grab your gun and coat from Mr. Charles. He will show you to your bunk."

A few hours passed, and ten people ended up on the docks. The articles were read to them, and all but one accepted and boarded the ship. The last man left on the dock could barely stand. He had a rosary around his neck and was squinting as if the moon's light was blinding to him.

"Hey! You there!" the man slurred. "You think you can just walk in here and recruit more for your devil crew? After what you did to my home? Thish is what I think of yer crew!" The man charged at Sheepbeard and took a few swings at the captain who took a step back from each one.

"I ain't got a clue who you are. I can promise ye that you don't want this fight. Never heard of a man that makes a storm look stable beating a sober man in a fight. Be a shame if you met your Maker after a fight you caused. Don't think He would view that too kindly," Sheepbeard barked at the drunk in front of him.

"You stole anything that washn't nailed down and burned down my monastery. He would understand," the drunk said, before taking another swing and nearly falling off the dock. "I'm gonna make you pay for what you did, you devil spawn!"

"I've seen actual devil spawn, boy, and let me tell you, I am much worse."

Sheepbeard threw a right hook that caught the man square in his jaw and sent the drunk tumbling to the dock. He planted his foot on the man's chest before kicking him down onto the beach and jumped down after him.

"I'll give you one last chance," Sheepbeard said, drawing his pistol and placing it on the man's temple. "Leave or you will be leaving much more than just this beach."

The drunk grabbed Sheepbeard's shirt. "I know I am being smiled down on, Sheepbeard. Can the same be said about you?" he said before spitting on the ground.

"Save a spot for me down in hell."

A loud crack could be heard before a small stream of smoke rose up into the sky.

"Time table is changing. We ship off now. Let the rest of the crew know, Mr. Williams, and goodnight," Sheepbeard said, while climbing aboard and heading into his quarters.

The sun was a third in the air when the bell on board rang, signaling the crew to their stations. They quickly filed onto the deck to await instructions and to find out what score they were going after this time. The new crewmates stood in the back, so they could learn proper order for how things worked on the *Twin Moon*.

"Listen up, you sea dogs," Sheepbeard called out, quieting any chatter between the crew. "Today we head out for a voyage unlike any we have gone on before. Today we go after one of Blackbeard's hidden caches!"

Some of the crew gasped, while others stood slack jawed.

"Once we get this treasure, we will all have enough gold to pay off our bounties three times over!" Sheepbeard said, while looking right at John. "All old hands go to your stations, and new hands go to Mr. Williams to see what you need to do. We raise anchor in five minutes. Mr. Greg, double time if you'd please."

A man tall as a mountain, and almost as wide, with a red striped bandana across his forearm took Sheepbeard's place before addressing the crew. "Aye, Captain! You heard him, louts! We ain't got time, so work twice as fast! I'm thinkin' a few of you had one too many grogs last night. So what do we do with a drunken sailor early in the morning?" he called out.

"Put him in the long boat, make him bail her," the crew answered.

"I said double time, you salmon. What do we do with a drunken sailor?" he said faster this time.

"Shave his belly with a rusty razor!" the crew called back matching Greg's speed.

"There you go, boys, now get to work! What do you do with a drunken sailor?" he called out again.

"Put him in the guard room till he's sober!" the crew answered while lowering the sails in unison. They continued singing until the ship was ready for sailing.

"Good work, lads. If we keep this pace, we will be back home before the next full moon," Sheepbeard said, emerging from his quarters. "Mr. Greg, go below deck and get a drink, need your voice to be in top shape."

Sheepbeard walked down the stairs to where John was standing by one of the cannons, making sure it was polished and had plenty of powder in it. "Williams says you are adapting well. This is your last chance to turn back if he is wrong. Another couple minutes and not even the best swimmer would be able to get back to shore from here."

"I'm doing fine. A bit odd not having much space to walk around, but comes with the territory, don't it? I've been wondering, Captain, why is the ship named the *Twin Moon*?"

"It was an idea by my original first mate. The ocean reflects the light of the moon and stars making a second moon. We usually have so much plunder on her that she shines enough to make a reflection like a second moon even in the darkest of nights," Sheepbeard said, while patting the side of the hull. "Another name for her was the Neptune's Lighthouse for the same reason."

"Doesn't all the light attract other pirates though?" John asked.

"If it does, so be it. We will just sink them and take what they have like a flame eating through a town, going from house to house until all that remains is ash. That actually reminds me, we should probably go check on my friend in the brig. Ms. Kelly, could you please get our friend from the brig? I think she has been in there long enough."

"Aye, Captain!" came a shout in return.

A few minutes passed before Ms. Kelly came back. Behind her was a woman who looked like it took all she had to keep standing.

"So, Ms. Ashley, think you have spent enough time in the brig?"

"No, Captain, please keep me in there. At least, I'm not completely seasick there," Ashley said, eyes shut tight with her head facing the deck.

"So it would be more of a punishment if you had to stay above deck, would it?" Sheepbeard chuckled. "If you are that messed up by it, you can stay working below deck, but if you hurl once, I'll stick you on the crow's nest for a week."

"Thank you, Captain," Ashley said, before quickly running back down below deck.

The *Twin Moon* sailed on for four days before reaching the island on Sheepbeard's map. They pulled into a small cove on the northeast side of the island with a waterfall on each side of the entrance.

"Spread out, boys. We're looking for a large statue of a snake on the highest point of the island. When you find it, make a fire so the rest of us can follow. Don't forget, a bonus share to the person who finds the statue," Sheepbeard called out. The crew gave a shout before they ran off the boat and into the forest of the island. After a few hours, as the sun lowered to the horizon, a smoke stream rose up, and, like moths, the rest of the crew scurried up the hills of the island to where John was sitting, tending to the fire in the shadow of a stone cobra curled onto itself.

"I knew you would work well. Good job, Mr. John," Sheepbeard said coming up the hill. "Now we just need to head seventeen paces south-southwest, and we should be on the chest."

Sheepbeard took his compass and took each step as if he was carrying the sky on his back, toe to heel to toe. "One, two, three, four...fifteen, sixteen." He counted out, before taking the shovel off the loop on his belt. "Now let's see what old Blackbeard hid away from us, lads."

With a jab that would make a knight jealous, John broke the earth and kept pushing the shovel until a large THUNK could be heard. "Oh oh, that's one of my favorite sounds," Sheepbeard said.

John and a few other sailors continued digging for ten minutes before the fire's light reached the latch of an old, worn, and wooden chest. They pulled the box up from the hole and set it down in front of Sheepbeard.

"He thinks this little lock is going to stop us? I don't know, boys. It looks pretty tough. Might just have to give up and head back to port. Or..."

He opened up his coat to show a large hammer with an engraving of a shark along the side. He lined up the tool with the top of the chest, raised it above his head, and, with both hands, brought it down like he was trying to push it back into the earth. It fractured the half rotten wood, but instead of hitting the gold or silver coins below, it hit only air until landing against the bottom of the box.

"What is the meaning of this?" Sheepbeard snarled before looking into the chest. "Mr. John, bring a light."

John brought over one of the branches from the fire with a small flame on the top and held it over the chest.

"There's only a roll of paper in here. I'm going to flay that man when I next see him. This isn't treasure!" Sheepbeard yelled out in rage.

Some of the crew started to mumble and talk amongst each other about what that meant for their payment.

"This paper better have a map to an island made of solid gold after all the trouble I went through to get the first map."

Sheepbeard grabbed the paper from its shattered housing and unfurled it. The parchment showed nothing more than a single Island, shaped not unlike the opal around the captain's left index finger.

"Williams!" he shouted. "You're well versed in unsung islands. Do you have any idea what this is?"

After looking at the map for a mere thirty seconds, William's eyes grew wide as cannonballs.

"This is Opal Isle, called that because there is always a fierce storm over it."

"What does that have to do with rocks?" John asked.

"Ye young pirates have no appreciation for anything that ain't gold nor silver. Opals are formed from rain water pickin' up minerals from the ground," Williams retorted.

"I still don't get it," John added

"The island has a constant rainstorm over it, which, if the light hits it in certain ways, will sparkle like a gem does. They picked Opal since, like I said, they are made from rain water taking minerals."

"Well then, where is this Opal Isle, if you know so much about it?" Sheepbeard interjected.

"It is a short sail east from St. Francis, sir."

"We better get sailing then. We are already running some of our supplies thin as is. We should go back to the ship. We leave in the morning at first light."

The crew returned to the *Twin Moon* empty-pocketed and angry at their lack of immediate payment.

"Quit your complaining; we'll have the treasure in just a few more days. I've seen Brits with more conviction than some of you are showing now," Sheepbeard barked.

At first light the ship came back to life, as they pulled back from the cove where they nighted. Once they were a good bit past the furthest rocks, Mr. Greg started up a song about what he would do once he got some treasure. The song would pass from one man to the next, each making his own verse about his dreams. Some sang about a golden hat; some about getting a ship and crew of their own; some wanting a simple life with a nice house. As the last few got their turn, someone near the front had noticed the water wasn't quite the right color. He tried to say something, but no one would listen to him. They just focused on the song and the current one singing. It wasn't until Mr. Greg noticed the water was much darker than it was before and he called out for quiet, that the crew started to notice.

John looked over the side of the boat and in return was met with a glimpse of a large pink thing slinking underneath, before an ear piercing scream echoed across the ocean. The now silent boat sat there for a few seconds before forty foot tentacles sprouted up on each side.

Brought out to the deck by the scream, Sheepbeard shouted, "All hands on deck! We got a kraken!"

The cannon crew sprang to life and rushed to a barrel. The rest grabbed a gun or ran ammo for those on cannons.

"Don't go firing wildly, boys. Aim for the base of the tentacle. Won't feel it if you hit too high!" Sheepbeard shouted.

The sound of cannons was nearly deafening. As one reloaded, another two would fire. The first tentacle took twelve cannonballs before it slumped back below the depths riddled with holes and charred from the gunpowder.

Sheepbeard took the wheel and turned the ship to face two of the remaining tentacles before the volley of iron repeated. Before one of them could slink back, a cannon got a good hit on it. The split part crashed onto the deck, dividing the top deck into two halves.

Sailors on both sides hacked at the tentacle in an attempt to rejoin their crewmates. The kraken's deep purple blood stained the deck like wine before they were able to throw the now smaller chunks back into the ocean. They kept firing until only one tentacle remained above the water.

Sheepbeard turned the ship to face it. The *Twin Moon* rammed into the flailing appendage at full speed, causing the kraken to slither back under the water and away from the boat.

"Good job, boys. I've seen royal galleons split in two by one of those hellspawn. You all fought well and here we stand on a still intact deck with not only our lives, but also a story for the ages," Sheepbeard said grinning from ear to ear. "When we next get back to land the first round for all of you is on me."

The crew cheered before a few of the cannoneers slumped down along the railing, too tired to stand after the fight of their lives.

"Mr. Williams, see to it that the men that were on cannons and running cannonballs get a half day of rest. They did a fine job and deserve a break."

Much to the relief of the crew the next five days of sailing went without event, beyond having to steer around the odd island or rock outcropping. It was the dawn of the sixth day when the lookout spied an island with a storm right on top of it while there wasn't another cloud in the entire sky. She quickly slid down the rope ladder that ran along the mast down to the wheel where Sheepbeard was.

"I think we're here, Captain. There's an island surrounded by a heavy storm. Might even be able to smell the lightning if we get a bit closer," Ms. Kelly said.

"Go ring the bell and wake the crew and tell them we make land in three hours. We will need a high sun to have hope of cutting through the storm to find this treasure," Sheepbeard replied, not taking his eyes away from the ocean, a smirk forming on his face.

"Before you go," he said, stopping her from leaving, "what do you think is on that island that even Blackbeard had to have two maps to keep it hidden? Someone like him wouldn't care if a single chest went missing. I think it is something more than gold. You don't become as famous as him for just having a good eye for targets. You have to have something more to make you known from the Colonies to Kiev. He has something hidden up his sleeve, and I intend to find it," he said with a wide toothy grin.

"Maybe he just spends a lot of his gold on people who go around talking him up?" Ms. Kelly wondered. "He could pay a couple guys to talk about him in the local tavern and exaggerate some of the details so he sounds even better, and people start to pass on stories of the captain that took on twenty Man-O-Wars with only one ship. He could do that at every port he stops at, and he could be more well-known than water." She finished, starting to walk down below deck.

After half a minute, Sheepbeard could hear pans being clanged together along with a ringing bell.

After a few more minutes, the crew gathered on the deck. Some were still under the previous night's grog, but most were glaring daggers at the lookout for her "unique" way of waking them. They neared the island as rain started to land on the deck.

Sheepbeard addressed the crew, "I want three of you to stay

behind and bail water. Looks like the storm gets worse the closer to the island you get, and I don't want to come back with a chest full of treasure only to find half the mast above water and everything else kissing sand.

"The rest of you will come with me and scour for four trees that share a trunk. Call down the line if you find the trees."

The rain pounded the crew, and gave everything a sheen, as lightning crashed above and around the ship.

"Now get below deck and get ready. Won't be long before we reach the beach and get us one of Blackbeard's treasures."

The crew dispersed back into the hold and each man grabbed a gun, a handful of bullets, a jacket, and a hat in a desperate attempt to keep the endless water off of them. By the time everyone was ready, the rain fell so thick it could hardly be seen through. Already the bailers were at work bringing buckets full of water up and over the side of the boat. Sheepbeard gave the order to drop anchor and the ship stopped a few feet from the beach.

Sheepbeard was the first to jump down. The crew spread out and covered the island until each man had about one hundred feet between him and the next man in the line. The entire landmass was almost liquid from how much rain had fallen, and only the toughest stones were solid enough to establish good footing. Anywhere else would cause a man to sink a few inches into the soup of dirt, sand, and bugs. The crew tried to walk the island in hope of finding the trunk as soon as possible, but the ground itself fought their every step and it was after midday when one finally found it.

A shout went down the line as each man told his neighbor until all the crew had gathered at the four trees coming from one tree stump. Sheepbeard took his shovel and gave it his best shove, but it did nothing but stir the ground like a ladle in a soup pot. After trying and trying again, he finally hit the wood on the top of the chest.

Realizing that digging it out wouldn't work, he tried to lift the chest with his shovel like he was fishing out the last apple in a barrel with an oar. Some of the crew followed suit and produced their own shovels to help lift the chest out of the gripping slurry it was stuck in.

Sheepbeard was finally able to get a hand on it and set the box onto a nearby rock. With one heavy swing, the wood yielded and inside was an amulet with a large blue stone inside, hung on a chain. Sheepbeard turned it over in his hand a few times before putting it on.

"All this trouble for a necklace? What a tremendous waste of time." As he yelled, he threw up his arms and two waves formed and followed the motion his arms took. "Now THAT changes things. Everyone back to the boat. We might have just gotten something that can set us up for life one way or the other."

Once everyone was back on the boat, Sheepbeard slowly raised his right arm. As he did, a small wave formed off the right side of the ship. He moved his arm and guided the wave so it slowly pushed the *Twin Moon* to face away from the island. As the crew dropped the sails, they had to cover their eyes as the clouds broke and the sun blinded them.

"Williams, I thought you said that there is always a storm around the island," Sheepbeard barked.

"Well, sir, you know what I say about absolutes. They will always be proven wrong," Williams weakly offered. "Although it looks like the storm isn't gone, just moving, sir."

Sheepbeard turned his head to follow his point. The storm clouds had not disappeared, but instead had shifted to gather atop a ship in the distance.

"I want three sets of eyes to keep watch on that ship: one for course, one for signals, and one for if either of the others misses something."

Both ships continued on their courses until a small flashing glimmer could be seen from the deck of the other ship.

"Sir, we have a message from the other boat. They said they have letters home and they want us to take them. They are set to cross the ocean and want us to take them back home for them." One of the crew members on lookout called out.

"Tell them that we will take the letters as long as there are at least three hundred gold coins in the barrel too. A ship of that size has to have more than fifty people on board, so only a couple coins per person shouldn't be unreasonable," Sheepbeard said.

After a brief set of signals sent over a barrel was placed into the ocean off the side of the ship, and it slowly floated in their wake. The *Twin Moon* slightly raised their sails, and fished up the barrel, and, just as the letters were onboard, one of the other lookouts spoke up this time.

"The other ship looks like it's turning around, sir. I don't think I have seen a ship that beat up still sail. I don't know how they're going to get across the ocean," John called out.

"Wait, how broken is it?" Sheepbeard asked before taking out his spyglass. When he looked through it and saw a ship with tattered sails, chunks taken out of the hull every few feet, and the figurehead broken in the middle with only the bottom half of a person still on the bow, he started yelling.

"Turn this ship around and get us out of here! That ain't a normal ship! That is the *Flying Dutchman!*" Sheepbeard screamed.

At the mention of that name, every sailor on deck felt the cold hand of death run down their backs before the storm started to grow and get more intense. The *Twin Moon* and her crew gave it everything they had, and Sheepbeard stood at the wheel trying his best to use the new magical amulet to push them forward, but no matter what they did, the *Flying Dutchman* kept gaining on them inch by inch, foot by foot.

The ocean itself seemed to be fighting to give them to the *Dutchman,* as the waves rose above the deck and crashed against the hull with everything they had. The ship shifted from crests to troughs, never at the same level for more than half a second. As the Dutchman got closer, the crew could swear that they heard laughter from the souls trapped on board. Laughter that soon the *Twin Moon* would be added to the Devil's fleet for all eternity and would never see land again. Just as the crew started giving up hope, at the crest of one of the waves they saw the buildings of St. Francis.

"Hold on lads!" Sheepbeard shouted. "Don't give up yet. Safety if we make it and our souls if we get caught. She was cursed to never be able to go to land, and there is some nice land in sight now."

The *Flying Dutchman* had gotten so close at this point that the storm clouds around it were now over the *Twin Moon* just as it was on the island. The wind whipped both crew and ship. The main mast bent. As the *Twin Moon* raced into the harbor, the *Flying Dutchman* pulled away. As it did, the crew heard a chorus of blood curdling screams as the Devil lost his prey that day.

Now in the safety of St. Francis, they cracked open the barrel and inside were scraps of paper with letters from people that someone in the crew knew and were long dead. The crew stepped off the boat glad to have solid earth below them. A few even kissed the ground.

"I am a man of my word, so the first round is on me!" Sheepbeard said, pointing at a tavern near where they had anchored.

The crew cheered, before leaving Sheepbeard and a few of the new recruits.

Before John could step off, Sheepbeard put his hand on John's shoulder. "Fought a kraken and stole a magical artifact from the Devil himself, not bad for your first voyage. I knew you would make a great pirate, and now, not a thing will be able to scare you if you did all this on your first trip off land. Quite the adventure you had huh, lad."

"I'm not here for the adventure. I'm here for all the treasure we can get now that you can control the tides," John said with a wide grin.

"Atta boy, now let's hurry up. I think half the crew is already under the table by now," Sheepbeard said returning the smile.

Meet Ben Collins

Ben Collins likes boats, so when the opportunity arose to write a story about a journey, he immediately knew it would involve the high seas. He chose to focus on swashbuckling scoundrels instead of an admiralty ship, as he felt pirates would be more likely to go on some ocean spanning voyage for the chance to look at some gold, and that he would be able to do much more with people considered lawless than a strict "by the book" crew under a crown. Should ye ever want to join in on the Twin Moon's adventures all you need to do is answer, "What do you do with a drunken sailor?"

The Outnumbered

Stephanie Dare Adams

*T*HUMP......THUMP...... *THUMP.*

Every hair on Juniper's neck stood up.

"What was that?" she whispered anxiously. She looked over at Conrad.

He was frozen in place, his brows furrowed. "Footsteps."

He looked at the window on the other side of the room. "We don't have time to escape...we have to hide. Now! Go!"

He gently, yet forcefully, guided Juniper to the closet behind them. They slipped inside and hid in the corner, trying to quiet their frantic breathing.

The footsteps grew louder. The awkward gait and smell of the creature made Juniper sick to her stomach. She didn't want to think about the creature they belonged to. She tried to think of Lulu and the others who were depending on her. Suddenly, she was jolted back to reality when the heavy footsteps stopped directly in front of the dark closet. The creature's large form blocked the light that had been streaming in under the door. Its raspy breath was sickeningly loud.

2 Days Earlier

Juniper skillfully dug through an especially muddy patch of earth. She had become adept at determining the difference between a pebble or something edible. She sat back and looked down at her hands and sighed. Her nails were caked with mud. Dirt had settled into the cracks and lines in her skin, creating little brown rivers and deltas. Months of scavenging for food had honed her skills, but it had also wreaked havoc on her body.

"Got one!"

A small, squeaky voice chirped from a thick bramble behind Juniper. She turned to see her little sister Lulu proudly holding up an especially fat, wriggling grub.

"Nice one! Where did you find it? You can usually find more around the same spot."

Juniper scampered over to her sister. Lulu was much younger than Juniper. She was a "happy accident" as her parents had liked to say—a phrase that couldn't be more true. Lulu embodied joy and charm. Her crystal blue eyes sparkled when relaying a juicy story to Juniper. She loved life, never seeming to have a care in the world. Juniper secretly envied her little sister. Even before Lulu was born, Juniper had been a very serious child. She didn't bother herself with unproductive play or frolicking. She was driven by achievement and notoriety.

"Looks like we have enough of what we need. Why don't we go ahead and pack up what we've got and head home? It will be getting dark soon." Thistle, another member of their scavenger party, was standing up and gathering baskets of their forage. She was a little older than Juniper, but a lot more rough around the edges. Though she was quick to anger, she had a gentle heart and everyone respected her.

"Agreed." said Juniper. Her hands were numb from digging in the dirt, and she was starting to get cold.

Everyone was busying themselves with gathering up the supplies when Juniper heard a rustle in the thicket to her left. Her hearing was the keenest of the group, and she was usually the first one to notice something approaching. Startled, she whipped her head around to get a better look. Although there were very few things that scared Juniper, a disembodied rustle at dusk that could possibly belong to a wildcat was one of them.

"Did anyone hear that?" she asked.

"I didn't hear anything." Concerned, Lulu looked at her sister.

"What did it sound like?" asked Thistle.

"I don't know. Just kinda like a rustling sound, I guess?"

"Juniper, dear, we're in the forest. There are a lot of rustling sounds out here." Conrad, one of Juniper's long-time friends—and lifelong smart ass—was flashing her a sly grin.

"Shut up, Conrad."

Thistle shot a stern glance at Conrad. "Look, let's just get out of here. Juniper, if you hear anything else, let us know. Everyone, please stay vigilant."

The group had soon packed up and began their trek back through the woods to their camp. Juniper was tired and dirty. She fell back on her normal routine of lustful thoughts to get her through the long walk home: a hot bath, a warm bowl of food, a crackling fire, a soft cot with fluffy covers. Focusing on what was waiting for her back at camp made her aching limbs a little less painful.

They were over halfway home when Thistle abruptly stopped in the middle of the trail. She stared straight ahead intently, her body blocking the view from the rest of the group. Juniper pushed past her sister and up to Thistle.

"What is it?" she asked.

Thistle didn't move. The color had drained from her face.

"Something just walked across the trail."

"What did it look like."

Thistle shook her head.

"Thistle, what did it look like?" Juniper asked more emphatically.

Thistle paused. "It... it looked like a ghost."

"A what?!" Juniper's hushed voice quickly became loud.

"Shhhh! It's still up there," hushed Thistle.

There was a long pause, then a male voice called out from the bushes ahead of them, "I'm not going to hurt you."

A pale figure slipped out of the bushes. He was as silvery white as the moonlight that had begun to trickle down through the gaps in the forest leaves. Although he was standing at least ten feet away, Juniper couldn't help but notice that his eyes were red and bloodshot.

"My name is Bruno. I'm not going to hurt you."

Lulu gasped at the sight of him, but then quickly weaved through the group and skipped up to him.

"Hi! I'm Lulu. Where are you from? Why are you so pale?"

So naive. So stupid. Juniper rolled her eyes.

"Lulu, wait," she called as she trotted after her sister.

Thistle and Conrad quickly followed.

"Lulu, back away from him," demanded Thistle.

"I told you, I'm not going to hurt you. I just need help. I'm not sure where I am. I... I just." His voice shook.

"Oh, no! It's ok. Please don't cry." Lulu reached out and took Bruno's hand.

"Where are you from? What village?" Thistle narrowed her brow skeptically.

"I... I'm not sure. What's a village?" Bruno looked embarrassed at having to ask the question.

"Seriously, dude?" Conrad aggressively took a step toward Bruno, but Juniper held out her arm to stop him.

Flustered, Bruno continued, "I'm sorry. The creatures have held me and my family captive since my mother was pregnant with me. Until today, I had never seen trees or the sun."

"Ok." Juniper paused as she processed everything Bruno was telling them. "But how did you escape? Where is everyone else?"

Bruno looked off in the distance for a minute and tried to regain his composure.

"Our captors were very careful, they rarely made mistakes. Every time one of us would decide to fight back or try to escape, they were quickly caught and killed or punished then returned to their cell. That was until one day when somehow, one of the creatures screwed up and opened all of our cells at the same time. We all tried to escape at once."

"Didn't they come after you?" Lulu looked up at Bruno through her long lashes."

"Well, no. They were absolutely terrified. One of us wasn't a problem, but when we all came at them, they ran. They actually *ran* away from us. The room was put on lockdown, but a few of us made it out the door and ultimately out of the whole compound. We were all running away so fast, we got separated. I'm not sure where anyone else went or if they made it."

There was a long pause amongst the group. Conrad finally broke the silence.

"Yeah, well, our camp is at max capacity. I'm not sure if we have room for you. And to be frank, I'm not interested in letting an outsider in right now. Especially one so... unique."

Conrad eyed Bruno cautiously, then turned to Juniper. "What do *you* think we should do?"

Juniper paused and let out a long sigh. "I think we should take him to Oscuro. He should at least hear his story and see what he thinks."

Thistle chimed in, "Juniper's right. We should take him to Oscuro and let him decide what to do."

Oscuro was the elder and head of their camp. He had found each one of them and brought them together to make somewhat of a homestead for them. The campsite consisted of a few tents and lean-tos made of branches and leaves. The dwellings surrounded a gathering place and an area for cooking. A few of them had even managed to bring some useful items from home like pots to cook in, bedding, and first aid kits. Everything was shared, and no one went without. It wasn't much, but it was home.

Juniper had known Oscuro before the invasion, but not very well. He had lived in their village, and she saw him in passing on occasion. After losing her parents, Oscuro filled the role of guardian for her. Juniper loved that he not only looked like a wise old grandpa, with his weathered, whiskered face, but also showed the same insight and tenderness of a family patriarch.

The group trudged the rest of the way back to the campsite with Bruno in tow. It was pitch black by the time they reached camp, and Bruno's pale body stuck out like a sore thumb in the inky night. Juniper felt multiple eyes glaring at them as they made their way to Oscuro's tent.

Thistle peeked her head into the tent. "Old man, you in here?"

As she backed out, Oscuro's black and gray peppered head followed. He hobbled the rest of the way and blinked in the bright campfire light. Oscuro silently eyed Bruno up and down as the rest of the group remained silent, waiting for one of them to say something.

Lulu finally piped up, "This is Bruno. We found him in the woods. He looks funny because he's been a prisoner of the creatures for a really long time. He escaped, but now he doesn't have a home or family."

Clearly satisfied with herself and her explanation, Lulu flashed a toothy grin at Juniper. Juniper patted Lulu on the head.

"I see," pondered Oscuro, still eyeing Bruno up and down, "tell me more."

Bruno went on to recount his story. Oscuro listened intently. When he was finally done, Oscuro sat and quietly stroked his whiskers.

He took a deep, tired breath before talking, "You're saying that when you attempted to escape *as a group,* that's when the creatures retreated?"

"Wait!" interrupted Conrad. "You actually believe this guy?"

Oscuro responded tenderly, "Although Bruno is indeed a stranger, I believe he is trustworthy, and the evidence of him being quaran tined and kept from the light is more than obvious. If what Bruno is saying is true, I cannot in good conscience pass up an opportunity to return us to our village, regardless of how dangerous it might be."

Thistle scrunched up her face in disbelief. "What are you saying, Oscuro? Do you think we actually have a chance with those monsters?"

"Again, if Bruno's story is true, there is strength in numbers. And one thing we definitely have here is numbers." Oscuro turned to Bruno, "Bruno, would you say there are more at this campsite than when you tried to escape."

Bruno's eyes scanned across the campsite. "It's pretty dark right now, but as far as I can tell there's at least triple the number here than what I escaped with."

"Wonderful!" piped up Oscuro. "We will come up with a plan in the morning."

"Oscuro, slow down!" Conrad nearly shouted in desperation. "Think about what you're saying! It's not a short hike through the woods back to the village. And even if it were, half the camp hasn't even set foot in the woods since they got here. Only those of us who are trained and able bodied go out. Even if we were to get the entire campsite to the village, we don't even know how many creatures will be there."

Juniper tenderly laid a hand on Conrad's shoulder. "Conrad, don't you remember sleeping in warm bedding, the feeling of a full belly, real shelter during a rain storm, living together happily in our village. We have a chance to get all of it back. You can't tell me you don't miss it."

Conrad dismissed them with a wave of his hand and sulked off.

Oscuro frowned, and addressed the rest of the group, "We will make arrangements in the morning to assemble a scouting party. Conrad is right, the hike back to the village will be dangerous. We will need a group to go ahead and make a clear, safe path for the rest of the campsite. In the meantime, go get some sleep. You have had a long day. I will tend to cleaning and storing the food you have found."

As the group dispersed to get cleaned up and fill their bellies before turning into bed, Oscuro held his hand out to block Juniper from following them.

"Juniper, dear, I would like a quick word with you before you go. I know you are tired, but I will be quick." He motioned to the baskets of food they had brought back. "Would you be so kind as to help me carry these inside?"

Juniper wanted nothing more than to eat and go to sleep, but she loved Oscuro and couldn't refuse his request. Besides, Oscuro had made so many sacrifices for their group, it was the least she could do.

They carried the baskets into his tent. It was cozy and smelled of herbs. She loved visiting his tent and listening to his stories. It was different this time though. There was an obvious tension in the air. She gently laid the baskets out and began organizing them.

"That's not necessary, dear. Come, sit and rest over here for a minute." Oscuro motioned to an empty spot next to him on the blanket.

"Juniper," Oscuro paused for a minute, carefully crafting his words, "I would like for you to lead the scouting party."

"What?" Juniper nearly levitated off the blanket. "Are you crazy? I'm probably the worst person to lead the scouting group. You know what happened to me, Oscuro, what *I* let happen to my family. I can't... I won't."

Although Juniper's parents had been gone for over a year, the pain of their loss was still fresh. Despite everything she had done, everything she had accomplished, her parents' death was still a defining failure for her. And although the creatures had ultimately killed her parents, she took responsibility for their death.

Her family had once lived in a beautiful, secluded farming village out in the country. Fresh air was plentiful. There was always enough food, and though her mother would occasionally tell them the "grub" was ready, she never imagined actually eating a real, live bug like they did now. Her days on the farm were typical of any other teenager's: full of friends, complaining about chores, and sleeping in. It was a simple life, but a good one.

The first encounter with the creatures was short. Lulu had been on the floor playing, while Juniper was reading one of her melancholic books. Both girls were startled by a cacophony of loud noises followed by her mother running into the room, grabbing them both, and herding them into a back room to hide. Juniper tried to ask their mother what was going on, but was quickly hushed. They seemed to have been hiding there forever when Juniper finally heard what would come to be the most disturbing, gut-wrenching sound she would ever hear.

THUMP.......THUMP.......THUMP.

A loud, unsteady barrage of heavy footsteps headed their direction. At first, there was only one set, but then another, and another—three in total. Her mother covered her and Lulu's eyes. Although she could not see the creatures, she could smell them. The stench grew stronger as the creatures inched closer. Juniper expected the worst, but as quickly as they had approached, the creatures retreated. Her mother would never discuss what had happened, but she heard her and her father whispering fearfully at night when they thought the girls were asleep. But sleep was elusive for Juniper. Her dreams were haunted by whatever image her brain attached to those repulsive creatures.

It wasn't long before the creatures came back. This time there were four. This time, she caught a glimpse of them. They were huge, thin, and gangly with flat faces and small eyes. Their skin was shiny and tight. But as grotesque as the creatures looked, the smell was infinitely worse.

Juniper and her family watched the creatures intently. One of them had brought implements with him - bright lights and large metal probes. He walked throughout the entire village, examining each and every space. He seemed to be searching for something in the lesser known nooks and crannies.

Their appearance became more and more common. At first, it was enough for everyone to hide, but soon, the creatures began their attack. It wasn't just Juniper's family who was targeted, but the whole village. Initially, the creatures directed their attack at their food supply. The villagers were unsure where they were spreading the poison, and exactly what it was, but many of the family's close friends began getting sick and inevitably perishing. The attacks became more and more vicious. Traps were laid. Some of Juniper's friends and neighbors were killed, others were taken away and never seen again. Her family eventually decided to retreat into the nearby countryside. Though they had taken everything from her, Juniper took comfort in the fact that her family was still alive. That was, until the night they decided to escape into the woods.

It was an eerily quiet, cloudless night in late fall. The moon was bright enough to act like a giant nightlight, casting a silvery glow on the field that separated them from the woods. Juniper's family had gathered a few of their belongings, and were preparing to cross the field when her mother remembered she had left a silver thimble her grandmother had passed down to her. Although her father strongly urged her to forget the trinket, she talked him into going back with her for it. Juniper's father instructed that she stay outside with Lulu. She and Lulu waited for what seemed like forever when Juniper decided to go back inside to make sure they were okay.

Much of what happened next was a blur. She remembered seeing her mother cornered by one of the creatures, her foot stuck in one of their traps. Father stood a few inches from Juniper. She vaguely remembered her father telling her he wanted her to quickly strike the back of the creature in order to distract it long enough for him to rescue her mother. She remembered him calling her name over and over again as she was frozen in fear. She recalled the warmth of his hand on her shoulder and his soothing voice as he said it was ok and that he was expecting too much from her and that she should go to Lulu. She remembered being unable to move as she watched her father rush the creature. It easily crushed him and then picked up both her mother and the trap and ambled off with them.

She didn't remember how long she stood there until running out to Lulu. She didn't remember what she told Lulu or how they made it across the field. She didn't even remember the next few days. The first thing she felt—*truly* felt—was the icy cold of winter setting in and the urgency to find Lulu and her a safe place. She was all Lulu had now. Her mother was no longer there to gently tuck Lulu in at night. Her father was no longer there to make Juniper laugh when she was stressed and taking things too seriously. She would never see her mother's beautiful, warm smile again or her father's worn, strong hands. Lulu and her were on their own.

Oscuro readjusted himself on the blanket. "I know what you *think* happened, Juniper, but you were not responsible for your parents' death. You are a good person. A kind person. You have trusted me thus far; I don't see why you would stop now."

Juniper stared down at her hands and shook her head. "Oscuro, I know you think I can do this, but I can't. I'm not like you; I'm not a leader. You're brave. You make decisions with conviction and follow through with them. People respect and trust you. Make Thistle the head of the group. She would be a better choice to lead them."

Oscuro reached over and took her hands. "Juniper, you see yourself as one who looks in a mirror. You are all too familiar with your flaws. You have an intimate knowledge of everything you hate about yourself. Your misfortunes and shortcomings stick out at you like a grotesque scar."

Tears visibly welled up in Juniper's eyes.

"It's OK, love. Everyone sees the vulnerable, unadulterated version of themselves. Here's what I want you to know, though. We may look at *ourselves* in a mirror, but when we look at *others*, we see a snapshot of them. We see what they want us to see: their bravery, their confidence, their humor, their talent. We don't see the turmoil and the scars underneath that. We don't know what they see when they peer into the mirror of their soul."

Juniper wiped her eyes and nodded.

"I can tell you, dear, that I have my fair share of scars I want to hide from the world. I have spent much of my life perfecting my snapshot. But I'm old now, and I don't have time for unachievable facades. I want you to know that life is about balancing both the mirror and the snapshot. It has taken a long time, but I have learned that I am not only the bad I see in myself, but also the good others see in me. You have much good in you, Juniper. You just need to believe it."

The tears that Juniper had been stifling finally spilled out onto her cheeks. She sat by Oscuro's side for some time crying out all the guilt, anger, and regret she had pent up for so long.

"Oscuro, I'm not ready to do this, but I do trust you. If you think I can lead them, I'll do my best to make you proud. But, please, send Conrad and Thistle with me. I need them."

Oscuro gently stroked Juniper's head. "Of course, my dear. Now it's time for you to go get some rest. We've had enough excitement for the day."

Juniper hugged Oscuro and trudged out of his tent. She washed herself up, ate some food, and got ready for bed. As she walked past Conrad's tent, she peeked in. He was already asleep. She knelt down beside him and studied his face. Conrad had been there for Juniper longer than anyone else. She knew him before the invasion and was relieved when they had found each other in the woods. Juniper reached down and held his hands. She stroked his long, calloused fingers.

"Thank you for seeing the good in me, Conrad," she whispered.

"Of course, doll." Conrad sleepily blinked and stared up at Juniper.

"Oh my gosh! You're awake!" Embarrassed, Juniper dropped Conrad's hand and stumbled back.

"Well, I was asleep, but I woke up when you started playing with my hands."

"I wasn't *playing* with your hands, Conrad. I came in to make sure you were okay and your arm was hanging off the cot. I was afraid it would fall asleep, so I was putting it back up."

"Uh, huh. Sure you did." Conrad laughed then paused for a minute. "But here's the real question, what the hell are you doing still up? Aren't you exhausted?"

"Well, yeah, but Oscuro needed to talk to me. He wants me to lead the scouting party tomorrow. I don't know if I can do it."

"He wants *you* to lead the scouting party? Really?"

"Wow, Conrad. Just, wow. Thanks for believing in me." Juniper rolled her eyes and stood up to leave.

"Wait!" Conrad grabbed her hand. "In all seriousness, Junie, I can't think of anyone else I would follow into the creatures' territory. I'm here for you, and I'll follow you anywhere."

Juniper lovingly looked into Conrad's dark brown eyes. "Thank you, Conrad. That really means a lot to me. Now, I'm going to go to bed before I pass out right here."

Juniper turned to go, but Conrad tightened his grip on her wrist. "Wait, come back, I have something else for you to play with."

"Oh my gosh, Conrad. You're so gross. I'm going to go pray for you. Only God can save your wicked soul."

Conrad laughed and let go of her wrist. "Night, Junie."

"Night, heathen."

The next morning, Oscuro gathered everyone in the middle of the campsite to share Bruno's story and brief them on his plan to attack the creatures. A scouting party, led by Juniper, would be sent out that morning. Their job was to find the safest path back to the village for the others to follow. Later that day, the rest of the camp led by Oscuro would follow the path they had set out. If Bruno was right, they would need everyone involved. Juniper figured that there would be some resistance, but everyone seemed to be on board. Their eagerness to help showed how ready they were to get back to their normal life, even if it meant death.

Juniper's scouting party consisted of Conrad, Thistle, and Bruno, along with Nezumi, the leader of another food scavenging party, and Russa, an engineer. Juniper was happy to have both of them on her team. Nezumi was decisive. He knew the woods like the back of his hand and was quick on his feet. Russa was sharp. She could think and build her way out of any problem.

With the help of everyone at the camp, the scouting party quickly gathered their supplies and was ready to go. Juniper had plenty of food, an incredible team, and the confidence of their leader, but there was one thing holding her back.

"Lulu, stay close to Oscuro the whole time, OK. He'll take care of you."

Tears welled up in Lulu's eyes turning them into a glassy ocean of sky blue.

"Juniper, I want to go with you. Why can't I go with you? I've been on so many food scavenging parties. I know the woods; I know how to stay safe. Please."

"I know, sweetie." Juniper cupped Lulu's small face in her hands. "This is different though. This is so much more dangerous. I'll meet up with you when we get there though, okay? I promise."

Lulu nodded and nuzzled Juniper.

"Junie, it's time to go." Conrad placed his hand on Juniper's back. He was already carrying his rucksack.

Juniper gave Lulu one last squeeze and kiss on the head. She turned to follow Conrad and didn't look back. She knew if she did, she wouldn't be able to leave. They met up with the rest of the scouting party, who had already said their goodbyes, and set off into the woods. Cheers and whoops rang out behind them. Everyone in the party seemed energized and confident—everyone except Juniper. Juniper felt like she was going to throw up and cry at the same time.

It was the afternoon. Juniper could tell because the sun was straight up in the sky. She was thankful for its warm sun rays streaming down through the tree canopy. The rest of the camp would be leaving soon if they hadn't already. She had marked the trail with bright pieces of fabric tied to limbs and branches so the rest of the camp could easily spot it. She was proud that they would have an easy path to follow. She and her scouting party had blazed a simple, straightforward trail for them.

Not much had been said while hiking. There had been a few warnings to "watch that root" or "briars to your left," but nothing substantial. Even Conrad was quiet. Juniper figured everyone was caught up with their own thoughts of leaving loved ones behind like she was.

They had walked easily on the path a while until they came to an especially overgrown area of vegetation.

"Careful here," she called back.

She was ducking under a low hanging tree branch when she heard Nezumi's urgent whisper from behind her.

"Juniper, stop."

She froze and glanced up through the leaves. At first, she didn't see or hear anything. Then, about six feet away, something moved in the brush ahead. Juniper couldn't quite make out what she was seeing, then fear instantaneously flooded her body like ice water in her veins. A massive wild cat was stalking just ahead of them. It was crouched down in the bushes ready to pounce.

"Do not move." Nezumi was right behind her, fixed in place as well.

While Juniper was frozen with fear, she knew Nezumi was quietly working out a plan to escape the cat. He turned and whispered something to the others behind her. Juniper couldn't quite make out what he said. Then he turned to her.

"I want you to slowly turn your head to the right, Juniper."

She followed his instructions.

"Do you see that small hole in the rocks over there? It's big enough for us to squeeze through, but small enough that I don't think the cat can follow us. I'm going to throw a stone in the opposite direction to confuse it, and we are all going to book it over there. Understand?"

Juniper shook her head. "I can't."

Conrad's soft voice called out from behind Nezumi, "Junie, I know where your mind is right now. You aren't that scared little girl anymore. Do this for Lulu. She needs you."

Juniper hesitantly nodded.

A second later she heard the rock crashing through the woods to her left. There was a loud *yowl* and the clamoring of feet behind her. A hand grabbed hers and jerked her out from under the tree branch. Before she knew it, she was bounding through the woods toward the rocks. They were so close. Then came the loud *crack* of tree branches breaking behind them. The cat was after them. Bruno, Thistle, and Russa had all made it safely inside the rock formation. Juniper swore she could feel the cat's hot breath on them. Nezumi was squeezing in when Conrad and Juniper caught up to him.

"Get your ass in there, Nezumi!" Conrad called.

In one fluid motion, he pushed Nezumi in the rest of the way, dove through the hole, and pulled Juniper along with him. Juniper felt the cat's giant paw swipe at her foot as it cleared the hole. The cat *yowled* again and tried to squeeze into the hole.

"What are we going to do?" cried Russa over the cat's screams. She had the least experience with the woods and all the lovely creatures it held.

They looked at Juniper.

"I... I don't know. Just let me think for a minute."

Nezumi sighed. "Juniper, it's ok. This is what we're going to do. Russa and I will stay behind—"

"What?" interrupted Russa.

Nezumi looked at Russa sternly, and continued, "Russa and I will stay here. Someone needs to stay to make sure the cat is detained before the rest of the camp gets here. I'm the fastest, so I'll distract the cat while Russa sets a trap. When it's ready, I'll lead it into the trap."

Juniper shook her head vigorously. "No! No, we have to stick together."

Nezumi disagreed. "You have to keep going on. It will be dark soon, and we have to reach the village before nightfall. You have to keep working on finding a safe way there."

Juniper looked to the others. They all reluctantly nodded their heads in agreement.

Juniper paused and chewed her lower lip. She knew they didn't have a choice.

"Ok."

Russa and the others worked together to finalize a plan and design a trap for the cat. By the time they were finished, the cat had wandered from the entrance of their small cave. Nezumi and Russa instructed everyone else to stay put until it was safe. They took a few supplies with them and quietly disappeared out of the mouth of the cave.

The others waited for a while, then Bruno poked out his head to make sure they were clear to leave.

"We're good. Let's go."

They quietly and cautiously crept out of the cave and continued on the path they were on. Thistle and Bruno constantly glanced behind them to make sure the cat wasn't following them. Juniper jumped at every rustle in the woods. No one talked, but this time it was for a different reason.

The sun was beginning to set, and the air was getting chillier. They had walked without any breaks for hours now, but Juniper knew they were getting close. She also knew there was one more deadly barrier they had to pass before they got to the village—an icy cold, rushing river. They had planned to have Russa craft them something to make it across more easily, but she wasn't with them now. Juniper had been trying to think of a way to get through it for the last hour without success. It wasn't long before she could hear the roar of the water passing over rocks.

"We're almost to the river." Juniper let the phrase hang in the air for a minute. "Does anyone have any ideas?"

Thistle piped up. "Let's look for a log or something to cross. There really isn't any other way."

Upon reaching the river, they searched for the smallest part to cross. It didn't take long to find it. Bruno found a large log to place into the water to serve as a bridge. There was only one problem. When they placed it into the water, it didn't stretch the whole way across.

Thistle addressed the group, "Someone's going to have to hold it while everyone crosses the log. You'll have to jump to the other side when you get to the other end."

"But that means someone will have to stay behind again." Juniper nervously chewed her fingers.

"That's okay," smiled Thistle, "I'll hold it. Honestly, I'm exhausted and this looks like a great place to rest until the camp catches up. Russa and Nezumi should be with them. Russa can give us directions to build something stronger and more efficient for us all to cross safely."

Juniper could tell that, although Thistle was tired, she didn't want to give up. She accepted her offer though; she didn't have the strength to argue with her.

They dropped the log in the water, and Thistle struggled to hold it still. She forced her words through gritted teeth, "Okay, who's up?"

Bruno stepped forward, but Conrad stopped him.

"Ladies first." Conrad motioned toward the log like a gentleman offering his seat to an old lady.

"Seriously, Conrad? *Now* you decide to act like a gentleman?" Juniper pursed her lips. She knew Conrad was only letting her go first so he and Bruno could be in a good position to help her in case she got in trouble, but it was still annoying.

She cautiously stepped out onto the log, but got only a few steps out before it started wildly rocking back and forth in the water.

"Whoa, whoa," cried Conrad as Bruno jumped to help Thistle steady the log.

Juniper quickly backtracked and leapt for the riverbank.

"What are we going to do now?" she said frustrated.

"Two people are going to have to hold it," Conrad stated the obvious.

"I'll stay." Bruno knelt down next to Thistle and braced the log.

"No! Absolutely not. We're not leaving anyone else behind. We'll find another way."

Thistle softened her face and tried to comfort her. "There is no other way, Juniper. We don't have the time now. The rest of the camp will be catching up to us soon, and we need you both to go see what's up ahead. We can't risk going ahead blindly, not when the whole camp is involved. Just go and take a look and then you can come back here and wait with us." Bruno placed his pale hand on her shoulder. "You and Conrad know the village better than any of us. It has to be you two."

Juniper once again couldn't hold back her tears. She nodded. Bruno and Thistle steadied the log as best they could as Conrad and Juniper crossed to the other side of the river. They waved at each other, and Juniper and Conrad continued on. The village lay just beyond the river and they reached the field separating it from the woods quickly.

They had easily crossed the field, climbed a tree, and snuck into Juniper's room through a side window. After a close encounter with one of the creatures which resulted in them hiding in a closet, Conrad crouched down in a safe corner to talk to Juniper.

"It's too dangerous with just the two of us. We've done as much as we can. Let's leave and wait somewhere safer for the rest of the camp to get here."

"Yeah, okay. We can go back across the field to Bruno and Thistle. At least, we know the best way to get into the village now."

They were climbing up into the window to leave when Juniper noticed movement in the moonlight from across the field. At first, she couldn't make out what was going on, but then Oscuro, Lulu, and Thistle stepped forward. Their smiling faces shone in the moonlight like a beacon.

"Conrad, look!" Juniper pointed in their direction.

"Holy crap. They made it." Conrad was incredulous.

Juniper and Conrad were so ecstatic that they forgot they were balancing on a window sill. Conrad went to hug Juniper, but lost his balance and fell back into the room.

SNAP.

Juniper knew that sound. Her stomach sank. Conrad cried out in pain. She jumped back into the room and softly landed beside Conrad. His foot was caught in the same type of trap that her mother's had been.

"No, no, no, Conrad!" She reached down to see if she could free him. "How did we not see this when we came in?"

"We must have gone right by it when we were running to the closet. We were so focused on hiding that we didn't notice it." Conrad moaned and grabbed at his foot.

Thump...thump...thump. The creature had heard the commotion and was coming back.

"Juniper," Conrad said softly.

"You're going to be okay. I'll find something to pry it open." She looked around the room frantically.

"Juniper."

"Ugh, there's nothing useful in here."

THUMP...THUMP...THUMP.

"Juniper."

"Look! The others are almost here. They're coming across the field."

"Juniper!" Conrad's soft voice had turned loud and urgent. "You have to go distract it until they can get here."

"No, I can't. I can't do it." Juniper cradled her head in her hands.

"Juniper, what happened to your parents... it's not your fault. Even if you did do what your father asked, it could have turned out the same way. Or worse, you could have died as well, and Lulu would be on her own. You have a chance now to save Lulu and everyone else. If you don't distract it now, it will see our ambush coming and kill us both. They'll lock down the village, and we'll never get back in. You can do this. Oscuro believed in you enough to send you first. We all believe in you, Juniper."

The creature was in the hallway now. Juniper looked out the window and saw Lulu's innocent, smiling face.

THUMP...THUMP...THUMP.

Suddenly she felt something hot welling up inside her, coaxing her to action. She recognized the creature's smell. She would never forget it. It was the same one that killed her parents.

Screw it.

She quickly jumped up and dashed toward the door. She sidled up to the wall it was connected to, just out of view, but ready to attack. The creature's foot appeared first. Without hesitation, she sunk her teeth into it. The creature screamed in pain and quickly withdrew. It hobbled back down the hallway. She had gained them precious moments.

Within a few minutes, two sets of footsteps came toward them. Juniper ran over to Conrad and stood between him and the two creatures coming in through the doorway. As they inched closer, Juniper suddenly heard the whole camp streaming in through the window like a tsunami.

"R..R..R..Rats!" the creature shrieked.

Juniper turned toward the flood of rats coming in through the window. They were her friends, her family, her mentors. They had been through so much together.

The shrieking creatures began to retreat, but Juniper wasn't going to allow it. Emboldened by their fear, she addressed her fellow rats.

"Look at them! Look at the fear on their faces. They've poisoned us, trapped us, experimented on us, chased us from our homes, and even killed our loved ones. But now, we have the upper hand. We can show them we've had enough, that we're stronger together."

The group cheered.

"We're here to take back what's ours."

More cheering.

"We're *all* here...and they're outnumbered."

Meet Stephanie Dare Adams

Stephanie is a pharmacist turned stay-at-home mama with a love of organizing all the things. She has too many hobbies—one of which is writing—but not enough time to do any of them consistently. When she's not following everyone around cleaning up their messes, she can be found reading web comics, painting, or bullet journaling. Stephanie lives in North Carolina with her talented husband and hilarious five-year-old son.

Acknowledgments

Committing to a charity drive sounds like a major undertaking. Admittedly, big undertakings make me a bit nervous. When we at the Legion of Dorks started considering a charity stream, we figured we would be able to collect a few hundred bucks for a charity we loved and that would be good enough for us. What we didn't take into account was how many people wanted to come along and support our efforts for four years and counting.

One of those people was our friend and author, Kelly Lynn Colby. She floated the idea of all of us pooling our creative resources and putting some stories together for a book. We had one in us, sure, but two? Absolutely! You hold in your hands the efforts of some wonderful writers to bring some brand new worlds and characters to life.

I can't begin to express how grateful I am for everyone who has been a part of building the Legion of Dorks that we have today. We're a group of random people who simply love caring for the people around us and making sure everyone has a place to feel safe on the internet. We're all on different epic journeys of our own, but when we focus our efforts on a common goal, the horizon is ours for the taking.

Within these pages, you'll find stories of grand adventure. Tales of ocean voyages, cowboys, mermaids and flying castles will surely delight. Have fun and know that you're helping children everywhere. Thank you for making a difference.

Stephen Adams

Legion of Dorks Co-Founder

www.ingramcontent.com/pod-product-compliance
Lightning Source LLC
Chambersburg PA
CBHW050525190726
48284CB00003B/950